DELTA FORCE | CANNON

KRIS NORRIS

OTHER BOOKS BY KRIS NORRIS

SINGLES

CENTERFOLD

KEEPING FAITH

IRON WILL

MY SOUL TO KEEP

RICOCHET

ROPE'S END

SERIES

'TIL DEATH

1 - DEADLY VISION

2 - DEADLY OBSESSION

3 - DEADLY DECEPTION

BROTHERHOOD PROTECTORS ~ Elle James

1 - MIDNIGHT RANGER

2 – CARVED IN ICE

3 - GOING IN BLIND

COLLATERAL DAMAGE

1 - FORCE OF NATURE

DARK PROPHECY

1 - SACRED TALISMAN

DELTA FORCE: CANNON

WAYWARD SOULS

KRIS NORRIS

Delta Force: Cannon

Copyright © 2019, Kris Norris

Edited by Chris Allen-Riley and Jessica Bimberg

Cover Art by Kris Norris

Published by Kris Norris

To you…
Thank you for joining me on my adventures.

Look for Colt's book, next.

CHAPTER ONE

Damn, she's fine.

Master Sergeant Rick "Cannon" Sloan, Army retired, eyed the blonde across the bar. V-neck crop top, tight black skirt and biker boots—the lady was dressed to kill. She had her elbows propped on one of the bar tables, showing off a healthy dose of pale cleavage as she leaned forward, dainty fingers absently skimming up and down her cooler. She'd hooked the heel of one black boot in the lower rung of the chair, her other foot tapping the floor. If it weren't for her steady hands and even expression, he'd have pegged her as being nervous. And she should be. She was seated next to the reason Cannon was at the bar. Biding his time. Hunting.

Nigel O'Mally. The bruiser in the leather jacket, who seemed determined to get his hand on her crotch. Cannon had to admit, she was good at deflecting the asshole's advances without pissing him off. Just enough to make O'Mally work harder—shift tactics. Up his game. Too bad he wasn't going to score tonight. And just as well. Most of

2 | KRIS NORRIS

the women he ended up leaving with didn't make it home alive. And the ones who did, wished they hadn't.

Not that anyone could connect him to the murders. Bastard seemed to have a horseshoe shoved up his ass. That, or he'd bought enough blue uniforms he didn't need luck. But, he'd been caught trying to pull off some lame-ass robbery—had managed to trip just about every security measure in the process—and was currently out on bail. Of course, he'd missed his court date, giving Cannon the excuse he needed to drag O'Mally's ass back in—profit in the process. And if there was any kind of justice, the U.S. Attorney's office would find a way to pin the murders on him while he rotted away in a cell.

"Hey, buddy. Are you going to order a drink or just sip soda water all night? This *is* a bar, ya know."

Cannon glanced at the bartender, keeping his eyes narrowed. Mouth pinched tight. He didn't answer, just stared at the guy until the other man took a step back. He swallowed—hard—then moved down the bar.

Good. The bartender recognized that Cannon was dangerous. Could sense he was someone accustomed to death. To fighting. And the guy had acted accordingly. Even now, he didn't make eye contact. Barely looked Cannon's way. Which suited him, because the last thing he needed was a scene. Something to out him before he was ready. The night was slowly coming to a close, about twenty patrons still left in the bar. He'd hoped more would leave once midnight had come and gone, but at least it wasn't still overflowing with bikers and gang members.

He looked over at the blonde, again. While her clothes definitely blended in with the other women in the room, something about her seemed...off. And it was more than just the color of her hair—her piercing green eyes begged for auburn locks, not blonde—it was her mannerisms. She didn't move like the other women—loose. Unsteady. Her actions felt calculated. And there was still that tapping foot...

Nigel wrapped an arm around her while twisting in his chair and dropping his other hand onto her thigh. Blondie's lips quirked, and her fingers tightened on her cooler bottle.

Shit. Cannon was good at reading body language. And the lady was about ten seconds away from smashing the bottle over O'Mally's head. If Cannon didn't intervene before that, it could ruin the entire takedown—cost him the fifty-thousand in bond money.

A bounty hunter.

If his teammates had told him he'd end up tracking down scum for money, he'd have flattened them. Punched them in the face then walked away without a second thought. He'd spent his entire adult life in the Army. Had worked his way up from a lowly recruit to lead in his unit. Was trained in hostage rescue, extreme weather survival, hand-to-hand-combat. There wasn't a vehicle he couldn't drive. A threat he couldn't address. And here he was, sitting in a bar that smelled like old beer and stale peanuts as he waited to make his move. One that wouldn't put the remaining patrons in danger.

Or her.

Fuck, he needed to stop focusing on the woman. She was lucky Nigel wouldn't get more than a grope out of the evening. Cannon couldn't waste his time worrying if she might get shoved aside. Maybe knocked down. Just as

4 | KRIS NORRIS

long as the asshole didn't have the chance to take her as a hostage, the night would end pretty much as Cannon had expected—Nigel cuffed and unconscious in Cannon's truck. The money he needed to start his own company all but in his pocket. Everything else was just a roadblock. And he had a way of dealing with those—he just hit the gas and barreled right through.

Blondie shifted in her seat, and he knew she was giving herself a better exit strategy. A way to slip out without getting caught up in Nigel's arms. Which meant, it was time to end this charade.

Cannon eased off the chair, scanning the bar, again. Not much had changed. Two redneck boys were still playing pool in the far right corner. A handful of college-aged kids bumping and grinding on the dance floor. There were two men at a table close to O'Mally. Similar clothes, though, they hadn't so much as looked at the man all night. Still, Cannon made a mental note to continue tracking their movements. He needed to be ready to react if they turned out to be the asshole's bodyguards.

That left only blondie as a wildcard.

Cannon walked forward, seamlessly shifting into warrior mode. Gone was the unobtrusive observer. The guy who'd blended in for the past two hours while waiting to strike. Now—he was primed. Muscles ready. Every sense honed on his progression across the bar. The feel of the floor beneath his boots. The slide of his jacket across his gun. He wouldn't draw unless forced. He planned on getting close to O'Mally. Too close for the bastard to get the jump on him, but perfect for taking the creep down. Bare-handed.

Oh yeah. He'd enjoy that part. Giving the man a taste

of what he dished out. If there was one thing Cannon despised it was men like O'Mally who preyed on women. Who thought, because they were bigger and usually stronger, it was their right to treat them however they saw fit. O'Mally was a threat. And Cannon had made a career out of eliminating threats.

He stalked across the floor, senses alert. The two men playing pool started shoving each other, voices raised. No doubt one of them would throw a punch. Though, based on the size difference, it would be over in all of two seconds. Not that he was in the habit of judging an enemy's skill by their size—he'd witnessed guys fifty pounds lighter than him and a good six inches shorter take out a bar full of bikers—but... He'd studied their mannerisms, too. The short guy didn't stand a chance.

Something clattered to the floor by the pool tables, and O'Mally looked over. Perfect. The asshole wasn't even watching Cannon. Sizing him up. If he had, O'Mally would have been puffing out his chest—making himself look bigger. Maybe scowling, showing a hint of teeth. Guys like him knew threats when they moved in close. Not that he'd necessarily peg Cannon as a lethal one but possibly competition for the blonde.

The one Cannon couldn't seem to get out of his head. There he was, about five seconds away from confronting his target—when all his attention *should* have been on the mission, on all the ways this could go down. Ensure he was in complete control—and a part of him was focusing on her. On the slight rustle of fabric as she slid one leg over the other—tights. Flesh colored. Nearly invisible against her skin. Or how a light flush had crept across the upper swell of her breasts. Not arousal. More frustration or anger, considering there was also a slash of red across her cheeks. She was sizing up O'Mally, the way he should be looking at Cannon—her eyes narrowed. Lips a thin line across her face. One hand slipped inside the purse hanging at her side, and Cannon saw a glint of something metallic on the inside.

Shit.

His instincts had been right. She wasn't like the other women here, after all. She was a plant. Maybe a cop or a fed. Hell, he wouldn't rule out assassin. Though, more likely another bounty hunter. Not a lot of women chose that route, but she definitely had the "calm and collected" vibe going. Now that he was closer, he picked up on more. Her muscles were primed, much like his, ready to strike. And she hadn't positioned herself for an easier exit. She'd turned so she had a clearer opening to grab O'Mally— slam his head into the table. Get behind him before he could react. She'd most likely been waiting until the crowd thinned out enough she could make a move. Cannon just wasn't sure if she was an ally or another mark he'd have to deal with. If she wanted O'Mally dead or alive.

Either worked for Cannon, but damn it—he could really use the bond money. Allow him to rent a space, hire a buddy or two to start expanding his services. Men he trusted—who he'd bled with. And if she was a threat, a hired hand... Shit, he wasn't sure he could take her out. Just the thought of hurting her...

Another step, and her head whipped around, her green eyes finding his and staying. Christ, she was beautiful. Made his damn chest tighten, his lungs fight to inflate. She was all smooth, pale skin, with full lips and high cheekbones. She wore more makeup than anyone needed, though, he suspected it was all part of her cover—to look the part. Blend in.

He had to hand it to her, she was a hell of a distraction. As long as she struck at the right time, she'd have a real chance at bagging the bastard. *If* she had backup. Surely, she hadn't come alone. Getting the jump on the guy was one thing. Dragging his ass out to her car —facing any possible company the creep might have hiding in the crowd. Like those two guys sitting behind her—it was suicide.

But, she hadn't so much as made eye contact with anyone else in the bar since Cannon had sat down. Hadn't focused on anything other than O'Mally and her phone when she'd gotten what he assumed were a few texts. Cannon knew. He'd been watching. But no one had been busy with their phone at the same time she had, which suggested...

Fuck. She *was* alone.

But, it was too late. He was already past the point of no return—inside his strike radius. Ready for battle. O'Mally had turned back, had finally caught sight of him. The bastard immediately straightened. Fisted his hands— one on the table, the other across the back of her chair. A fucking game changer just waiting to happen. It put her within reach. A possible target. Or a hostage. Either was bad.

Blondie read O'Mally's intentions—swiveled a bit more. Just enough the bastard would have to lunge out to grab her shoulder.

She's got good instincts.

Too bad it might not be enough. Unless she was a

professional. Then, he might end up on the wrong side of a gun. He was ready, but there were too many variables, and he didn't have enough intel. He'd just have to go in. Adapt.

He'd spent the past ten years adapting. If he'd learned one thing during his time in Delta Force, it was that no plan ever truly translated into the field. Sure, his team made a best guess. Tried to account for all possible outcomes. But there was always something that wasn't on the schematics. That hadn't been factored in. A family member when the mark should have been alone. Weapons that hadn't been accounted for. Murphy was always out there, just waiting to fuck things up.

And he was sure as shit sitting on Cannon's shoulder, right now—itching to throw a wrench into the entire mix. One with stunning green eyes and a killer smile.

Cannon stopped in front of the table instead of simply grabbing the guy, knocking him on his ass then carrying him back to his truck. The short confrontation—letting the jackass know, not to mention the woman, that Cannon was there to take him in—would give him some useful information. How she reacted, consciously or not, would be just enough to tailor the rest of his takedown.

He hoped.

It could also blow the entire op right out of the water. If she made a move right then… He'd be adapting to some deadly changes. The kind that might get one of them killed.

No doubt about it. Adapting was a bitch.

O'Mally sneered at him, gaze clearly assessing him. "Fuck off."

Cannon stood still, hands at his side—within reach of

his M9. Or the Ka-Bar on his thigh. Fuck, the asshole looked wasted enough Cannon could probably go for the twenty-two in his ankle holster and still out draw the creep. "Nigel O'Mally?"

"Whatever it is you want, I ain't interested. Now, fuck off, before I get nasty."

Cannon's lips twitched, and it took him a moment to realize he was smiling. Fuck, he couldn't remember the last time he'd smiled. Maybe Indonesia in '14. It felt odd, tugging at muscles he rarely used. But just the thought that the bastard would throw a punch—or, better yet, draw—it warmed Cannon's chest.

He took a moment to glance at the blonde, but she hadn't reacted. Not so much as a twitch of her lips or a raise of her brow. Stone. Cold.

So much for getting a read. Gaining the upper hand.

He palmed the table. Showtime. "There's nothing I'd enjoy more than having you get nasty. But… I don't have all night. And your bounty isn't getting any higher. So, you can either come quietly or—"

O'Mally moved. Reached inside his jacket as he lunged for the girl. But she was already sliding right, slipping out of the chair. Two seconds, and she was out of reach, backing toward the wall. Cannon shifted left. A quick swing of his fist, and O'Mally's arm was knocked away, his gun clattering to the table. A step, a reach, and the bastard was in his hands—squirming, trying to find purchase.

Cannon twisted, brought the fucker's head down on the corner of the table. It cracked hard, left a bloody smear, then he was falling. Crumpling on the ground at Cannon's feet.

Four seconds flat.

Until the men behind O'Mally's table jumped up. One grabbed Blondie—yanked her against his chest. His beefy arm wrapped around her shoulders, a fucking Sig Sauger pointed toward her head. The thing was massive—more firepower than the bastard looked like he could handle. But it didn't matter. No one missed a target that close.

His buddy was still drawing—the silencer on his gun catching on the pants. Another two seconds, and he'd have it free. Possibly firing off rounds in a panic, because his eyes were like white saucers. Huge. Unblinking. He most likely had tunnel vision—couldn't see past his boss getting slammed into the table. That made him dangerous. Unable to process whether he *should* fire, only that he *could*.

But Cannon was already working through steps four and five. Already had his M9 in one hand, his knife in the other—his sights on the asshole holding the woman. A quick shot, and he'd clip the man's shoulder—or better yet, peg him right between the eyes—eliminate any chance of the jerk shooting her. Cannon would have to be quick—catch the prick's buddy with his knife before the idiot fully drew. Started shooting whoever moved.

Until the woman punched up her arm, caught the creep holding her in the chin. A drop of her weight, a twist and shove, and she had him spread out across the table, face smashed into the top. She pivoted just enough to kick the other guy in the knee, buckle his leg. Another shift, and that gun Cannon had glimpsed was in her hand —pointed at the guy stumbling against the wall behind her.

Her hair fluttered around her face, tilting off a bit to

one side as she huffed, one hand holding the asshole to the table, the other leveling her Beretta at his friend. She spared Cannon a quick glance before focusing on the guy she'd kicked. "Freeze, asshole."

The guy blinked, glanced at O'Mally, around the bar, then nodded.

She motioned to his weapon. "On the table."

He all but dropped it, wincing when it nearly clattered to the floor.

"Gently. Now, unless you want to go to jail with your two buddies, here, I suggest you get lost. Fast."

He nodded, again, looked over once at Cannon then took off. Bumping into several people on his way to the door. It bounced off the wall, a cool swirl of air breezing through the bar.

She waited until the door closed then focused on Cannon, slamming the guy she was holding against the table, again, when he shifted. "Move, again, and I'll let him deal with you."

The asshole looked at Cannon, paled, then stilled.

Blondie smiled, finally gazing up at Cannon. She studied him for several moments then arched a brow. "Pretty sure I know most of the local hunters. You're new. You got a name?"

"Most people call me Cannon."

"Cannon? That's it?"

"It's enough. And you are?"

"Nash. Deputy U.S. Marshal Jericho Nash. And it looks like we just collared the same guy."

CHAPTER TWO

Jericho Nash cursed as the guy—Cannon—smiled. He shouldn't smile, not like that. It did something to his face —morphed it from bruiser to pure sex appeal in under a heartbeat. One second, he resembled something out of a slasher movie—hard. Lethal. Ready to wage war. Then the next, his lips lifted, and his eyes softened, and—he was 007. All suave, handsome features with a body that looked as if he could tackle a tank. Tackle a tank and win because his muscles had muscles. His arms were as thick as most men's thighs, but he carried it off. Managed to appear athletic and graceful, and she didn't doubt he could vault over the table. Maybe parkour off the wall and land behind her.

But the last thing she needed was to get involved with a bounty hunter. Even if *involved* only meant a few rounds of sex. A night. Maybe two.

Butterflies scrambled in her stomach as a warm feeling settled in her core. Damn, one stray thought, and she was practically drooling over the guy. Not her best night.

Though, based on how the evening had just played out, she should have expected it. Adrenaline rush aside, getting rescued—by a bounty hunter, no less—had pretty much landed her at rock bottom. Other than getting shot or punched, her collar had gone as wrong as humanly possible. And all because she'd been stupid enough to believe her partner might actually show up, this time.

She was going to kill Dave. Long and slow. And she was going to enjoy every second of it. *After* she cleaned up this mess.

Cannon's muscles eased as he holstered his gun and knife, crossing his arms and standing there as if he had all the time in the world. As if he hadn't just taken O'Mally out in about five seconds flat. Christ, she hadn't even seen him draw his weapons before she was staring down the barrel of his M9. She would have been worried she'd read his intentions wrong—was in serious danger of getting shot—if he hadn't been focused on the spot just over her left shoulder—right where the bastard's head was who'd grabbed her. And she had no doubts this Cannon guy could have landed a shot right between the idiot's eyes. That only left the knife. She wasn't sure she wanted to know what he'd intended to do with it.

Throw it at the other guy. Pin him to the wall with it. Gut everyone in the building for fun. Anything seemed possible.

Cannon swept his gaze down the length of her, absently kicking at O'Malley when the bastard attempted to push onto one elbow. Cannon bent over, grabbed the creep and bodily planted the man's ass in the chair, securing his hands before banging O'Mally's head on the table. "Marshal? That's...unexpected."

She snorted as she retrieved a pair of linked zip ties out of her purse—slipping them around the bodyguard's wrists. "Please. I knew you'd made me the moment I saw your eyes."

"True. But I was thinking more along the lines of a cop. Fed. Maybe another hunter. Marshal didn't even make it on the list, sweetheart."

Her lips twitched at the endearment. No one had called her anything other than ma'am or bitch in a long time. It sounded...dangerously intimate.

"You thought I was a bounty hunter? What part of this outfit screams hunter?"

"The gun in your purse."

She laughed. Damn, it had been forever since she'd been surprised. "You saw that?"

He shrugged, motioning to the guy still pinned to the table. "So, when did you realize those two creeps sitting behind you were his bodyguards?"

"I..." She'd suspected—had been pretty damn sure O'Mally didn't go anywhere without a few armed thugs to do his bidding—but she hadn't positively identified which of the men still scattered around the bar were his. In fact, she'd bet her money on the two guys playing pool until they'd started shoving each other.

Cannon grunted. "You hadn't."

"I knew he'd have some men. And I was watching them, but your little takedown kind of threw a wrench in my plans."

"Which plan was that? The one where they knocked you out? Or maybe where you didn't make it home?"

Jericho straightened. "I'm a federal marshal. I can handle myself. This isn't my first rodeo."

"Never said you couldn't or that it was. But three against one?" He shook his head. "Not great odds for anyone. And since when do marshals go after felons on their own? Don't you have a partner or two?"

"He...must have got detained."

"He ditched you?"

"I didn't say that."

"You didn't have to. It's written across your face. In the rigid line of your back. The way you scrunch your nose. Fuck... So, why didn't you back down? Let O'Mally go?"

"Did you miss the part where I'm a federal marshal? It's my duty—"

"To not get yourself killed over some lowlife like Nigel O'Mally. You can always hunt his ass down, again—assuming you keep yours in one piece."

She hitched out one hip. "So, you expect me to just turn a blind eye when I see a wanted felon because it's dangerous? Sorry, I don't operate that way. Being a marshal isn't something I turn on and off."

He pressed his lips together—damn, he had a perfect mouth—giving her the once over. "You didn't come *here* dressed like *that* on a chance. You were fishing. You knew he'd be here, and you were planning on reeling him in."

"How do you know this isn't my usual attire?"

He snorted. "Call it a hunch if it makes you feel better. Am I wrong?"

"You'd like it if I said no."

"You just did." He arched a brow. "Does your absent partner know he could have gotten you killed tonight?"

"I'm sure there's a reasonable explanation for why he didn't make it. And no one's dying here, tonight."

"Damn straight. Not on my watch." He rolled his shoulders, glancing between the two men. He looked as if he was mulling something over before he shook his head and smiled—that same killer tilt of his lips that did odd things to her chest. Made her heart kick up against her rib cage. "Do you have a vehicle outside?"

"Wrangler. Why?"

"Unless you were planning on dragging him across the floor, you'll need a hand. I'm betting he's at least two-twenty."

"I'd guess two-forty, and I can just wait until he's conscious enough to stumble."

"And chance he might try to escape or worse? I'll carry him for you."

She shook her head. "Who are you? And why are you being so...nice?"

"Already told you my name. And you're a marshal, and O'Mally's a wanted felon. I'm just doing the right thing."

"A felon with a fifty-thousand dollar bounty on his head. The one you were obviously hoping to cash in on."

"Don't remind me."

"So...you're just going to give him to me? No whining or begging? No trying to outsmart me? You'll just hand him over?"

"You sound surprised."

"Maybe because that never happens in these situations—when I cross paths with other hunters. Usually, I have to threaten to throw a few asses in jail for obstruction of justice before I get a begrudged collar."

A chuckle. All gravelly and deep. Like the hum of a bass speaker. "Sounds like you've been dealing with the wrong guys, sweetheart. Don't get me wrong. I had plans for the money—"

"What kind of plans?"

"Excuse me?"

"For the money. What were you going to do with it?"

Another glance up and down her—as if he was measuring her up. Deciding if she met some secret criteria in order to know the answer. Not that she blamed him. She was being more than a bit intrusive, but—there was just something about him. A sense of honor she hadn't come across with other bounty hunters. It piqued her curiosity, not to mention her damn libido. The one she needed to get control of before she did something she'd regret.

Silence.

Awkward, numbing silence.

"Forget I asked."

"I'm hoping to expand my business. Hire a few... friends."

"You're starting a bounty hunting business?"

"Trust me. Being a Bail Bond Recovery Agent isn't my dream job, but... Let's just say there aren't that many venues for my particular skill set."

"Your particular skill set? Christ, please tell me you're not former CIA?"

Another low laugh. "No."

"Whew." She relaxed a bit, shoving at the guy still bent over the table. "Good. You had me worried for a moment. But if you're not CIA..."

She studied him more closely. Short dark hair, a healthy dose of scruff. He was dressed in jeans, shirt and a jacket—nothing out of the ordinary. She glanced at his feet—boots. Black. Worn. They'd seen some mileage. She skipped her gaze back up to his face, noting the hint of silver around his neck. Crap.

She groaned. "Ex-military? Really?"

"Were you hoping for assassin?"

No wonder he seemed to have honor shoved up his ass. Which meant his "friends" were most likely ex-military, too. Guys he'd fought with. Brothers. It also explained the hard edge that only faded when he smiled. The sense of death that hung around him like a shroud. She'd been too focused on O'Mally—on not getting shot—to pick up on it before. But now... There was no escaping it. This guy was definitely a class-A predator.

She'd bet her ass he hadn't been doing run-of-the-mill grunt work in the service, either. He'd seen action—the kind that screamed Special Forces. She just wasn't sure which branch.

"Can you do me a favor? Keep an eye on these two while I make a quick trip to the ladies' room? I'll only be a few minutes."

"You need to pee? Now?"

"I've been knocking back sparking water for a couple of hours without a break. Is it too much for you, or do you have somewhere else you need to be?"

"Fine. Go. I'll be waiting."

She shoved the bodyguard into a chair then headed for the restrooms, resisting the urge to glance over her shoulder. While she hadn't been lying about the water, she hadn't really needed to use the facilities. In fact, she was too wired to even sit. But...

She needed some air. Standing that close to Cannon—nothing seemed to work. Her lungs, her brain, her mouth.

It was as if they'd all just shut down. Turned to mush and dripped onto the floor. At least in here, she could splash some water on her face—get out of the wig, clothes and makeup she'd had to parade around in all night. If she was going to take in a couple of felons, she should look like a marshal. And if Cannon also got a chance to see that side of her—the real side—it wasn't a bad thing.

Not that she cared. She didn't, did she?

She lost the wig then grabbed a towelette out of her purse and wiped it across her face, removing the caked foundation and extra thick eye liner. She didn't have time to reapply even a fraction of what she'd had on, but she'd rather go without. Cannon had been right. She'd come to the bar knowing O'Mally would be there—a tip from an informant who still owed her a few favors. A fact her boss would figure out if she showed up as she had to the bar. And the last thing she needed was him cornering her as to the whereabouts of her absentee partner.

She was definitely going to kill Dave. If Cannon hadn't turned out to be one of the last few good guys out there...

Jericho rolled her shoulders, took a deep breath, then quickly changed—thankful she'd put some jeans and a tee in her purse. She was jumping the gun. Making assumptions about a man she'd just met. One who could have wrestled O'Mally into the back of his vehicle and taken off, by now. Which was another reason she'd ventured to the restroom. She was curious if his offer only lasted until she was out of sight. Or if he'd simply wait the five minutes she'd spent in the ladies' room—guard the men as he'd promised.

She had a habit of trusting the wrong guys. One she was itching to break. Better she figure that aspect out, now. If he intended on starting his own business, they'd likely run into each other, again. And she wanted to know if he'd have her back if things went sideways. Or if she'd have to spend every encounter watching that he didn't stick a knife in her back, instead.

The door creaked as she walked out, rounding the corner before nearly tripping. Cannon was standing behind the table—just like he'd been when she'd left. O'Mally was slumped in the chair in front of Cannon, barely conscious. The bodyguard hadn't moved, his gaze focused on the top of the table.

A smile tugged at her mouth, but she managed to keep it to nothing more than a small lift of one corner. Cannon glanced over at her, turned then snapped his head back. He didn't hide his obvious perusal, those hard eyes finding, then holding, hers.

Copper. How had she missed what color they were before? How they practically shimmered in the light? Not quite brown or hazel. Not even a combination. They were...stunning.

She stopped a few feet back, chest tight, breath held. The man was huge. She'd realized that before, but she'd been caught up in the takedown. In keeping the guy pinned to the table. After spending a few hours next to Nigel O'Mally, she'd grown accustomed to feeling small. But Cannon had at least twenty pounds on O'Mally and a few inches. She wasn't short at five-eight, but Cannon dwarfed her.

He raised a brow, motioning to her. "I knew that blonde color was all wrong."

"Not sure red is any better—"

"It goes with your eyes."

He'd noticed her eyes?

She pushed at a few strands tickling her face, questioning if she should have kept it up in the ponytail. "Thanks for waiting."

"Wouldn't want to fail the first test you gave me, sweetheart, now, would I?" He snorted at her sharp inhalation. "You were wondering if I'd take off with O'Mally."

"That's silly. I was just—"

"It's impolite to lie to my face, Jericho."

God, the way he said her name. That deep voice—the lingering echo of it through the air. It made the room heat, her damn pulse quicken. If she didn't know better, she'd swear this was some kind of instant attraction. Lust at first sight. Maybe a moment out of time, just like in the movies.

But she knew better. She didn't have moments. Didn't have much of anything outside of work. Becoming a marshal had taken more than simple dedication and hard work. It had taken sacrifice. Her love life being at the top of the list.

She swallowed past the lump in her throat—the one making it insanely hard to do anything other than stand there and stare at Cannon. Hands trembling slightly. Her gaze locked on his. "You're right. It was a test. But I'm starting to think maybe I'm the one who failed it."

A gravelly laugh that didn't help her breathe easier. "There's still time for a retake."

"I suppose there is. So, Cannon—"

"It's Sloan. Rick Sloan."

"I think I like Cannon, better. It's what I assume your buddies call you. Makes me think of this as more of a partnership. Dare I say, budding friendship? Either way, I was going to ask if you had a vehicle outside."

"Chevy's gassed up and ready to go. Would you like me to follow you? Just in case?"

"Actually, I was wondering if you could handle O'Mally on your own?"

For the first time since she'd spotted him, his armor cracked just a bit. His eyes widened, followed by a furrow of his brow. "Is there a reason I'll have to?"

She took a few steps to the side, studying both men before smiling up at Cannon. "Here's the thing. I wasn't really the one who collared O'Mally. If you hadn't stepped in..." She shrugged. "Chances are I would have gotten myself into a bit of a bind. Had a few tough choices to make. Seems only fair you get to cash in on that."

He frowned. "But...you're a federal marshal. He's a wanted felon."

"I'm a federal marshal who happens to be off-duty. Whose partner ditched her and is lucky she didn't end up another victim. You were right. I should have let O'Mally go. Caught up with him another night. Or just left him for the bail bondsman to deal with. It's not my money at stake. But I guess I just kept hoping my backup would show. And O'Mally's the kind of scum I take personal offense to. The idea of him loose, hurting other women, really boiled my blood. Not something I could easily let go of."

She walked over to him, stopping a bit closer than she normally would have. "I love Seattle. But there're a lot of wayward souls who call this place home. Thinking this city could use a few more men like you. Just do me a favor? Keep this between us. I can't have everyone thinking I've gone soft."

Cannon watched her, leaning in even closer. "Wouldn't dream of it."

"Guess this means I'll be seeing you around. Oh, and you might want to consider expanding your practice. Maybe look into personal security. Overseeing corporate events. Consulting with companies. In fact..." She reached into her purse, rummaging around until she found the card she'd been searching for. "Take this."

Cannon accepted the offering, brushing his fingers across hers in the process. "Admiral Jonathan Hastings? You know him?"

"You could say that. Give him a call. Tell him I sent you. I'm betting he has the kind of clearance you can talk about your background without worrying about national security. I'm sure he'll have a list of people who could use your services. *If* you were serious about starting a business."

"I was, but..." He huffed. "You don't have to do this."

"I know. Consider it that retake we talked about."

She headed for the door, stopping when Cannon called out her name. She glanced at him over her shoulder.

He pointed to the bodyguard. "Aren't you forgetting something? Or did you already call the cops for him?"

"The bodyguard? I knew he looked familiar. I just remembered. His name is Jason Stanwick. He missed his court date, too. And the twenty-five thousand dollar bounty on him went live..." She looked at her watch. "At midnight. That should be enough to get you started. You *can* handle both of them, can't you? See you 'round, Cannon."

"Jericho."

She turned back one more time. "Yeah?"

"You tell your partner if he ditches you, again, I'll be paying him a visit."

"In a completely non-threatening way, seeing as he's a Deputy U.S. Marshal."

He smiled. "Right. Non-threatening. And I *will* see you, again. Soon. That's a promise."

"Then, that'll be your second test. Keeping your promise. See you don't fail it."

"Haven't failed a test, yet. Consider it a date, Deputy Marshal."

Date. She hadn't had anything like that in...

She snorted, heading for her Jeep. She'd taken another leap of faith, tonight. She only hoped this one would turn out better than her previous encounters. That maybe Cannon was a man she could trust.

CHAPTER THREE

So, this was where Jericho worked. It didn't look different than any other federal office Cannon had been to. Though, he couldn't quite overlook the fact that there were only a few women scattered amidst a dozen men.

Seemed the Marshal Service was still predominately male. Though, it was nice to see they were, at least, making an effort. In fact, more than a few of the higher ranking positions were women. Not that he was looking for anyone other than Jericho.

And her dick of a partner.

After spending the night babysitting O'Mally and Stanwick, Cannon had finally hauled their asses into the station a couple of hours ago. He'd wanted to give Jericho time to change her mind, not that he'd thought she would. But, he'd been ready in case she'd returned to the bar, cuffs in hand. Half of the local marshal service in tow. But, once sunrise had come and gone, he'd decided to hand the men over—get his reward.

Seventy-five thousand dollars.

Seemed surreal, even for him. And he knew it wasn't typical of what he'd normally get—that he'd essentially lucked out by bagging two extremely dangerous felons at once. Both with abnormally high bounties. But he had to admit, it was just what he needed. What had turned the tides on his venture. Made his decision to retire look viable, when he'd secretly been wondering if he should go back to the Army. If he'd jumped too soon. Given up the only lifeline he'd had.

But, now, he had options. Possibilities that had been nothing more than wishful thinking before. And he'd already made arrangements to visit a few available spaces —see if any suited his needs. He'd also put in a call to a couple of buddies. Brett "Colt" Sievers had jumped on board before Cannon had done more than ask the man if he might consider switching to a new line of work. Said he would meet up with Cannon within the week.

And all because Jericho had taken a chance on him. Had broken ranks. Though she'd brushed it off, he knew she could catch serious shit over letting him claim the reward when she'd been on scene. Could have brought both men in without having their bounties paid out. Cannon owed her, and payback started with the cup of coffee he'd gotten at the small café across the street.

He scanned the room, finally spying her at a desk shoved into the far corner. She had her back to him as she leaned against the inside edge, chair off to her left, her head bent as she focused on the folder in her hands. He started toward her, stopping when some shithead in a cowboy hat stepped in front of him, blocking his way. Though, Cannon respected the guy's vocation, there was just something about him that immediately put Cannon on edge. And he was good at judging people. At reading their intent by the shift in their eyes, the line of their back. This guy wasn't even polite about nearly knocking him into a desk, choosing to stand there as if the jerk owned the place. Cannon was pretty sure he didn't—not when he could see the station's supervisory deputy pacing inside his office.

Cannon eyed the man—the guy's head barely reaching Cannon's nose—waiting to see what move he'd make.

The jackass rolled his shoulders, exposing the gun on his hip—Glock. Looked like a twenty-six. What he guessed was standard issue for Deputy U.S. Marshals, though Cannon hadn't missed that Jericho had chosen a Beretta, last night. Most likely her personal weapon or maybe a backup. Of course, the fact this jerk was already alerting Cannon to the fact he was armed and, apparently, ready to draw simply by Cannon walking across the room didn't bode well. Not when the guy seemed twitchy. Almost as if he was coming down off of a high.

The man eyed Cannon. "Can I help you?"

Cannon fisted his hands, reminding himself he was just another civilian, now. That he didn't have his ranking behind him. Wasn't Special Forces—couldn't demand answers or assume he'd get a pass. That there was a new order he needed to follow—even if he could have snapped the prick in two without breaking a sweat.

Instead, Cannon took a calming breath, never losing eye contact. The guy paled a bit, swallowing hard before crossing his arms over his chest. A clearly defensive move. Cannon hadn't realized how much his ten years in Delta Force had changed him until he'd helped out a few friends a couple of months back. One of his buddies had gotten involved with a narcotics officer suffering from conversion disorder, leaving her temporarily blind. She'd all but crawled out of her skin when they'd first met. Had been able to smell death on him, or so she'd claimed.

It had been part of the reason he'd decided to retire. Knowing he couldn't even wash the stench off him—that it had become etched in his DNA—had hit him hard. And he'd made a choice to get out before he lost any chance at having a life. One beyond insurgent cells and war. Where he didn't spend years of his life pretending to be the very thing he hated, only to have it all go sideways on him.

But, apparently, he still had the mercenary vibe going because the guy lowered his hands, his right brushing over his pistol. It struck him, then, that Jericho hadn't reacted to him. Hadn't seemed the least bit intimidated by him or his actions. If anything, she'd held her head a bit higher. Had looked completely comfortable standing toe-to-toe with him. Just another quality to add to the list of reasons she intrigued him.

Cannon met the man's expectant stare. "Actually, no, you can't. I'm just visiting a…"

Fuck, what was Jericho to him? A friend? A stranger with possibilities? A potential lover? He hadn't had one of those in quite a while. It hadn't been an option while he'd been undercover. And he'd been too busy getting the paperwork for his hunter's license to think about dating since retiring.

Not to mention he wasn't sure he was dating material. That there was anything left inside worth sharing.

The guy sidestepped with him. "This isn't a bar, and

unless you have official business, I'm going to have to ask you to leave."

"Look, buddy, I'm not in the mood to dance, right now, so unless you want to go a few rounds—"

"Easy, Dave. Cannon's with me."

The guy—Dave—spun, nearly tripping sideways as he looked at Jericho. "You know this guy?"

"Didn't I just say that?" She smiled at Cannon, and fuck if his heart didn't give a hard kick. Made him inhale as his breath stalled. That smile was exactly as he'd been picturing it all night.

She glanced at the two cups clenched in his hands. "Did you bring me coffee?"

He grinned, hoping he wasn't simply baring his teeth or snarling, because he hadn't truly smiled in years. Other than maybe last night—with her. Shit, this was quickly becoming something more than just a nice gesture...and he had no idea how to stop it. If he even wanted to stop it.

He offered her a cup. "Thought you could use a pick-me-up. I wasn't sure how you took it, so I got one of those salted-caramel latte drinks."

Her eyes widened as she cradled the paper cup in her hands. "You brought me caffeine and sugar? Together? You're a damn godsend." She took a cautious sip, moaning around the lip. "Oh my god. This should be illegal."

Cannon clenched his jaw when she made another low moan. Christ, it was bad enough he'd spent the rest of the night thinking about her. Now, he had sound effects to go along with the sinful smile. The sexy sway of her hips. And it was the kind of noise he bet she'd make if he kissed her just right. Slid into her ever so slowly.

Dave huffed. "Jesus, Jer, get a room, why don't you?"

Jericho arched a brow. "You're just pissy because no one brought you coffee."

"I can buy my own damn coffee. Besides, we've got work to do. You can socialize on your own time."

Her smile faded as her eyes narrowed. "Maybe I'd have more of that if my *partner* actually showed up for a bust, instead of making me wait half the night, only to ditch me."

"I already explained what happened. No one made you sit there. You could have left, anytime. Or called nine-one-one."

"We're talking about Nigel O'Mally. Scumbag and wanted felon. Besides, I only went there because you said you'd show. Do you know how much I hated walking out of there empty-handed?"

The guy replied, but all Cannon heard was a dull roaring inside his head. *This* was her partner? The fucker who'd *stood* her up? Left her there to handle not one, but *three* dangerous men on her own? Who hadn't been assed enough to give her an hour of his time to bring in a known thief and suspected murderer? And he had the fucking gall to bitch about it? Make it seem as if it was Jericho's fault?

Cannon took a step, only stopping when she palmed his chest. He glanced down. Her hand was half the size of his. She couldn't keep him from moving if she grabbed him and used all of her weight. Christ, he bet he was double her weight. But there was something about the way she touched him—a tingle of awareness that shot through his torso and into his heart—that kept him from pushing past her. Punching the smug smile off of her partner's face.

She met his gaze—stunning green eyes that made his pulse race. It never raced. Not in the field. In the two years he'd been undercover. When he'd been forced to take down six armed men with his bare hands. Yet, one look from her, and it tapped wildly against his ribs.

"Down, boy."

"Don't worry, sweetheart, I won't do anything permanent to him."

"He's a federal marshal, and we're standing in the middle of the Marshal's office."

Dave drew himself up, glaring at Cannon. "Did you seriously just threaten me? Who the hell do you think you are?"

"Dave—"

"Who am I? I'm the guy who *didn't* ditch your partner last night. Who didn't leave her to face a bunch of armed felons on her own because I couldn't pull my head out of my ass long enough to give a damn."

"Tough talk coming from...what? Christ, are you a bounty hunter?" Dave turned to Jericho. "You're siding with bounty hunters, now? And did you leave and let this asshole claim the bounty? Damn it, Jericho—"

"Nash! Faraday!"

Cannon glanced up. The man he'd seen pacing was standing in the doorway of his office, his deep booming voice cutting through the room. Most of the peripheral noise died off, leaving an odd quiet throughout the space. He moved toward them, stopping in front. He eyed the two marshals, mouth pinched tight, brows furrowed.

Jericho plastered on a small smile as she nodded at the guy. "Art."

"The U.S. Attorney's office just called. Jeremy Brenner's over at the West Precinct. He has a possible security request. I'll know more in about ten minutes. I'd like you both to handoff anything you have to Taylor and Watson. In case this stretches out over the next few weeks."

Dave nodded, glaring at Cannon one more time before excusing himself then heading for his desk.

The guy—Art—frowned, glancing down at Jericho. "Is everything okay between you and Faraday?"

"Fine. Why?"

"You never were a good liar, Jericho. And it's no secret he's been...off a bit, lately. You two have always worked well together, and I'd hoped having you along would keep him grounded. But if that's not the case..."

"He's just having a hard time at home. We're fine."

He looked up, as if just now noticing Cannon's presence. He nodded, extending his hand. "Art Collins."

Cannon shook his hand. "Rick Sloan, though, my friends all call me Cannon."

"Cannon. That's funny. My brother-in-law did a few tours with a guy nicknamed Cannon. That wasn't you, by chance, was it?"

"Could be. What's his name?"

"Jackson Perry."

Cannon snorted. Small fucking world. "Jacks? Hell yeah. Afghanistan about five years back. Guy knocked down more doors than I care to remember. Hell of a soldier. Heard he retired a couple of years ago. Joined local law enforcement. How's he doing?"

"Doing fine, thanks to you. He said you pulled his ass out of a nasty firefight. Took a bullet to the leg for your troubles."

"It wasn't much more than a graze. Had worse."

"So, are you still enlisted? Delta Force, right? Alpha squadron?"

Cannon glanced at Jericho, smiling at her wide eyes and slightly gaped lips. He hadn't divulged much information about himself for a reason. Though, the look she was giving him made him long to share a few more details. "I was until a couple of months ago. Decided to hang it up. Let the younger guys do the heavy lifting for a while. Just started up my own security business."

Collins chuckled. "You're the Sloan who brought in O'Mally and Stanwick this morning. Hell of a collar. You're obviously still sharp if you were able to bag both of those felons at the same time. I just wish we had the manpower to hunt down a few more, ourselves. But...we have to prioritize. Even then, it feels like a never-ending task."

"Happy to help out."

Collins looked over at Jericho. "It's odd. I heard a rumor that Stanwick claimed a female deputy marshal was at the bar where he was caught, last night. Blonde. Black skirt. That she just walked out. He couldn't seem to recall the name."

She grinned. "Don't look at me. When's the last time you saw me in a skirt?"

"Right." He shook his head, turning back to Cannon. "Great finally meeting you. I hope we run into each other, again."

Cannon nodded toward Jericho. "I don't think that's going to be a problem."

Collins eyed them then smiled. "Excellent. Hey, does your venture have a name? Never hurts to have quality help available—in case someone asks."

"It's called Wayward Souls." He looked over at Jericho. "A friend mentioned the phrase, and it stuck."

"Wayward Souls. I'll keep that in mind." He nodded then turned, making his way back to his office.

Cannon inhaled when Jericho slapped him in the chest. "What was that for?"

"You're ex-Delta Force? Seriously?"

"You knew I was military."

"You could have told me you were Spec Op, instead of me having to guess. And not any branch. Delta…" She whistled. "Explains the takedown. The knife."

"I didn't do anything with the knife."

"It's what I imagined you might do. All of it possible, by the way." She blew a few stray strands of hair out of her face. "Wayward Souls?"

"Thought you'd be happy I took your advice."

"I am. I just didn't think you'd name your company after something I said."

"Guess you're a hard lady to forget."

A light blush crept along her cheeks then down her neck, and he couldn't help but wonder if she'd look like that after a night of tumbling in the sheets.

Jericho chuckled. "Anyway, thanks, again, for the coffee."

"I had a promise to keep."

She inhaled, holding it for a few moments before

slowly exhaling. "Careful, Cannon. You might just change my opinion of men."

"God forbid." He took a step closer, leaning into her. "You sure you'll be okay partnering up with Faraday? Collins is right. Even I can tell something's off about him, and I just met him."

Jericho sighed, glancing over at Dave. "He and his wife separated six months ago. I'm sure it's just the fallout from that."

"Doesn't matter what it is, if it puts your safety in jeopardy."

"I'm not in danger. Promise. But..." She held up her hand to stop him from interrupting. "I'll call him on it if it happens, again."

"You might not be alive to do anything if he leaves you hanging, again."

"What's wrong? Gonna miss me?"

"I don't buy coffee for just anyone, sweetheart." He looked at Faraday, noting the slight tremble in his hands, the beads of sweat on his forehead. Call him crazy, but Cannon swore it was more than just some stress from a relationship gone wrong. And, while he'd compared it to the guy coming down off a high, he might not be far off.

He held out his hand. "Your phone."

"Excuse me?"

"Can I please have your phone? Unlocked?"

She pursed her lips, looking incredibly sexy and unsure all at the same time, before reaching into her pocket and retrieving her cell. She unlocked the main screen then handed it to him. "Don't tell me. You have a shitty service plan so you want to borrow mine to make a long-distance call."

He snorted, opening her contact list then inputting his information before handing it back to her. "That's my personal cell. The one I pretty much never give out. Promise me you'll call if you find yourself in a dangerous situation, again. Doesn't matter what time. Where you are. What's going down. Just call."

She stared at her cell then slowly drew her gaze up to him. "That's... Thank you. And I will."

"Promise me."

"Scout's honor." She glanced over his shoulder when Faraday called her name. "Gotta go, but...how about coffee tomorrow morning? That same café. Say around seven? Even if I'm on guard duty, I should be able to make it before my shift starts."

"I'll see you there."

"Great." She turned then looked back at him. "And thanks. For the number."

"My pleasure. See you tomorrow, Jericho."

She smiled then headed for her desk, talking with a couple of other marshals who gathered around her. Cannon gave her one last sweeping gaze then turned, walking out the door and back to his truck. He made a mental note to call in a few favors—have his buddies dig up whatever they could find on David Faraday. Not that he didn't believe Jericho. It's just...

Cannon was good at seeing beyond the surface. And everything about Dave Faraday suggested there was something darker going on. Something more dangerous than a rocky marriage. The kind of secret that got people killed. And, with Jericho in the crosshairs... Cannon couldn't afford to give the guy the benefit of the doubt. Not with her safety on the line.

He cursed under his breath. He'd just given her his cell number. Not any of the burners he kept—the ones he normally used for contacts, in case he wanted to lose the person, later. His personal number. The one only a few of his brothers knew existed. And he hadn't thought twice about it.

She was quickly becoming an itch he couldn't seem to scratch enough. He just wasn't sure if it was temporary, or the kind of trouble that lasted a lifetime. That he'd managed to avoid, until now. Until...her.

CHAPTER FOUR

He was late.

Jericho glanced at her cell for what felt like the fiftieth time since she'd arrived at the restaurant, waiting for a text she wasn't sure would come. It had been a month since Dave had left her hanging at the bar, and she'd been hesitant to trust him other than during regular hours. But he'd asked to meet her for dinner—said he'd explain everything. That he wanted to make it up to her. And she'd stubbornly agreed.

Now, she was sitting at some obscure table, watching people come and go as time just ticked past. A waiter walked by, refilled her water, waited to see if she was going to order, only to sigh and say—yet, again—that he'd come back in ten.

She'd be in her Jeep driving home in ten, unless Dave called. Or showed up.

God, she was gullible. Trusting. Which so ironic considering she rarely trusted anyone. But Dave was her partner of sorts. They'd been watching each other's back on assignments since she'd joined the Marshal Service eight years ago. It was an unspoken chain of trust, wasn't it? A default that came with the badge and title. Partners trusted each other. Period.

She scrubbed a hand down her face. Obviously, she was a terrible judge of people—except where Cannon was concerned. He'd never let her down. Had always showed up on time for their coffee dates—which had been nearly every morning since they'd met at the bar—and he'd never once given her a reason to think he wouldn't drop everything and ride to the rescue if she needed it. Of course, he'd made a point of telling her that every time they met—casually slipping it into the conversation that she had his number. Could call anytime. Day or night. He didn't care if it got him arrested. Hell, got him killed. He'd be there.

Which was precisely why she *hadn't* called him. Chances were, he'd just ping her location and show up— guns blazing. Knife cutting a swath through whoever was in the place. She'd done a bit of researching. Okay, so she'd casually asked her uncle—Admiral John Hastings, or Jack to his family. The closest thing she'd had to a father since her own had been killed on a mission overseas. And she'd been floored by what Jack had told her.

Purple Heart. Silver Star. Medals with titles she couldn't remember. Cannon had them all. A shoebox full of them. And those were the ones on record. That were public knowledge. She knew he had more—for missions even the President didn't know about.

Cannon was one of the last true warriors out there. And one of the few good guys left.

So, she'd avoided calling him, keeping any

communication to either texts or in-person meetings—which were getting more frequent. She'd wanted to call. Pretty much every night since he'd given her his number. Just to hear his voice. To feel that gravelly tone wash over her—make her feel...

Safe. Hot. Some weird combination of both. It was like being aroused and soothed all at the same time. And she didn't know whether she wanted to pounce on him or close her eyes and sleep.

Who was she kidding? She wanted him. In every way possible. She wanted to gaze over her coffee mug and see his face. Watch how it changed whenever he smiled—which seemed to be whenever he looked at her. Listen to how his business was coming along—which buddies had jumped at the chance to come work for him. How many felons he'd collared this week. Fall into bed at night wrapped in his arms—his large firm muscles above her. Driving her into the bed. Then, wake the next morning, still entwined. Do it all over, again.

Another reason she hadn't called. While he'd given her clear signs he was interested, he hadn't—once—made a physical play. Hadn't tried to kiss her. Push her against a wall. Strip her down. It was just coffee and talk and...

Crap. Why hadn't she realized it before? She was stuck pushing thirty in the friend zone. She didn't want the friend zone. Didn't want calm and collected. She wanted crazy. Wanted insane speeds and huge leaps of faith. Wanted her chest tight, breath held, muscles primed—balancing on the edge, never knowing if they'd make it or just fall.

And she wanted it with Cannon. Rick Sloan. Ex-Delta

Force soldier and the guy haunting her dreams. Waking and otherwise.

Her phone chirped, and she looked down.

Sorry, Jer. Shauna showed up, and we're actually talking. But, I'll be there. Just hold out a bit longer. An hour, tops. I want to make this right.

Damn it!

How was she supposed to reply to that and *not* come across as a bitch? Become the asshole in their unofficial partnership?

Jericho tapped a token reply. She'd give him one hour. Exactly. Then, she'd leave—kick his ass in the morning if he didn't show up. Or, better, let Cannon do it. The guy was itching to—had it in his head that Dave was putting her safety at risk. Which, honestly, maybe he was—a bit. He was definitely distracted. Brooding. Lacking in any real form of communication. But...she owed him the benefit of the doubt, didn't she? Wasn't that what partners did for each other? Had their backs when shit went sideways? Gave them a chance at redemption?

Endless chances where Dave was concerned.

I want to make this right.

That's why she'd stay. Loyalty. On the chance he really did want to talk—confide in her. She knew, firsthand, how hard that was. Making yourself vulnerable. So, she'd order a drink—wait it out. Then, at least she could say that she'd given it her best shot.

She glanced at her phone, wondering if Cannon was back in town, yet. He'd been away for the past three days —had it only been three? If felt as if she hadn't seen him in weeks. Years. Maybe it was like being in some alternate reality where time passed differently. Cannon space.

Either way, he'd been helping some buddies in Montana or something. Brothers, he'd said. But he'd planned on being back tonight.

She could text him. Or call. No, not call. Not going there. She'd already decided that. Not unless it was an emergency. Life or death. Even if she wanted to call. Listen to the way he said her name—god, it shouldn't turn her on that much.

Alcohol. That's what she needed. A stiff drink to take her mind off of waiting. Off of needing to call Cannon— see if he could stop by for a nightcap. Give him a chance to make a move. She really wanted him to make a move.

The waiter stopped at her table, again, refilling her water. She thanked him then grabbed her purse. An hour's worth of water and pop required her attention. Especially if she was going to be waiting another hour. And she knew Dave would take the full hour, if he showed, at all. It was a given. The same way she knew Cannon would bust down the door if she needed him to. Knowledge that went soul deep.

She headed for the restrooms, thankful that it was a private room and not some multi-stall bathroom. She appreciated the solitude—a chance to splash some water on her face. Get her head on straight. Ever since she'd met Cannon, she'd been floundering. Distracted. As if there was a part of her always trying to tune into his frequency. Hear it above the white noise. A romantic version of a dog whistle only she could detect.

Which sounded crazy. But fitting since the man made her feel exactly that. As if her skin didn't quite fit without him touching it. No matter how innocently. She'd be sitting there at coffee, feeling edgy, one foot tapping the floor until he'd put a hand on her arm. Or shoulder. Or simply brush his fingers against hers. And everything would settle. Like bringing an image into focus.

Maybe Dave wasn't the problem. Maybe it was her. Maybe she was the one who was putting both their safety at risk. Not that she had any idea how to fix it. What she felt for Cannon—she doubted it would ease any time soon.

She hung her head, breathing slowly in and out, when shouts arose beyond the door. Something clattered to the floor, glass breaking in the distance. She placed her purse on the sink then grabbed her gun, badge and phone. She slipped her phone into her back pocket, clipped her star and holster on her belt, then headed for the door, gun drawn but at her side. She dropped her purse against the wall behind the door, so it wouldn't be visible if someone checked the area after she was gone. More shouts sounded from the dining area, followed by footsteps down the hallway outside the restroom—the one she knew led to the kitchen area and the rear entrance.

Which only increased the twitchy feeling in her gut. She'd been involved in enough takedowns to recognize the makings of a bad situation. Either the cops or the feds were raiding the joint, or something else was going down.

Jericho cracked open the door—slowly, so the hinges wouldn't creak—then took a quick peek out. The hallway was dark. Deserted, despite the fact she knew there had been two lights on when she'd entered the restroom. Voices echoed from the dining room. Male. Harsh. What sounded like threats.

A hint of movement flashed in her peripheral vision, and she inched back in, ducking behind the door. Gun poised at her shoulder. Back pressed into the wall. Footsteps outside, then the handle rattled. Twisted. The door opened, not quite touching her as it stopped at a forty-five. Heavy breathing sounded on the other side, some guy muttering a few words she couldn't make out.

She didn't move, breath held, finger inside the trigger guard, until the door closed, someone shouting, "Clear."

More steps away, then the din of a man talking loudly in the background. God, she hated being right. But she needed more intel before she called for backup. Before turning this into a hostage situation if it wasn't already heading that way.

The door didn't make a sound as she opened it, checking the hallway then slipping out. The dining area was ahead of her, on the other side of a short wall. She made her way to the archway, using the reflections in the glass to evaluate the situation. A number of men were spaced out amidst the patrons, arms crossed—handguns shoved down the front of their pants. They hadn't drawn, but she had no doubts they would, if given a reason.

"Is that everyone?"

Damn. She recognized the voice. The southern drawl mixed with more nasal than was pleasant. She shifted sideways, getting a glimpse of the man in the mirror behind the bar area. Patrick Wilson. The guy was a known arms dealer, drug runner, and was suspected in over a dozen murders, including two officers. But he'd been picked up on a petty breaking-and-entering charge. Had either bought or threatened his way into a fairly low bail then simply ditched his court date. Some new evidence had upped the charges against him to manslaughter, aggravated assault, and grand larceny. He was one of the few felons on the U.S. Marshal's Most Wanted list. She'd nearly caught his ass two months ago, but he'd disappeared.

Until now.

Jericho surveyed the dining room. Two families were shoved into a couple of booths over by the kitchen entrance, with a handful of couples scattered around the floor. Maybe twenty people, and way too many for her liking. No way she could take a stand and not risk anyone getting hurt.

Patrick grabbed one of the waiters and shoved him against the bar. "I said, are you sure this is everyone?"

The man gulped then nodded.

"My colleague said he saw another woman in here."

"N-n-n-no. No one, else."

"Then, why is there a glass of water at that table?"

Crap. If the server admitted she'd been there, they'd scour the place. Maybe start shooting people until she stepped out.

The waiter shook his head. "She left. Got stood-up by her date. I saw her grab her purse."

She focused on Patrick. On the way his hands fisted at his sides and how his head kept twitching to the left— ready to do whatever was necessary if he decided to open fire. She could clip at least four or five of them before the rest finished drawing. Which still left more than enough men to kill everyone in the place.

Patrick sneered. "Left, huh? You'd better not be lying."

The waiter shook his head, crumpling to the floor when Patrick punched him.

"I have some business to attend to. If everyone just sits quietly, this'll all be over soon. But, if I get even an inkling that you've called the cops. If I see any lights. A uniform. So much as a big black van pull up either in front or out back, I'll kill everyone in the room."

He waved a gun around then disappeared through a door. Office, maybe.

Jericho made her way back to the restroom, clearing inside then removing her phone. She hit Dave's number, cursing when it went directly to voicemail. She left him a detailed message then called Art.

The man answered on the second ring. "A bit late for a social call, isn't it, Jericho?"

"I'm at Malone's. Between ten and twelve armed men. Patrick Wilson's in the back. Says he'll kill everyone if he even thinks he sees a cop or a SWAT truck. He's not bluffing. I saw his face."

The man mumbled something in the background as a chair scraped out. She heard boots against a wood floor, a door creak. "Where are you positioned?"

"Ladies' room. They came in while I was washing my hands. I've got two families and another dozen people. Looks like the front door's been locked. Lights heading to the rear entrance are out. I'm betting he has men stationed in the alley. Maybe on the roof or across the street out front. Alert him if anyone remotely officer-like even breathes on this place. I'm alone."

"Well, shit." Was that a car door chime? "They know you're there?"

"Not yet. Hoping to keep it that way."

"Sit tight. I'll rally SOG. But it'll be a good twenty minutes before we get there."

SOG. The Marshal Service's Special Operations Group.

A unit of highly trained and disciplined officers. The kind that didn't back down.

"First off, those boys are exactly what he'll be looking for. Second, I don't think we have twenty minutes. I won't engage, but if he looks like he's going to start shooting…"

"Don't do anything rash. You hear me?"

"Me? Do something rash?"

"Where's Dave?"

"Hopefully on his way. He was supposed to meet me here. I couldn't reach him. Left a message."

"We'll be there as soon as possible. I'll notify local law. Keep them at a safe distance. Make sure some rookie doesn't accidentally drop by for a drink."

"Get here soon, or this is going to end bloody. Though, I doubt it'll go any other way."

He snorted then hung up, the dead silence on the other end of her phone feeling like an omen of what was to come. She cursed when more shouting echoed through the door, something else falling heavily to the floor.

None of them were going to last twenty minutes. While she'd never do anything to endanger civilians, she knew Patrick Wilson well enough to understand that he didn't leave witnesses behind. She'd have to stay out of sight. Wait until he was getting ready to leave then try to buy more time.

She removed her Beretta from her ankle holster. Two guns. More than enough firepower. But, ironically, not nearly enough to get her out of this. Neither was suppressed. They'd know she was there the moment she fired. So hunting them down one-by-one wasn't going to work. She palmed her phone, again, hitting Cannon's contact.

"Jericho? Everything all right?"

God, just hearing his voice. It calmed the fluttering in her stomach. Stilled the slight tremor in her hands. "Where are you?"

"Just closing in on my office. Why?"

"I'm at Malone's. It's bad, Cannon. Epically bad."

Tires screeched in her ear, the hum in the background revving higher. "Lay it out for me, sweetheart."

"I've got ten, maybe twelve armed men. More in the alley out back. Probably across the street or on the roof. Along with Patrick Wilson."

A pause then a huff. "I'm familiar with the name. You safe?"

"For now. There's close to two dozen people in here. I'm alone. I've called in the cavalry, but it's twenty minutes out. And, if he sees anyone, and I mean anyone, he thinks is a cop..."

Not that Cannon looked like a cop. Mercenary, maybe. Assassin, definitely. But not a cop.

"Understood. I'm five minutes away. Try not to engage, but if you do, torso shots. Take out Wilson and the men nearest to him. He'll keep his best guys close. You might get lucky. Have the others scatter when his main force starts dropping. Keep something between you and them if you can. You can't save folks if you're dead."

"There are kids, here, Cannon. I'll try to buy time if he looks like he's going to start killing people, but... I can't..."

Had he just sworn under his breath?

"Guys like him like to hear themselves talk."

"If he sees you, he'll open fire."

A snort. "No one's going to see me until it's too late. Four minutes."

"Counting down."

She ended the call, just as a gunshot boomed through the air. She cursed then headed out, sticking to the shadows. Sobs sounded from within the room, then Patrick's voice.

"I told you all to stay still. Do you see what happens when you don't listen? Seems like you all might have a hearing problem."

She glanced in the room. Only the two men next to Patrick had their guns drawn, the others still standing idly around the room, chests pushed out. Arms crossed. They seemed amused. The window near the front door was splattered with blood, a body lying in a heap behind a toppled chair.

She checked her watch.

Three minutes.

She started mentally counting, drew a deep breath, then eased forward—gun leading the way. "I'm going to have to ask you gentlemen to remain calm."

Gasps lit the air, the men's heads snapping up.

"Ah, ah, ah, the first person to go for their gun gets dropped." She stepped out just enough to see the five men standing close to Wilson. "So, just keep your hands where I can see them."

Wilson focused on her, a smug smile tilting his lips. "Deputy U.S. Marshal Nash? Well, I'll be damned. What are the chances you'd be here? Haven't see you in... what?"

"About two months. Since I chased your ass down that alley. Nice touch. Running into that bar. Knowing I wouldn't risk an armed assault in a crowd. Thought you might have had the good sense to leave Seattle. Guess I was wrong."

She huffed, watching the reflection of one of his men edging his way along the small wall separating her from the right side of the dining room. "I swear, if the man on the other side of this wall takes one more step, I'll shoot him through it."

Patrick waved his hand—stopping the guy. "That was your table. The one with the water glass."

Two minutes.

"In the waiter's defense. I did get stood-up, and I did grab my purse. Now, as I see it, there's three ways this can go down."

He arched a brow. "Is that right? Why don't you explain them for me."

"One, you all surrender, and I arrest you. Very civil. No one else gets hurt."

He laughed. "Two?"

"We all draw down, and very few of us leave here alive."

He glanced around, nodding at his men. "Or three?"

She motioned toward the door. "You and your men leave. We continue this conversation another day."

"Leave? You're just gonna stand there and let me walk out of here?"

"That's right. And I bet by the time I follow you out that door, you'll be long gone."

"That doesn't sound very marshal-like. Letting me go."

"I'm off-duty. Do we have an understanding?"

"I've got ten men with me."

"Pretty sure I counted eleven." She focused on his face, firing off a round through the wall when his man lunged toward the side. The bullet hit him in the side, dropping him to the floor.

She smirked. "Sorry. You were right. Make that ten men."

Wilson looked at the guy then back to her. "You can't kill all of us."

One minute.

"Nope. But I'll kill at least four of you before any of your men finishing drawing. Clip another two before I go down. Is this really worth dying over?"

"Who says I'll be dead?"

"You'll be the third person I kill, after those two men at your side. The ones with their guns already out. Who are itching to fire, again. But their hands are shaking. You don't let them use, do you? Drugs might make them fearless, but it affects their reflexes. Their aim. That kind of spoils the whole fearless part."

"Maybe they're just anxious to get this show started."

"Anxious to die?"

"We all die, Marshal."

"I wasn't planning on doing it, today. Were you, Mr. Wilson? Because that's the only way this is going to end if you don't take option number three."

Patrick looked at the men standing next to him—the ones with their guns clasped in front of them by their waists. Hands trembling ever so slightly. Eyes wide—a bit glazed. "Can I think on it for a minute?"

Zero.

"Something tells me we might not have that much

time before one of them makes the decision for you." She stared Wilson directly in the eyes. "So...what's it going to be?"

CHAPTER FIVE

Three days.

That's how long Cannon had been gone. Only seventy-two hours. Barely a blip in time compared to any other mission he'd been on. Case. He needed to remember he wasn't military, anymore, and he didn't have missions. Just cases. Which, this time, had involved a couple of fellow servicemen. Brothers. They'd needed some extra muscle—someone they could trust with their lives. Who could shoot. Fight. Take a beating, if necessary, and keep going—and Cannon had been happy to help out. Hell, he owed Ice, one of the guys working for another company, his life. Russel Foster, aka Ice to his buddies, had needed some intel, and Cannon had jumped at the chance to remove a bit more of the red ink from his ledger. Even the score a bit.

Not that he'd come close, yet. Ice had dragged Cannon's ass—literally—for miles through hostile territory to a landing zone. Had nearly gotten killed more than once in the process—not to mention having to eliminate several tangos along the way—just to bring Cannon back. That kind of debt didn't go away with a few token good deeds. Maybe not a lifetime's worth. But he'd give it his best shot. Be the kind of man that could shake Ice's hand—look at himself in the mirror and like what was staring back.

The kind of man Jericho would be proud to stand beside.

Jericho.

That was an entire nest full of vipers Cannon didn't know how handle. Not without getting bitten. Though, part of him suspected he'd already succumbed to the poison. The kind that messed with his head. Had him tied in knots. Wishing for things he'd never considered.

Thirty-two days since she'd rocked his world inside that bar. Jumpstarted the heart he thought he'd left in the desert. Burned and buried under a shit ton of sand, blood, and death. Yet, there it was, beating inside his chest. Threatening to stop every time he saw her. And that smile…

It was like standing in the midst of a storm, only to have the sun break through for one mesmerizing heartbeat. All its light and warmth just shining down on him. The eye of the hurricane. It made him feel…

He scrubbed a hand down his face. Feel. How long had it been since he'd felt anything? Had given himself permission to indulge in thoughts that went beyond the mission? Beyond keeping his teammates alive? Beyond the next five minutes?

He wasn't sure he ever had. Yet, after a month of having coffee with her damn near every morning, he couldn't hide from the truth any longer. He was crazy about the lady. Her courage, her honor. She was smart and compassionate and so damn beautiful, his chest physically hurt just being around her. He couldn't remember what it was like to go to bed not thinking about her, smelling her perfume on his clothes, hearing her voice inside his head. Or to wake up without having spent the night dreaming about all the ways he wanted to touch her. Wanting to hear her voice, even if all she said was his name. She was quickly becoming a drug he couldn't live without.

Not that he'd told her, yet. At first, he'd been convinced it was more mutual respect. She'd helped him get his business off the ground, and she was a hell of a resource. Had offered him insight into viable office locations and how to obtain a few special permits from local law enforcement.

But the more time he spent with her, the more he needed to spend. It wasn't enough to simply meet with her for an hour every morning. Now, he was texting. Was dropping by her office on his way home—ensuring she was okay. Offering his aid if she ever needed it. Anything and everything to be around her.

The jig was up. He couldn't pretend any longer. At least, not if he wanted to stay sane. Hell, even Ice and Rigs—another buddy Cannon had teamed up with the past three days—had recognized that something was different about him. That he was distracted. Not to the point it compromised the mission—case—but enough they'd mentioned it. Had asked if he was "okay"? If there was anything he needed to "talk" about? Soldier speak that was loosely translated into them questioning his focus.

He'd gotten the job done. Had kept a bullet from

finding Rigs' head, but... They knew. And it seemed about time Jericho knew.

Cannon took a deep breath. God, here he was, nearly back at his office—the one Jericho had helped him find. Perfect for his needs, and in a part of town no one would question his undertakings—and he would have sworn he was scared. Actually fucking scared.

He hadn't blinked when he'd had to out himself to save a fellow soldier—a SEAL who'd somehow survived a firefight. Had managed to drag his ass across a mountain, only to get captured. Cannon had been stone cold steel taking the men out with only his hands. Hadn't felt much of anything killing the rest of the cell. But the thought of telling Jericho he had serious feelings for her—that he wanted more than coffee dates and late-night texts. That he fucking needed her in his arms, his bed, his damn life if he had any hope of breathing—*that* sluiced ice down his veins. Made his palms clammy, his damn pulse race. And all because he didn't know for sure she felt the same.

Which was stupid. He hadn't been removed from society to the point he didn't recognize mutual attraction. The way her skin blushed, or how her breathing sped up. The flutter of her pulse at the base of her neck. The waver in her voice. The dreamy look in her eyes. He knew she wasn't meeting with him out of obligation or platonic friendship, even if he had kept her on the other side. The non-physical one. She was interested. He just needed a plan.

Good. He excelled at making plans. Strategizing. All he needed to do was treat this like any other op. Figure out the steps required to take their relationship to the next level then execute them. He already had her attention. Her number. Next, he needed to ask her on a real date. Dinner. Maybe some dancing. A walk on along the wharf would be nice. Give him an excuse to hold her hand. Lend her his coat. He'd invite her inside. Make sure he had her brand of cooler on hand, then...

His phone rang. And not just any ringtone. One he hadn't heard before. The one he'd reserved for her. That he'd practically been begging her to use.

He glanced at his watch as he hit the accept button on his navigation screen. "Jericho? Everything all right?"

Was she breathing hard? Because she sounded winded even before she'd said anything. "Where are you?"

He read the road sign as he crossed over Holgate Street. "Just closing in on my office. Why?"

Shit, she was definitely breathing hard. And there was a waver in her voice—fear. It was definitely fear. Not a lot. In fact, he doubted anyone else would pick up on it. But he did. He'd spent the past month hanging on every word she said. In putting her pitch, her tone, her damn intonation into his memory. He'd recognize any change in her voice, subtle or otherwise.

"I'm at Malone's. It's bad, Cannon. Epically bad."

He hit the gas, fishtailing his truck around the next left. Somehow avoiding the curb and taxi idling on the side as he accelerated toward the outer section of the warehouse district. What the fuck was she doing at Malone's? Only local gang or mob families ate there. No sense getting into a gunfight just to eat a burger—no matter how great it was. Not if there wasn't a friend's life or bounty involved. "Lay it out for me, sweetheart."

She breathed into the phone. Calm but just knowing she was in danger... "I've got ten, maybe twelve armed men. More in the alley out back. Probably across the street or on the roof. Along with Patrick Wilson."

Fuck. He knew Patrick Wilson. Asshole was bad news. Wasn't much the man wasn't involved in, including killing a couple of cops. They'd nabbed him on some lame-ass charge, and he'd bought his way out. Cannon also knew the charges had gotten harsher over the past couple of months. That Wilson was on more than one most wanted list. Which meant he had nothing to lose. Cannon had planned on going hunting for the man after he'd gotten back. "I'm familiar with the name. You safe?"

"For now. There's close to two dozen people in here. I'm alone. I've called in the cavalry, but it's twenty minutes out. And, if he sees anyone, and I mean anyone, he thinks is a cop..."

"Understood." He barreled around the next corner, cutting through a paved path along some small park then jumping onto the next street—dirt spraying across the asphalt. Birds squawking as they scattered into the air. "I'm five minutes away. Try not to engage, but if you do, torso shots. Take out Wilson and the men nearest to him. He'll keep his best guys close. You might get lucky. Have the others scatter when his main force starts dropping. Keep something between you and them if you can. You can't save folks if you're dead."

Jericho. Dead. Fuck, he couldn't think that way. Couldn't say the two words together, because if he thought, for a second, he wouldn't get there in time—that he'd arrive to find her limp on the floor, her blood pooled beneath her —he'd lose it. Right there in the cab of his truck.

"There are kids, here, Cannon. I'll try to buy time if he

looks like he's going to start killing people, but... I can't..."

Shit. Which was her way of saying she'd do anything—sacrifice herself without hesitation—if there was even a remote chance she could save a kid. Not that he blamed her. He'd do the same.

"Guys like him, like to hear themselves talk."

"If he sees you, he'll open fire."

See him? No. That wasn't going to happen. "No one's going to see me until it's too late. Four minutes."

"Counting down."

She disconnected, the sudden silence making his throat close tight. His hands fisted around the steering wheel. He was only a minute out, but depending on how much resistance he faced, he could still be more than a couple away from breaching the dining room. From being close enough to save her. Take down whoever was aiming at her—take a bullet meant for her. He'd take one for a stranger. For her...

He'd face Hell for her.

Cannon pulled up a block away, already sliding out of the truck as it rocked to a halt. He circled around to the flatbed, opening the tailgate then the black bag stashed in the back. He quickly donned a vest—patting down the pockets as he double checked his weapons. Ka-Bars. Two on each side, another two strapped to his shoulder blades. Handguns—M9 with suppressor left holster, Glock 19 right. Walther in his ankle holster if the situation got desperate. He had three extra clips for each in the pockets spaced around his waist. One more in his left boot. He rounded out the items with a couple of smoke bombs, a flashbang, some duct tape, zip ties, and a small amount of C4—he was ready.

He glanced at his watch. Three minutes since she'd ended the call. That gave him one minute to deal with Wilson's men positioned on the outside and make his way to Jericho before he was pushing the time frame he'd given her. Time she didn't have. Hell, it could already be too late.

Fuck that. He'd never failed a mission, and he'd be damned if he'd start, now. Jericho was his. Anyone who messed with her had to go through him, first. It didn't matter that he hadn't told her. Hadn't made a move. She'd been his the moment they'd met, and everything between then and now had just been him learning how to be human, again. How to be the kind of man she deserved.

As opposed to the one who was quick-stepping down the alley. Blending in with the shadows. Narrowing in on the back entrance. He spotted Wilson's first guy standing by the door. Asshole wasn't even trying to hide. Probably had something to do with the second guy patrolling by the dumpster off to his right. The sniper Wilson had poised on the roof. The one who seemed to think his head wasn't visible above the edge of the building.

He checked his watch. Thirty seconds.

Took him two more to eliminate the sniper—move into position on the opposite side of the door. The guy by the dumpster turned, went down without making a sound. Another two seconds, and Cannon was at the door, watchman in a choke hold. Fingers clawing at Cannon's arms—trying to loosen his grip.

At ten seconds, the asshole was unconscious on the cement, hands zip-tied. Mouth taped shut. One leg twitched, but it didn't matter. It would be over by the time he came to.

Cannon eased the door open, scanning the short hallway then darting inside. He got three steps in when another man popped out of the darkness, eyes wide, mouth gaping open. He turned then dropped, blood splattering across the wallpaper on the far wall. The suppressor keeping all but a dull whoosh from alerting the rest of the crew. Cannon grabbed a leg and yanked the guy back, leaving him in the shadows. Voices sounded from the other end of a long hallway, too muffled to make out.

He moved up the corridor, tossing a knife at another man standing in the kitchen door. The guy gasped as he stumbled back, tripping against a counter. Cannon slipped inside, silencing him with a quick jab to the side of the head. He crumpled, barely making a sound as Cannon caught most of his weight then slowly lowered him to the floor.

Sixty seconds.

Which meant Jericho was out of time.

He returned to hallway, cursing when her voice echoed through the air. She was laying out the options—buying him more time. Smart lady. He hadn't been joking. Men like Wilson liked to be in control. Show off. And that was their downfall—talking when they should be shooting. There was a single shot that damn near stopped Cannon's heart until he heard her voice, again. Then, he was moving. He was zoned in. Primed. He took four steps and was at the corner. Saw the assholes standing next to Wilson raise their guns. Saw Jericho off to the left, half-hidden behind a small wall. Her reflection in the glass mapping out her actions. The flex of her muscles as she pulled the trigger.

She caught both men before they could fire, bodies flipping backward. Hitting a counter then falling to the floor. She was aiming at Wilson—was a breath away from shooting him, when two men she couldn't see aimed at her.

Cannon moved. Capped both men before they got their fingers inside the guards. Took out two more as they turned—attention divided. In less than ten seconds, it was over. Wilson was on the floor. Bloody patch on his shoulder and chest. Gun lying useless beside him.

Jericho twisted—aimed her gun his way before inhaling. She stood there, frozen for two heartbeats before nodding and lowering her arms. He scanned the room, slowly moving toward her, gun at the ready. He kicked some guy lying beside a wall when he looked as if he might be reaching for his gun—or maybe he was trying to shift to breathe better. Didn't matter. Movement meant a possible threat, and he didn't leave any of those alive or unbound to bite him in the ass later.

Jericho glanced at his gun then back to him, brow arched as she motioned toward the children cowering in the far corner. He sighed, slowly holstering it, when something flashed behind her.

"Jericho. Move."

She reacted instantly, dodging left as the report boomed through the room. She spun as she hit the set of windows, but Cannon already had his knife drawn. Had tossed it at the fucker behind her, catching him in the throat. The guy's feet shot forward as he reeled backwards, landing in a spray of blood. He made a muffled gurgling sound then stilled.

Cannon had his gun back out and was at Jericho's side before she could do more than stare at the downed man. He knew she didn't want to scare the patrons in the room, the kids, but they'd have to deal with it until backup arrived. He shouldered up to her, still watching the room. "Area's not clear, yet. At least, not that we know for sure. Stick to my back until your unit arrives."

Another nod, followed by a hiss. He glanced at her, noting the patch of blood on her arm. Not big but just seeing the red highlighted against the white made his stomach roil.

"You hit?"

She looked at him then down at her arm—as if just now noticing—before motioning him off. "Just a scratch. I'm fine. Especially considering how this could have turned out."

He frowned at the raised pitch of her voice. The waver. Similar to how it had been on the phone. Again, it wasn't something most people would pick up on. But he wasn't most people. And he'd heard it. It wasn't fear, this time. Shock mixed with pain. Adrenaline dump. A combination of all three. Either way, she needed to decompress before it hit her any harder.

"Okay, we'll get everyone calmed down, then go room by room."

"I'll—"

The door crashed open, glass splintering through the room. Men dressed in black gear, the words U.S. Marshal printed out in yellow block letters across their vests, swarming through. They had assault rifles sweeping the room, yelling at everyone to get down. Four men circled him and Jericho, muzzles pointed at their chests, expressions hard.

Cannon raised his hands, allowing them to take his gun, turn him toward the windows. This was just part of the process. A way of keeping the unit safe, even if he was one of the good guys. But, having been in their shoes—not knowing who to trust. If one of the armed assailants was masquerading as help in order to make a run for it—he didn't resist. Jericho grunted as she hit the wall beside him, hands braced to either side.

Cannon glanced at the men over his shoulder. One guy seemed more edgy than the rest, even for a specialty officer. Someone caught in the current situation. It made Cannon antsy in return—wondering if the guy had something to hide. "Are you so damn blind you don't even recognize one of your own? Jericho's a Deputy Marshal, you dumb twats."

That guy grabbed Cannon's vest and rammed him harder against the windows. "If I were you, I wouldn't give me a reason to shoot you. The Supervisory Deputy will be here in a moment. He can clear everything up. Until then, everyone's a suspect. And, if you so much as twitch, I'll kill you. Both of you."

Cannon nodded toward the families cowering on the floor. "Pretty sure the ten-year-old isn't part of the crew."

"You'd be surprised."

"Actually, son, I doubt he would be. Not after all he's witnessed." Art moved into view. "They're both clean. And Mr. Sloan's right. You should recognize Jericho, Andrews. Show some respect."

Andrews eyed them then left, making the rounds of the downed men.

Art shook his head. "Sorry about that. SOG guys tend to take everything to the extreme. Andrews, especially. Guy's got a pretty short fuse. But that's kind of the point of having them around." He motioned to Jericho's arm. "You okay?"

She grimaced but nodded. "It's only a graze. I'll be fine."

Art waved a medic over. "See that gets cleaned and bandaged. God knows she won't do it, herself. Lest she admit she's not bulletproof." He turned to Cannon. "I'd like to say I'm surprised to see you here, but... I'm going to need statements. From everyone. And we'll all need to take a trip to the office. Straighten out the details. Afraid I'll have to keep your gun until we can run a ballistics test. Yours, too, Jericho. Strictly routine. You'll have it back tomorrow." He leaned in closer to Cannon. "You *do* realize you're not authorized to shoot people, don't you, Mr. Sloan?"

"Seemed like a good idea at the time. Authorized or not."

Jericho brushed off the medic's hand. "Art. This is on me. You know I called him."

Art waved it away. "Let's just get this cleaned up. We'll talk back at the office. I'll have someone drive your Wrangler. You can ride with Cannon—see you both make it there..." He paused when Dave stormed through the door. "Faraday. Nice of you to show up."

Dave glanced at Cannon then Jericho. "Jesus Christ, I pull up, expecting to have a drink, and all hell's broken loose. What the fuck happened? And why is he here?"

Art stepped in front of Dave, holding him back. "We'll figure this out back at the office. For now, just help with the statements. The cleanup."

Dave huffed but moved off, joining the other marshals working their way through the patrons.

Art turned to her. "Stop giving the medic a hard time. Once he's finished, have a seat. Catch your breath. I'll be back when it's time to leave."

Cannon snagged a chair then stared at Jericho until she begrudgingly sat. He pulled one over for himself, ensuring they weren't in front of the windows—just in case. He watched the marshals work the crowd, constantly checking on Jericho. She seemed distant. Strangely quiet. Not that he blamed her. What she'd just gone through...

Which was why he didn't ask her the multitude of questions racing through his mind. Why she'd been at Malone's. Why Dave was just showing up, now. If she felt half as edgy as he did. But not from the shootout. It was her.

Sitting there, worrying if she was really okay. If she'd somehow gotten mixed up in something dangerous without realizing it. If she wanted him to hold her as much as he needed to. That not putting his arms around her, taking her hand in his, was using up a year's worth of restraint. That he wanted nothing more than to hike her up over his shoulder and march out—take her home. Love away the shadows beneath her eyes. The white cast to her skin.

Instead, he sat there. Unmoving. Silent. Minutes. Hours. Days. It didn't matter. He'd wait. He hated waiting. Considered himself a man of action. That's what he'd been trained for. Constantly adapting. Staying ahead of the threat. Never giving the enemy time to regroup. But, sometimes, *that* required doing nothing at all. Staying in the same four-foot box for days on end, observing. Calculating. He didn't like it, but he was good at it.

So, he sat there, close enough she felt his presence— the heat from his body. The steady whisper of his breath— but not touching her. Stimulating her because that was the last thing she needed. Her eyes were still wide, overly white. As if the irises had shrunken down to small pinpoints of intense green. And he didn't miss the way she fisted one hand—banged it on her thigh as it bounced a bit.

She was edgy. Hyper aware. Of sounds, smells, sights. Touching her, now, would be the equivalent of scraping a knife across her skin. Which brought him back to where she needed to decompress. Somewhere quiet. Limited lighting. Not that she would probably get a chance. But he'd do what he could.

The medic gave her the okay then headed toward the gathering of people. Jericho gazed over at him, gave him a small smile, then tapped her phone. She stood, despite his encouragement to keep her ass on the chair, walking a few steps away as she spoke into the cell. He caught a name— Uncle Jack—before the background noise drowned out her voice.

Not exactly how he'd envisioned the night would go. Though, looking around, it struck him how much worse it could have ended. How easy it was to picture Jericho on the ground, her shirt covered in blood. Eyes dull. Unseeing. He'd seen ten lifetime's worth of death, and knowing he could have lost her...

He closed his eyes, opening them when her hand

landed on his shoulder. He didn't even need to see her to know it was her. The faint scent of her perfume, the way her fingers curled around his muscles. The distinct pattern of her breathing. He knew.

He smiled as he stared up at her—still so fucking beautiful—covering her hand with his. He waited to see if even that was still too much, but after her initial sharp inhale, she settled.

She motioned to her boss. "Art said we can head back to the office."

He stood, shifting her hand into his. He didn't care if people were looking. What they might think. All that mattered was her cold hand pressed against his. Proof he hadn't failed.

He palmed the small of her back with his other hand, still keeping his touch light. "I'm parked a block away. I'd suggest we go out the back but..."

"But there are probably a bunch of dead bodies in the way, right?"

"I didn't have time to be choosy on how I eliminated them. Just that they went down."

"God, Cannon. I'm not judging. I mean, you..." She swallowed. Noisily. As if it took more effort than usual. "We can walk around."

"Then, follow me."

CHAPTER SIX

God, his hand was so large. So strong. So...warm.

Jericho sighed when Cannon gave her fingers a squeeze, slotting them around his as he gave her one of his killer smiles then headed for the front door.

Killer. It took on a whole new meaning, now. Not that she hadn't known what he was capable of before. She'd talked to her uncle. Knew other veterans. Hell, her father had died in the service. But nothing compared to seeing Cannon in action.

He'd just appeared. Shadows one second, his body stepping out of them the next. He hadn't hesitated—taking the assailants down with his M9. One shot. That's all he'd used on each man. Though, he'd told her to go for the torso—something she would have done, regardless. Biggest target. Guaranteed to drop them unless they'd been wearing armor, which she'd been pretty damn sure they hadn't—he'd tapped them each in the head. And he hadn't even blinked.

Hadn't been sweating when he'd tossed the knife at

the guy who'd snuck up behind her. A flash of silver and a thump. That's all she'd seen or heard. Then, he'd been at her side—putting himself between her and any possible attack—all the while still scanning the room. Hands steady.

Her hands were steady, now, too. At least, the one he was holding was. The other...

She tucked it in her jeans' pocket. She didn't want to know if it was trembling. If she was merely cold because the weather had changed. Had started raining. Or if it was something else. She needed to believe she was just as calm, just as detached, as Cannon appeared.

For a moment, she'd thought he'd been worried. Had looked at her as if he hadn't thought he'd ever see her, again. Eyes wide. His skin slightly pale. Then, it had vanished. The way she knew he could if he wanted. That he could have been long gone before the SOG team had arrived. But he never would have left her. Not even if he'd been convinced the threat was over. He'd made that clear. He'd rather go to jail than leave her side.

He wouldn't go to jail. She'd seen to that, personally. Had done the one thing she'd sworn she'd never do. Had avoided since she'd decided to go into law enforcement. First, as a cop, then the shift to the Marshal Service. But... It was Cannon. And he'd saved her life. Had been willing to die for her. She needed to return the favor, even if it meant asking for help.

"Sweetheart?"

She gave herself a mental shake, coming back to her senses as he leaned toward her. She glanced around. They were at his Chevy. Though, she didn't remember walking down the alley. Wasn't sure how long they'd been standing beside the passenger door. Waiting.

She sighed. "Sorry. I was thinking."

"I'm familiar with the feeling. Let's get you inside and warmed up. You're shivering."

She was? His coat settled around her shoulders. Heavy. Warm. Infused with the aroma of pine forest and man. His scent. She frowned. Hadn't he been wearing a vest?

She arched a brow. "You don't have to give me your coat because you're a guy and I'm a girl, ya know."

Another smile that flip-flopped her stomach. Made her slightly lightheaded. "Then, I'll give it to you because I'm the boyfriend, and you're *my* girl."

Boyfriend? *His* girl? Had he seriously just said that? Or had she imagined it? Words wrought from stress and wishful thinking. She went to question him, but he had the door open and was lifting her in before she could get any words to form on her tongue. Then, his door opened, and the engine turned over—heat already pouring out the vents. Had it still been warm from when he'd driven back from Montana? How long had they been inside the restaurant?

Damn, she was zoning in and out. Losing track of time. Something she never did. It's not as if tonight had been her first firefight. The first time she'd had to shoot someone. Been shot at. There wasn't any reason that it should be different. Other than the fact she'd honestly thought she was going to die. That Cannon wouldn't make it in time. Or he'd decide she wasn't worth risking his career—his life—over.

Maybe that's why she felt off. Guilt, over not fully believing in him. Though it had only been coffee dates, a few stops by her office—he'd never, once, let her down. And she'd harbored doubts when it had mattered the most.

Looked like another test she'd failed.

His hand covered hers. "You want to talk?"

She gazed over at him. Lips pressed together, eyes narrowed—he looked lethal. No suave secret agent. He was pure warrior. A hard man who was accustomed to doing hard things. Yet, the way he held her hand—brushing his thumb along her knuckles... She wasn't sure any man had touched her that gently. As if he knew she was overly sensitive.

Cannon sighed, alternating his attention between her and the road—when had they started moving? "It's normal."

"What's normal?"

God, her voice sounded raw. All low and scratchy. As if it had taken all her strength just to get those two words out. But if he'd noticed, he didn't show it. Didn't react. Instead, he let go of her hand for a second to turn the heat up a bit more then clasped her fingers in his, again.

"Feeling disjointed. That wasn't your typical arrest. At least, I hope to hell it wasn't. That..." He shook his head. "That was a battle. Facing off against ten men on your own—"

"I wasn't alone. You were there."

"But you didn't know I'd arrived until you'd already confronted them. Drawn your weapon. Made peace with the fact you couldn't take them all out before they started shooting back. Watching you..." He focused on her. "I've never been so damn proud and scared in my life."

Jericho tilted her head, staring into those copper eyes. Had he really been scared? "Do you ever get used to it?"

"Being shot at?"

"Killing people. I know it was justified. That I gave them a chance to walk out, but..."

Crap. Her voice just faded. The words stuck on a huge lump in her throat.

"Fuck." Cannon swerved over to the curb, shoving his truck in park before unclipping their seatbelts then turning to fully face her.

She blinked a few times. "Cannon?"

He slid closer, his large body taking up most of the space. The air. "There are two ways a person can go. They can either wear their heart a bit too close to the surface. Have it bleed a little every time they have to make a tough choice. Work through a few night's worth of bad dreams and guilt before finally accepting that they did everything they could to alter the outcome. That, in the end, they did what needed to happen to save lives. Uphold justice."

She sat there, staring at him, mesmerized by the lines on his face. The look in his eyes. "Or?"

He swallowed. "Or, you become someone who's stone cold. Who was so busy shoving the bad shit down, they didn't realize it meant they couldn't feel the good. That happiness and love was the price they'd pay for not experiencing the pain. The guilt. That, somewhere along the way, they became the monster they were hunting." He lifted one hand—thumbed her chin. "Don't become the second. Don't shove it all down. Scream. Cry. Go a few rounds in the ring. Blow it off at the shooting range. Hell, talk it out with someone who's in the business. It doesn't matter what it takes, but allow yourself to feel. To express those feelings. Or you'll wake up one day and realize you haven't felt *anything* in a long time. And you'll wonder if you ever can, again."

She reached for him when he went to turn, waiting until his gaze was back on her. She wasn't sure what she wanted to say, only that she needed to say something. Anything to ease the shadows around his eyes. The firm line of his mouth.

She placed one hand on his cheek. "I want to go on a real date. Not just coffee or texting. I want to go out to dinner with you. I want to stare at you across the table. Smile. Flirt. Then, I want you to drive me home, ask to come inside for a nightcap. I'll play it cool, at first. Pretend like I'm not dying for you to kiss me. Take me to bed. But, once the door closes—once we're alone…"

He moved. Slid one hand up her back, into her hair. Tangling it around his fingers as he snaked his other hand around her waist—pulling her flush against him. He lowered his head, hovering his mouth an inch away from hers. Their breath mixing. Then, he was kissing her. Lips molding to hers. Lifting, repositioning, then claiming, again. His tongue delving inside when she moaned. All heat and spice and sinful pleasure. He didn't let up, tugging her even closer once they'd paused to catch their breath.

Her chest flattened against his, the hard ridge in his jeans pressing against her hip. She shifted, lifting into him when he cupped her ass, grinding his erection against her cleft. Sparks shot through her groin, coiling low. A few more seconds, and she might come.

Harsh breathing filled the cab. Hers. His. She wasn't

sure how long he ate at her mouth before he seemed willing to pull back—lift his lips from hers.

She stared up at him. Breathless. More aroused than she'd ever been. But it wasn't just the by-product of adrenaline. Of nearly dying. It was him. His honor. His strength. She'd spent her life trying to live up to her father's ghost. The expectation that came from his sacrifice. But Cannon didn't care about that. He was offering her more than comfort. He was offering her a chance to be defined by something other than her badge.

She closed her eyes as his forehead fell to hers. "Is that a yes to going out to dinner?"

He laughed. The rich sound easing the tight feeling beneath her skin. The one she hadn't realized was there.

Another soft kiss. "How about we get this meeting over at your office. Then, I'll take you home. Spend the next several hours just holding you. Keeping you safe while you sleep. After that, I'll go out. Get us each some coffee. Some of those maple bagels you insist on sharing. And I'll feed you in bed before spending the rest of the day pounding you into it."

She inhaled as heat poured through her body. He was going to get her off with nothing more than his voice. His promise. "I like the way you negotiate. You have a deal—"

A loud knock wrapped on the window. Cannon had a gun in his hand, her shoved back in the seat behind one muscled forearm before she could blink twice. Not that she knew where he'd been hiding the gun. He cursed, rolling the window down.

Dave leaned in a bit. "Are you going to drive to the office or do you two need to get a room, first? It's fucking cold and late. Let's get this done."

He turned and walked back toward his truck—the one she now noticed in the rearview.

Cannon snorted. "Not to sound like an asshole, but your partner's a dick."

Jericho sighed, clipping her seatbelt in place. "He's an acquired taste. But, he's had my back for years."

"Until recently. Tonight wasn't the first time he's ditched you. I know you've been covering for him, but it's getting out of hand, sweetheart."

"Tonight was different. We weren't there on a stakeout. We were meeting for drinks. Maybe a plate of nachos. He wanted to talk about all the shit that's been happening. Said he wanted to make it right."

"So, where the fuck was he?"

"He texted me and said his wife showed up. Asked me to wait. I imagine they were busy trying to patch things up. I honestly don't know but...he did show up. That's something."

"Timing matters. Arriving *after* you would have been killed doesn't mean squat." He waved a hand in the air. "I know. Not the time or the place. Let's just get this done." He glanced over at her and winked. "I've got big plans."

Jericho nodded, relaxing back in the seat. Butterflies rioted inside her stomach, but she was pretty sure it wasn't connected to the shooting, but the man sitting beside her. Who'd just severed all rational thought with that kiss.

She brushed her fingertips over her lips. Looked as if this night was finally getting better. All she had to do was wait for her uncle to do his thing, and Cannon would be set. Not to mention her official backup plan.

CHAPTER SEVEN

Cannon sat in the chair, hands clasped together, feet braced apart as he rested his elbows on his knees. He'd been waiting almost three hours inside the small room, watching events unfold beyond the glass door and large window. They hadn't handcuffed him—one positive in what could be a shit ton of negative.

It still amazed him how his life had changed. How he'd gone from unit leader—in charge of not only keeping his men safe, but ensuring no targets got past him—to just another cog in the proverbial wheel. Sure, he had the appropriate permits. Was licensed to carry, to conceal. Had his Bail Bond Recovery Agent's license. Had met with local law enforcement. Discussed as much of his background as he could without violating national security. But he wasn't an officer. Or agent or anything else that would brush this incident nicely under the mat.

He had connections. He wasn't all that worried. But, he'd hoped he wouldn't have to cash in on all of them within the first few months of going civilian. Not that he regretted it. Anything for Jericho.

That was his new motto. Should probably just get it tattooed somewhere because after the kiss in his truck... Yeah, he wasn't going anywhere, anytime soon. In fact, he was starting to think in very long-term plans. The kind that had them sharing living space. A shiny ring on her finger. A little girl that looked just like her.

Not now. Or next week. But... It was inside his head. Taking up valuable hard disk space. Showing him images of how their life together *could* play out. *If* he played his cards right. Didn't spook her.

He hadn't even thought twice when he'd called himself her boyfriend. He'd noted her surprise. But what had registered more was the accompanying hint of blush. The way her breathing had kicked up. Or how her pupils had dilated. She'd liked hearing it.

Then, her jackass partner had shown up. Killed the moment. And Cannon had pretty much been stuck in this chair ever since. Systematically working through what he'd do if they did decide to press charges.

He'd start with a call to Sam Montgomery, aka Midnight. Sam was an ex-Army Ranger. They'd trained and served together before Cannon had shifted over to Delta. Had done a few joint missions after, too. He was one of the men Ice worked with. But, more importantly, Midnight's fiancée was Bridgette Hayward. A former Assistant U.S. Attorney and a current badass lawyer. Cannon doubted it would take more than a single call to them to straighten everything out.

Of course, it meant he'd owe Midnight. But, Cannon could live with that. Would gladly help the guy out, red ink or not, when or if the man ever asked. Hell, even if he didn't. He was a brother. And Cannon took that seriously.

"Sloan."

He glanced up. It was Jericho's partner. Faraday. The man on the top of Cannon's watch list, quickly becoming a threat he hoped he wouldn't have to deal with. Though, the guy seemed clean—Cannon hadn't been able to dig up anything on him, despite calling in a couple favors—there was still something about him that grated on Cannon's nerves. And if he kept hanging Jericho out to dry...

Dave motioned to his right. "Art would like to see you in his office." He held the door open, clasping Cannon's arm when he went to walk past.

Cannon glanced at the other man's hand then up to his face. "Problem?"

Dave focused on his hand then huffed, lifting it to stab through his hair. "Look. I think we got off on the wrong foot." He sighed. "I didn't mean to ditch Jericho that night at the bar. It's just..."

He leaned against the door. "I've been going through some shit. Not that it's an excuse. It isn't. And I know I've let her down. I just wanted you to know that, if I'd had any idea she was in trouble, I would have risked messing up my marriage, tonight, to get there sooner. And I'm glad you had her back when I couldn't."

Shit. The jerk was trying to make amends. Cannon hated having to push his concerns aside. Tamp down the voices in his head that were still chattering away. Yelling at him that Dave Faraday was a threat to Jericho's well-being. But, if Cannon wanted a future with her—and he fucking wanted a future with her—he needed to play nice with her co-workers. And since she teamed up with Dave

Faraday the majority of the time—were the equivalent of partners...

Cannon nodded. "She has a lot of faith in you. It'd be nice if that wasn't misplaced. And since everything turned out okay..."

That had been about as nice as Cannon could manage with his senses still on high alert. The takedown still replaying inside his head. Not to mention the hint of blood seeping through Jericho's bandage—the one he'd been staring at for hours.

He motioned toward the large glassed office at the far end of the room. "I assume that's the Supervisory Deputy's office?"

"You can go right in. Guess Jericho really does have feelings for you. Never thought she'd call Jack, but..."

Jack? Hadn't Cannon heard her say Uncle Jack just before she'd gotten out of range in the restaurant? Not that he knew who her uncle was. The only thing she'd said about her family was that her father had died overseas while serving. And she was an only child.

Cannon headed for the room, smiling at Jericho when she looked over at him. She was surrounded by three other men. One had to be a lawyer. The other two... Could be internal affairs, or feds. Maybe counselors. But she didn't seem anxious, so he kept walking, knocking on the glass door before cracking it open.

"Supervisory Deputy Collins."

The man waved him in, offering Cannon a chair. "First off, we can continue with Supervisory Deputy and Mr. Sloan, or we can cut through the bullshit and just leave it at Art and Cannon. Your choice."

Cannon smiled. He liked Art. "I understand you wanted to see me, Art."

Art leaned his ass against his desk. "Well, you did leave upwards of eight bodies behind. Thought that might warrant a chat."

"Jericho called. She was in trouble."

"Yes. Deputy Marshal Nash has explained, at length, how and why you became involved."

"I eliminated the threat. It's that simple."

"Except for the part where this isn't Afghanistan or Syria, and you're not in Delta Force, anymore."

"No, it's not, because over there, we played as a team. Soldiers didn't leave their brothers to face threats on their own."

Art cocked his head to his side, hands lifting to shoulder level. "Stand down, Master Sergeant. Damn, you Spec Op guys are touchy. Jackson's the same way. Constantly breaking ranks to protect his team. I'm just not sure if that makes you exemplary men or dangerous ones."

"Both, I hope." Cannon raked his hand through his hair. "For the record, that wasn't exactly what I'd had planned for this evening."

"No, I assume you were hoping to meet up with Jericho. Share some more *coffee*."

Cannon studied the guy, but Art's expression was fixed. "Are you trying to tell me something?"

"No. Just making sure I understand the dynamic between you two."

"Not sure our *dynamic* is really anyone else's concern."

"Normally, I'd agree. But when it directly impacts this office—my job—I make an exception." He reached behind him and grabbed a piece of paper, handing it over to Cannon. "I guess it's a good thing you're part of it, now. My office, that is."

He read the sheet, an odd tumbling feeling building in his gut. He looked up at Art. "This is authorization for me to be a Special Deputy U.S. Marshal."

"That it is. Valid for three years, though, I assume as long as there *is* a dynamic between you and Jericho, and she's part of this office, it'll be renewed. You'll notice it came from the Director, himself, in Arlington. And that it's dated as of midnight yesterday. Which means your little OK Corral shootout tonight was covered by it."

"But…" He glanced out the door, studied Jericho, then focused on Art. "I didn't call in any favors. Not, yet."

"I didn't assume you would until you had more of an idea how this was going to play out. Though, if you had, I'm betting you would have started a little lower on the food chain."

He nodded. "You think Jericho called someone."

"Oh, I know she did, son. Her Uncle Jack, to be precise."

"That's the third time I've heard that name. Who's Uncle Jack?"

"You'd know him as Admiral Jonathan Hastings. He goes by Jack to his family and close friends. Betting you'll have to get used to calling him that, too, soon."

Cannon held up his hand. "Just…wait. Admiral Hastings is her uncle? She never mentioned that, nor did he when I met with him a month ago. I thought they knew each other because her dad had served with him."

"Jericho prefers to keep their relationship on the down low. She doesn't want people thinking she uses that connection to get preferential treatment. That's why she uses her mother's maiden name. In fact, she goes so far in the other direction that Jack has to hide any involvement he has in her professional life. If he wants to give her a recommendation or letter of reference. In the thirteen years she's been involved in law enforcement, she's never once asked him for anything."

"Then, why—"

"Because she cares about you. More than she might be willing to admit. It might also have had something to do with the fact you just saved her life. All without any concern to your own. Guess you can take the man out of the Army, but…"

Cannon scoffed. "What good is having all of this training—this skill set—if I can't help out the people I care about? The woman I lo—"

Fuck, he'd almost said it. Almost said he loved her. Which was ridiculous, wasn't it? Sure, he'd been getting to know her over the past month. Was enthralled by everything he'd learned. And he'd been damn near frantic at the thought of losing her, but… Was that love? He hadn't had a horrible childhood, but not a great one, either. His mother had loved him. He knew that. Had made a lot of sacrifices to see he had food, clothes. But, after fifteen years in the service, ten with Delta… He wasn't sure he really knew what love was.

Though, he had to admit the idea didn't bother him half as much as he'd have imagined it would. He'd already been considering something beyond tomorrow or next week. Wasn't too hard to believe that those thoughts stemmed from a deeper emotion. One that was suddenly bubbling up inside him. Boiling over.

He stood, pacing over to the wall then spinning. "I didn't ask her to call."

"Like I said, if you'd been involved, you would have started lower down than an Admiral. Not that it matters. If the Director of the U.S. Marshal Service wants to make you a Special Deputy Marshal, I'm not going to question it. I suggest you carry that around with you until I can get your ID made. Your badge. Shouldn't take more than a few days. Week tops."

"So, I'm in. Just like that?"

"There are limitations. Basically, you'll need to be asked, but yeah...you're in. Just like that. You are familiar with Wyatt Earp, aren't you? What being a deputy means?"

"That's not funny. And you're not forming a posse."

"No, we're not. But, yeah, it is. A bit. Anyway, ballistics will test your gun for a positive match. Though, I doubt it's a secret which ones were your handiwork. Single taps to the head. Knife wounds. That was very impressive."

"Time and resources are precious. Not practical to waste either. Not when you don't know if you're going to have to adapt before the op's done."

"Not sure I want to see what you do when you adapt. But, I'll see your gun's returned once we're finished with the tests. Though, I'm sure you have a few spares. Anything else?"

He released a slow breath. "I guess not."

"You do know that we hire a lot of ex-soldiers, don't you? With your experience and impressive record, I'm betting you'd be offered a permanent placement, as long as you scored well on the entrance tests."

Cannon chuckled. "The day I handed in my official retirement papers, two men were waiting in my CO's office. Said something similar."

"Feds?"

"CIA. Apparently, ex-Delta soldiers are their flavor of choice for their Specialized Activities Division. SAD for short. And, as much as I'd prefer the Marshal Service over the Agency, I think I'll stay on this side for a while. See what's out there."

"Understood. Drop by next week, and I'll get that badge and ID to you."

"Will do."

He left, pausing for a moment before heading to Jericho's desk. She was engrossed in a set of papers spread out across the surface. Most likely a report. She looked up when he stopped in front of her, her lips instantly lifting into a beautiful smile.

Damn, she shouldn't smile at him like that. Made his thoughts scatter. Made it impossible to focus on anything other than the tone of her skin. How smooth it looked, and how he couldn't wait to touch every inch of it.

He nodded at her arm. "How's the wound?"

"Stings, but...it's okay. They finally letting you go?"

"Looks like it. Funny thing. Seems I've somehow become a Special Deputy Marshal. Hadn't realized I'd filled out the paperwork."

She closed her eyes then sighed, slowly rising before joining him on his side of the desk. She looked up at him —all deep green eyes and pale pink lips. "I was hoping to talk to you before, but—"

"But you were busy calling your uncle."

"Meant to tell you about that, too. I just... I didn't want this to bite you in the ass."

"I do have a few connections. You didn't have to ask Hastings for something if it made you uncomfortable."

"Uncomfortable? Are you kidding? The man was practically beaming over the phone. Pretty sure I heard him mutter to my aunt about how I'd finally called on him for help. He's also a big fan of yours. Said you've done a few jobs for him. Off the record, of course. All top notch work." She gave him a slight hip bump. "Besides, you're worth it."

"This is crazy. You know that, right?"

"Actually, I thought I was merely taking your advice. You *did* tell me to make sure I was safe. Now, if I need you, I can just call. Ask you, officially, for help."

"Based on how trouble seems to follow you around, I should probably get a phone just for you."

"See? I knew you'd come around."

He leaned in close, his lips brushing against her neck. "Pretty sure it's you, who'll be coming. Repeatedly." He eased back. "You done? Can I drive you home?"

Her breathing roughened as she glanced at her desk. "Report's done. I can finish any other details later." She grabbed her purse. "Maybe we can pick up my Jeep tomorrow?"

"I'll have a buddy grab it, if you're okay with that? We might be a bit...busy to make the trip, ourselves."

"I like the sound of that—"

"Nash."

She turned. "Art. Everything okay?"

He sighed, waving Dave over to join them. "I know you're both tired, and Jericho should be heading home for mandated twenty-four hour decompression, but... Brenner just called. Turns out Patrick Wilson was connected to Ty Brown. Was allegedly carrying out a few jobs for him via some prison pipe line." He glanced at Cannon. "Ty Brown is—"

"A hitman for the Macmillan family. Was arrested a couple of months ago, and has been biding his time in the State Pen ever since." Cannon looked around at them. "What? I read."

Art shook his head. "Anyway, after tonight's showdown, they've decided to move Mr. Brown. And Brenner would like the two of you to do the honors. I guess there have been a few threats directed toward the guy."

Jericho scoffed. "That happens when you have enough information stored inside your head to bring down the Macmillan's empire. I thought Brown wasn't talking?"

"He's not. But the feds seem to think if they move him, now, make it look as if he's receiving preferential treatment after the untimely death of Wilson..."

"The family will think he made a deal. Possibly ratted out Wilson."

"And then, he will make a deal. Especially if the marshals moving him are the ones who brought him in then took Wilson out of the picture. I know it's shitty timing, but... You help keep our best Assistant U.S. Attorney happy, and I'll personally see to it your asses get the next seventy-two hours off."

Jericho groaned but nodded. "When are we leaving?"

"Got a car waiting for you downstairs. You should be able to catch a couple of hours in Walla Walla before you have to pick him up. I'll make reservations for you. Text you the info."

"This night just keeps getting better. Fine, but I'm turning my phone off after, Art. For all seventy-two hours."

"That's okay. I'll just call Cannon if I need to get through to you."

Dave snorted. "Great. Four hours with the love birds texting back and forth." He turned slightly. "We should head out. I have plans tomorrow night, and I'd rather not have to break them after fighting for six months to get a chance. I'll meet you out in the car."

Cannon watched Dave leave, nodding at Art before the man returned to his office. Just Cannon's luck. He finally realizes how much Jericho means to him—has plans to spend the day in bed with her—and she gets called away.

Jericho touched his arm. "Timing sucks, doesn't it? But, I'll be back tonight. We can still have dinner. It'll give you time to figure out how you're going to seduce me afterwards."

He laughed. "Oh, sweetheart. I already seduced you on the ride over."

"Oh, so you think us sleeping together is a done deal?"

"I don't know. Maybe I'll ask your Uncle Jack?"

She laughed—louder than he had. An adorable blush coloring her cheeks. "I'll call as soon as we drop Brown off."

"I'll be waiting." He snagged her arm. "You gonna be okay? Thanks to you, I could come if you thought you were in danger."

"Being in danger kind of comes with the job." She smiled. "I'll be fine. Moved prisoners a thousand times.

One-on-one is pretty routine. And no one ever knows the route until we file it with the service when we leave. It's about as safe as this job gets. Now, Con Air. Multiple prisoner vans and buses... That's another story."

"You have my number—"

"If anything goes wrong. Yeah. But it won't. I'll call once it's done. We restrict cell use during the actual transfer—just to be safe. In case someone tries to ping our location."

She took a step then moved back, reaching up and tracing one hand across his jaw and along his shoulder before tapping his chin. "See you tonight. And, in case you were wondering, I can't wait."

"Neither can I. So, see that you get your ass back in one piece."

CHAPTER EIGHT

Six o'clock. And they were just, now, getting into Seattle. God, it felt as if they'd been in the car for days, not hours, but...prolonged silence had a way of dragging the time out. Making each minute feel like ten.

Jericho leaned her head against the seat then glanced over at Dave. He'd insisted on driving the last half of their trip back from Walla Walla. Had said he wanted to make sure they made good time so he wasn't late for his meeting. He'd actually said that. Meeting. Which had struck her as odd. Hadn't he said he had plans with Shauna?

She'd asked him about it, but he'd mumbled something that hadn't made a lot of sense, then just shut her out. She'd been tempted to strike up a conversation with Ty Brown. She hadn't. The guy was a major creep. Had spent the entire time they'd been readying him at the prison then driving back simply staring at her. Never talking, just those dead eyes following her every move.

Even now, he was in the back, head turned toward her. Disturbing smile on his face.

Jericho rolled her shoulders. The bastard was just trying to get under her skin. Unnerve her. It happened all the time. Being female still had some drawbacks in this line of work, and one of them was having assholes like Brown focus on her. Maybe they thought she was weak—could be bribed or overpowered. Or maybe they just hadn't learned any manners. Either way, she wasn't easily intimidated.

Her phone buzzed against her side. She turned a bit, pulled her cell out of her pocket enough to read the text.

It's after six, sweetheart. We might have to jump straight to where I seduce you. Order pizza, later.

She smiled then stuck the phone back in her pocket. They'd be at the office soon—where Brown would stay in their lockup for a day until the feds decided where they wanted him. More fuel for their ruse. Just another twenty minutes, and she'd have three days off. Could text Cannon back.

Dave cleared his throat. "You're not going to answer him, are you?"

She glanced over at him, frowning. "Do I look like I just graduated from Glynco, yesterday? I know better than to text or call during a transfer. Jesus, Dave, give me a bit more credit."

"I don't know, Jer, This guy's different. I mean…you called Jack. Jack!" He shifted his focus to her for a moment. One of the only times he'd actually looked her in the eyes since they'd left Walla Walla. "You swore you'd never call him for anything."

Was there a tone in Dave's voice? Because it sure

sounded like it. Part jealousy, part anger. Not that it made any sense.

She shrugged. "I've never had to have a civilian rescue my ass, before. Extreme situations call for extreme measures."

Dave grunted. "I already apologized for not showing up sooner. Not sure what else you want from me."

"How about you level with me? Tell me what the hell is going on, because this isn't the first time. In fact, I've been covering your ass for months. You blow off meetings. You come in late, leave early. I've lied so many times to Art, I don't even know what the truth is, anymore."

She scrubbed a hand down her face. "Are you in trouble?"

He clenched his jaw, jumping the muscle in his temple. "I'm fine. This thing with Shauna just really knocked me for a loop. But... I'm dealing. Taking steps to fix everything."

"Is that what you were going to tell me last night? I mean, I didn't question why you wanted to meet at Malone's. You and I both suspect it's backed by the Macmillans. But, whatever. They have great burgers and nachos, so I brushed it off. But, you said you wanted to make things right. I'm still waiting to hear what that entails."

"I didn't know the place was going to get hit."

"I never said you did. It's just..." She paused. Took a deep breath. Losing her cool wasn't going to solve anything, and it sure wasn't going to convince Dave to be honest with her.

She forced her muscles to relax, making a point of staring out the window—giving him a chance to collect himself. "I just want you to be honest with me. We've been working together for eight years. Had each other's backs through some pretty nasty crap. You know I'm here for you, right?" She glanced at him then turned away, again. "If it's something...bad. If you're into something the service would disapprove of, we can deal with it discreetly. I have connections. I'll call in favors. All you have to do is talk to me."

"I... Wait. Is that black Suburban following us?"

She looked in the passenger mirror. "I've been checking. It joined on the last on-ramp. Haven't noticed anything odd."

"How would you when you're staring at your phone half the time?"

Jericho whipped her head around. "What is your problem? No, seriously? This isn't like you."

He met her gaze. "Maybe you just don't know me as well as I know you." He motioned toward the rearview. "It's definitely following us. I'm taking the next exit."

"What? Wait..."

But he was already swerving into the lane—cutting in front traffic, peeling off the interstate. Damn near flipping them over in the process while he alternated his attention between the road and the mirrors.

Jericho searched behind them. "It didn't follow us down. So, feel free to stop trying to kill us. We should head back out. Resume the route."

"And have them pick us back up? I don't think so. We can take ninety-nine or Colorado Ave."

"Through the industrial district? Are you high? Do you know how many places there are between here and the office that we could get waylaid?"

"Yeah, I'm aware. But, if someone is looking for us on the interstate, it's safer to stick to the small streets. We're not far. We'll be fine."

"We don't even know that the Suburban was following us." She huffed when he ignored her—kept driving. "Fine. At least, update Art."

"I know the protocol, Jer. I was a Marshall for two years before you joined."

He shook his head but didn't make a move to get his cell. Use the radio. An uneasy feeling built along her nape, raising the small hairs. She didn't know what was off, just that something was.

It wasn't as if Dave had done anything wrong, per se. If he thought they were being followed, he'd taken action. Was currently trying to avoid any kind of hijacking. But there was a slight waver in his voice, a tremble in his hands as they gripped the steering wheel. She studied his face. A few beads of sweat dotted his upper lip. The man was nervous.

Which made sense if he thought they were being followed. About to be jumped. Despite what she'd told Cannon, prisoner transfers were always risky. Always a crap shoot as to whether you made it back without having people shoot at you. Still... She slipped her hand into her pocket, unlocked her phone and swiped down from the top. Cannon's text would be on the main screen, now. She hadn't cleared it. So, touching it, jumping to their chat window was easy. She didn't even need to see the cell to make it happen. Then, she tapped on his name, went into his information. A quick shift of her hand, and a glance, and she was able to share her location. Send him a ping without actually removing her phone. Showing Dave.

It wasn't exactly illegal. After all, Cannon was, in theory, a marshal, even if it had limited powers. Was restricted to authorized cases. But... She didn't have time to worry about protocol. About whether she was being overly paranoid. And, if she was wrong, all Cannon would see was their last twenty-minute drive along the wharf.

She removed her hand, hoping Dave hadn't noticed. "Okay. We'll take Colorado. Stay off the main thoroughfares. Just do me a favor?"

"What's that?"

"Look me in the eye and swear you're not in trouble. After that, I'll let it drop."

He chuckled. "That's all? My word?"

"It's always been enough, before, so..."

He sighed, glancing in the rearview then over to her. "Fine. I'll level with you. It's not trouble so much as a revelation."

"Don't tell me. You found Jesus?"

He laughed. "Not quite. I... Shit. Is that the same Suburban?"

She glanced behind them. "I don't see anything."

"Not behind us. Up ahead on your right. We're just about to pass it."

She scoured the upcoming road—one hand resting on her gun. Just in case. But the damn street was empty. Not even an abandoned car sitting by the curb. "There's nothing there. What..."

Pain. Deep. Slicing through her side, stealing her breath. Her voice. Jericho looked down just as the knife pulled free—a small chip in the tip. Blood covering the silver blade. It blossomed on her shirt. A big red circle that started spreading—eating up more of the white. Like the spot on her arm, only brighter. She had a moment to look over at Dave—see him wipe the knife off on his pants —before his hand settled in her hair. Smashed her head down hard on the dash, then over into the window.

Black washed across her vision. Tiny dots that swam together until only pieces of the outside world showed through. A hint of the window to the left. Something shiny to her right. A voice sounded in the background. Muffled. The syllables all wrong. As if it wasn't English.

The dots tilted. Rolled. Swallowed the light, only to spit her back out. Pain thrummed through her temples, her side. She tried to speak, but her jaw wasn't working. Wouldn't open. Her forehead felt wet—was she sweating? She attempted to lift her hand—touch her skin—but the signal wasn't getting through. Nothing was getting through.

Breath against her cheek as hands patted across her body, tugging at her waist. "The truth is, Jericho, you were always a better marshal. A better friend. I knew you'd eventually find out. Trust me. This is kinder. What they'd do to you... It'll all be over soon."

That voice. She knew it. Her...partner? Was that right? It sounded so far away. Like those old phone lines. All hollow and dull. What was his name?

A beep, then the guy was talking, again. "It's done. I'm just pulling into the warehouse. Did you leave that body like I asked? No, I don't fucking trust you. But, if the damn Marshal Service doesn't think I'm dead, we're all fucked. You hear me? And, since I'm not your only source, you might want to consider that before you decide to make any changes in our agreement. I'm not stupid. I have an insurance policy on the off-chance you try to double cross me. Fine. I'll set the timer for five minutes. Give us enough time to get some distance. What? No, there won't be any issues. We're off the route, and she's out cold. No, I can't kill her outright. The ME has to determine she died in the blast. I'm chancing it enough as it is with a knife wound. It'll be a miracle if she doesn't bleed out before it goes off. I know what I'm doing. I have a car waiting. We'll meet in thirty minutes at our usual place. Don't be late."

A chiming. Like bells. Were they near a church? No, the door. Someone had opened the door. Voices. Two. Words she couldn't make out. Then, footsteps. Heading away. Fading into the pain. The darkness.

Was something ticking? Because it sounded like that. A clock counting away in the background. Jericho opened her eyes. Blinked. The dots were still there, only not as many. More like a gray film over her vision. She blinked, again. Cleared part of her view. She was in the car, leaning against the door. A man was slumped over the steering wheel, dried blood smeared across his head, down the side of his face. She couldn't hear him breathing. But she couldn't really hear anything other than the thready pulse echoing inside her head.

And that ticking.

She moved, nearly blacked out from the pain, but managed to clear her mind a bit. There was something dark stuck to the windshield. Numbers flashing with every tick. The first one was a three. That's all she could make out.

A bomb. It registered, now. As if her brain was playing catch up. The sound. The numbers. The words from before—set the timer for five minutes. That's what he'd meant. He'd set a bomb. Destroy any evidence. Kill her.

You're already mostly dead.

But she wasn't. Not yet. She looked down, thought she was going to puke from the motion. The slide of the world left then right. She held her breath, waited for the scenery to stabilize. Pain flared as she shifted in her seat, managed to unclip the seatbelt then lift her arm—place her fingers on the handle.

Two more breaths, and she pulled on the lever. Only engaged it halfway until she pulled, again. The door opened, and she tumbled out, landing hard on her side. Another wash of black. Of pain cutting out the rest of the world, until the ticking drew her back. She wasn't sure if she actually heard it or if it was playing in her mind. Her subconscious counting down until the moment she'd die.

Not like this. Not while she was still conscious. Still breathing. She did her best to roll, push onto her knees then stumble to her feet. She swayed, the floor of the warehouse tilting beneath her. It took a moment, then she was moving, tripping her way toward the back of the warehouse. Toward an entrance that led to the water. A few pallets were stacked near the wall. Not tall, but enough to deflect the blast. Keep her safe.

She used whatever was available to lurch her way toward the back. The wall. An old metal cabinet. A stack of cardboard boxes. Each item became another tether point. A place to brace one hand then launch herself forward. Each step felt painfully slow. As if she was wading through water. Just moving her legs made her vision erode at the edges. More of those black dots eating away the light. She tried to count off the seconds in her head but couldn't seem to get above seven before losing focus. Having to start, again.

Was the clock still ticking? She was too far away to hear anything. Her surroundings reduced to the drag of her legs. The bloody drops she left with each step. The rasp of her breath as she fought to keep walking. Had it ever been this hard to breathe? The pain in her left side flared with every inhalation.

So, she took shallow breaths. Just enough to keep her going. Keep from igniting the pain, because if she stopped —if she paused to try and push it down—she'd never start up, again. She knew it. She'd simply stand there until the blast either knocked her down or incinerated her. Maybe both.

It was taking too long. She was sure she'd used up all of the three minutes she'd seen on the clock, and she wasn't at the pallets, yet. Had it really been a three? She couldn't be sure. Everything was getting fuzzy. Where she was. How she'd gotten hurt. The only constant was the slow scrape of her feet across the pavement. The view of the pallets getting closer.

Another two counts of seven, and she was there. Stepping behind the wood. Leaning against the wall to prevent her knees from buckling. Water lapped in the background, the scent of brine heavy in the air.

She bowed her head, tried to get control of the pain, when the vehicle exploded. The rush of air knocked her sideways. If it wasn't for a window ledge on her right, she would have hit the ground. But she managed to stay upright. Avoid getting burned as smoke filled the room, the black cloud billowing to the rafters.

She coughed, doubled over from the pain, then pushed

back up. Heat blasted the air, burning a line down her throat as she tried to breathe. She wouldn't last in here much longer. The door knob rattled in her hand, refusing to turn. She frowned, realized there was a deadbolt, then focused on lifting her hand. Turning it then turning the handle—tumbling into the fresh air. A cloud of smoke followed her out, fading into the evening fog.

Jericho leaned against the wall, still trying to muddle through what needed to be done. But her thoughts were fuzzy. Not connecting like they should. An idea would spring to mind then just derail before becoming coherent. Maybe it was the pain throbbing through her temples. The one only slightly better than the burning sensation in her side. Had she hit her head?

She managed to brush her fingers across her forehead —stared down at the blood smeared on her fingertips. She'd definitely hit her head. Though, the bleeding wasn't bad. Not like her side. The bottom half of her shirt was soaked. The excess dripping onto the floor. Which meant, even if she didn't die from the blood loss, she was leaving a trail. A giant arrow pointing directly to her. To where she was heading. She couldn't remember exactly why she needed to remain hidden, only that she did. That someone might come back—kill her. She needed to stem the bleeding.

Of course, needing to and being able to were distinctly different. Just getting her hands to move—to slip off her jacket—took three tries. Unbuttoning her shirt was impossible, so she just ripped it open. Flung the buttons in all directions then got it off, too. She balled it up— layered it over the wound. Fought through the excruciating pain tying it in place with her jacket sleeves.

It wasn't perfect. Didn't completely stanch the flow. But it slowed it down. Prevented it from collecting on the pavement beneath her. It would have to do. Hopefully, she'd find something else to press against her side, or maybe a first aid kit.

There was one in the trunk of the car. She remembered that much. She glanced over her shoulder, staring at the fire burning inside the building. How had she forgotten the car had exploded? That her only resources were on her back—in her pockets?

She reached for her phone. Nothing. No badge, no gun. Just the shifting scenery and the wound on her side. The whirling feeling inside her head, making it impossible to focus. To think clearly.

More stabbing pain, which meant she still had time. Once it numbed—became indiscernible—it would be too late. She needed to move. Go...

Cannon.

The name broke through the haziness. The foggy feeling clouding her thoughts. Just appeared like a beacon in the dark. His office wasn't too far. A few miles. Surely, she could drag herself there. He'd know what to do. Would keep her safe. She was sure of that. Felt it settle inside her. Cannon was the answer. All she had to do was reach him.

CHAPTER NINE

"Are you sure we're in the right place, buddy?"

Cannon grunted a reply, scanning the street. A light fog crept in off the sea wall, highlighting the crumbling buildings and charred brick. The place looked more like a set from *The Walking Dead* than a section of the wharf. And definitely the last place he'd ever envision Jericho stopping during a prisoner transfer. "Industrial fire took out a city block six months ago. It's scheduled for demolition. Some shipping company bought the whole thing."

Jericho had shown him the plans for the new development. Definitely an improvement and part of the reason he'd gone with her suggestion and rented a space in the area for his office. It wasn't so trendy his crew would stand out—or the rent was too high—but it was slowly being gentrified.

His partner, Brett Sievers, aka Colt to his buddies, snorted. "Must have been one hell of an explosion."

"Took four days to put out, from what I've heard." He glanced at Colt. "This feels—"

"Wrong? Yeah. Who would use this route to transport a prisoner?"

"No one. Which is why we're here. Something's off."

Colt shouldered up beside him. "And you're certain her GPS pinged here?"

"Jericho's smart. She doesn't break protocol, and she doesn't make stupid mistakes. She told me, outright, that she couldn't text or call during a transfer. If she broke ranks so she could share her location—she did it for a reason. None of which are good." He gave Colt a slight shove. "And yeah, I'm sure. I checked it a dozen times. Signal began just off the interstate, traveling west then north. It seemed steady for a few minutes then stopped."

Brett nodded, still scanning the area. "Is that when the signal vanished?"

Cannon's chest tightened at the thought. That's when he'd gone into full soldier mode. He'd been...concerned when his phone had chirped—when he'd read the notice. *Jericho Nash is sharing her location.* Had instantly gone on alert. But it had seemed so benign, at first. Just her in what was obviously a vehicle, traveling in the primary direction of her office. Sure, he'd noted the area. Thought it odd that they'd ventured off the interstate, but...

What the fuck did he know about being a Deputy U.S. Marshal? True, he knew about routing. Had run enough convoys in his time to recognize a good plan from a bad one. Traveling the industrial area—definitely a bad choice. It opened them up to endless opportunities for someone to either hijack them or simply take them out. One RPG from the top of a warehouse, or a well-placed IED under a manhole cover, and it was game over.

But, he didn't have all the intel. Didn't know marshal protocol—an oversight he planned on rectifying—or if they were meeting up with auxiliary forces. Maybe local law enforcement. Fuck, for all he knew, the Marshal Service had a safehouse tucked away out here. Maybe Ty Brown had decided to make a deal, after all. Was being placed in Wit Sec.

It wasn't until the little blue blip had stopped moving for a couple of minutes, then vanished without any kind of text or explanation from Jericho, that he knew she was in trouble. The kind that left behind a bloody trail or mangled bodies.

That's when he'd grabbed Colt and jumped in his truck. He might not know marshal protocol, but he knew a damn SOS when he saw it—in any form. And he wasn't about to let her down. Worst-case scenario, he could say he hacked her phone—followed her. Lose his Special Deputy status. Hell, they could toss his ass in jail if he was wrong.

But he wasn't. He felt it. Sensed it like he had on countless missions. A shiver along his spine that had warned him of a pending attack. Or had stopped him in the middle of an op to just...wait. Outlast the ambush he'd known was there but couldn't see. Couldn't explain outside of the clenching in the pit of his stomach. The nagging voice in his head. This was no different. Jericho needed him.

Colt gripped his shoulder, looking him in the eyes. "Do you smell that?"

Cannon snorted. "The stench of brine or piss?"

"Smoke. Wind's blowing the wrong way, but...it's there."

Cannon inhaled, and fuck if Colt wasn't right. "Can you tell what direction it's coming from?"

"Must be close to the pier to mask it this well. It's probably blending in with fog. It's thicker over the water." Colt pointed at a broken down warehouse off to their left. "I'd guess on the other side of that line of warehouses. The row that backs onto the sea wall." Colt grabbed Cannon's wrist, when he took a step. "You sure this isn't a set-up? You've made a lot of enemies over the years."

"Jericho wouldn't set me up."

"Cannon."

"I know how to read betrayal, and she's clean." He scoffed when Colt just stared at him, fingers still digging into his muscle. "If she wanted me dead, she could have killed me at the restaurant, last night. Instead, she called her uncle and got me a pass. And that's not taking into account the kiss in my truck."

Colt chuckled. "You're risking our lives based on a kiss? Must have been one hell of a kiss."

"I am, and it was." He sighed. "She's...different."

Different. That was an understatement, and not nearly a suitable explanation. But...how did he explain what he felt for Jericho when it seemed crazy, even to him? A month of coffee dates, two takedowns, and a kiss shouldn't have him this worked up. Emotions didn't belong on missions. Had a way of getting good men killed. Every soldier knew to lock them in a box they could examine later—after they made it back alive. True, this wasn't a mission, but even trying to recon a place without his head fully in the game...

It made him a liability. And if Jericho was hurt...

He shut down that line of thinking. Couldn't go there. Not and be the man she needed him to be. He had to shove it all away—block out the images of her bleeding. Dead. Because that wasn't an option. Not after finally finding her. Admitting to himself she meant more to him than anyone else had. Ever. He hadn't labeled it love, yet, but damn it, if this wasn't love—this out-of-control, head spinning, need-to-hold-her-now feeling—then he wasn't sure what was.

Colt merely nodded. "Good enough for me. So, if this isn't a set-up, then this was her calling for backup. And you know how much I hate letting a lady down. We should go along the side of that building. Stick close to the walls. Re-evaluate from there. But don't worry. If she's here, we'll find her."

Damn straight they would. And, if there was so much as a scratch on her, Cannon would make catching the bastards who'd hurt her his sole vocation.

Colt crossed the street, heading down the south side of the building. He had his gun drawn, at the ready, feet barely making a sound. He was slightly shorter than Cannon, and about forty pounds lighter. But he moved like a damn cat. All grace and power. Cannon considered himself a stealthy guy. Could climb walls, vault over fences. Parkour with the best of them. But Colt made it look easy. Like walking down the street. Guy was crazy good at tracking, too. Had once followed a tango for five miles on nothing more than bent grass and a few scuff marks. Definitely the kind of teammate Cannon was happy to have on his side.

He just hoped he wouldn't need to put Colt's skills to

the test. Or his own. But, as they neared the rear edge of the warehouse, the scent of smoke increased. It could have been anything. Some teenagers setting fires for fun. Homeless people seeking shelter—trying to stay warm. But that feeling—the tight one in his chest...

This was bad.

Colt stopped Cannon with a raised fist as they reached the corner. The guy scanned the area, lips firm as he glanced at Cannon. "Something's burning inside the building across the street. There's some wreckage scattered on the pavement just outside the door. Thinking it blew up, first."

"Can you tell what it was?"

A twitch beside his left eye.

Fuck, Cannon knew that look. The silence saying everything Colt couldn't. "A vehicle."

"We don't know it was hers."

"She breaks protocol, and now, there're pieces of a car scattered where I lost contact. I think we both know it's hers." He checked his weapon. "Fuckers will pay if they hurt her. I'll hunt them down."

"I'll help, but let's not jump to conclusions, yet. Place looks clear, but..."

Yeah. Cannon knew the score. Which meant running through the possible threats. Snipers—check. Suspicious cars or items that could house explosives—check. Possible tangos hanging around—check. Took all of a minute to run through the various hazards. Feel confident they weren't going to get jumped straight off. Then, they were running. Weaving—just in case—as they headed for the partially open rolling door.

Cannon covered his mouth as they stopped just

outside. Fuck, the smell. Rubber, electronics and the unmistakable stench of burning flesh. And, for the first time in his life, he wasn't sure if he could handle seeing the other side of the door.

He'd watched his teammates—his brothers—die. Had faced more horrors than most people could imagine. Had the smell of death burned into his brain—apparently etched into his DNA. Surrounding him like a damn shroud. But just the thought of stepping inside—seeing her charred remains inside the vehicle…

Colt grabbed his arm when he went to duck under the door. "Let me go first." He shook his head. "Cannon. I'm asking as your brother. Let me have a look."

"Ten seconds. Then, I'm coming under this door. I won't risk your safety because I'm scared at what I might find."

Scared. He'd never admitted that before. Especially to a teammate. Thankfully, Colt didn't call him on it.

His buddy held up his hand, fingers splayed. "I'll be back in five."

The man darted inside, reappearing just when Cannon was about to follow. Colt coughed, blinking a few times as he shook his head. "Hard to tell what happened, but there's at least one dead. There's a blood trail leading toward the back. Thought we should check it out together."

"Could you…"

"I think it's male. Harder than hell to be sure, but it was on the driver's side. From what you said, it didn't sound like she was driving."

Cannon nodded. He couldn't do anything else. His throat seized. Fucking frozen at the thought that he'd have to accept that Jericho was dead. That he'd failed her. Instead, he took a deep breath then moved in behind Colt, shadowing the man's every move.

Two seconds and they were inside, circling the burning vehicle in opposite directions. His buddy had been right. Only one inside. Driver's seat. No one in the passenger or the rear. Which meant the bastard in the back had most likely orchestrated the escape. Ty Brown. Now at the top of Cannon's most wanted list, and a fucking dead man walking. It didn't matter if Brown had mafia connections. If Cannon had to take out the entire Macmillan family to get to the guy. The fucker would pay.

Another two seconds and they were on the other side —trying not to breathe in the smoke. The steady black mass filling the warehouse. Making it hard to see more than ten feet in front of them.

They headed to the back, following a line of blood. Whoever had gotten out was hurt. Bad, judging on the amount of blood. The steady trail along the floor. It led to some pallets then disappeared out a rear door that was partially open—one large bloody handprint smeared across the handle.

Colt held up three fingers, slowly counting down then shoving the door aside. Cannon went high, Colt low, as they cleared the exit, sweeping both directions before shutting it behind them.

Colt took a quick scan then went to one knee. He held up more blood and a couple of buttons. "Looks like our vic took some countermeasures. Blood trail ends. Though, this much means they were standing here for a while." He glanced up at Cannon. "I know it's not much, but these buttons are pretty small for a man's shirt. Let's assume this is Jericho. Any idea where she'd go?"

"She'd be worried about being followed or hunted. If whoever ambushed them, blew up their car, would come back. She'd go someplace she felt safe. Assuming she can think clearly. That's a lot of blood to still be functioning."

Her blood. God, how wrong was it he hoped it was hers? That she wasn't the body in the car? That being injured was the preferred outcome? Because based on the amount, she didn't have long before she died, too.

"Cannon!"

He blinked, scowled at Colt. "What?"

"Get your head in the game. We need to find her, so... where would she go? On the run. Bleeding. Scared. Maybe not thinking too clearly. Possibly concussed. Obviously, her phone was in the damn car, which is why it stopped sending a signal. We have to assume she only has the clothes on her back. Nothing else to keep her safe. Where would she go?"

"My head is in the game. It's just... I don't know. Maybe there's a safehouse around here."

"She sent *you* her location for a reason. She wanted *you* here. *You* helping her. That's the key."

"Fuck. The office. She helped me find it."

Colt frowned. "I know it's only a few miles away, but that's pretty far in what I can only imagine is her condition. You sure?"

"If she's conscious and has any form of rational thought, she'll head there. Guaranteed."

"Let's go. I'll see how far I can track her before we have to double back and get the truck. Might be hard, though. Not much to go on."

Other than her blood. Colt didn't say it, but it was there. Hanging between them. Sure, it looked as if she'd tried to stop the bleeding, but Cannon doubted she had the necessary supplies. So, the shirt or vest or whatever she'd tied around herself to buy some time would eventually bleed through.

He pushed down the doubt. It wouldn't help them find her. "There's a first aid kit in the truck. We'll need it."

"Roger that. Let's see if we can get a bead on her. Assuming your theory's correct."

Colt struck off, heading for the far end of the building. He stopped, went to one knee, placed a hand on the ground before glancing at Cannon over his shoulder. "There's a smudge of blood. Probably from a shoe. Not much but..."

"Follow it."

Colt took off, again, pausing every few steps to examine the ground or the side of a building. A stack of bins. He'd study something then move. Never stopping for longer than a few seconds. They were two minutes into it when he pulled up short, motioning Cannon to join him. He'd been staying back—keeping watch. Making sure that whoever had hurt Jericho wasn't still hanging around. Watching. Hunting her down. Would launch an attack against Colt.

Colt pointed to a few drops of blood. "We're at the edge of how far I want to go without getting the truck."

"You keep going. I'll get it. Follow behind you."

Colt snagged his wrist. "She can't be too much farther. Not with the amount of blood she's lost. I don't imagine she's moving that fast." He stared at the long strip of asphalt. "Any chance she might have tried to requisition a vehicle? Think she knows how to hot-wire a car?"

"I'm sure the Marshal Service taught her a few tricks. Either way, I still say she'll try for the office."

"You know her best. Okay, I'll keep—"

A noise.

Not much. Maybe someone bumping into a trash can. Or dropping a bottle. Breaking a window. But it got their attention. Had them both darting to the edge of the next building—seeking cover. It had been too soft, too damn low to pinpoint. But it was close.

Colt made a few hand signals. He'd go right. Cannon left. They'd clear the immediate area. Eliminate any threat. It would only take a minute. One they didn't have to spare with Jericho out there. Bleeding. Dying.

God, he hoped that was the case—that they were following her. That she was still out there. Hurt he could handle. Fix. Dead... That was beyond his help. Would send him spiraling to a dark place—far worse than any of the deserts or jungles he'd waged war in. His own personal Hell. Void of any chance at love. Void of Jericho.

Colt made another signal then disappeared behind the corner. Cannon made his move. Blended into the shadows lining the wall. Picked his way up the side. Another soft sound. A boot against the pavement. Not quite a scuff. More like a misstep. A stumble.

Was that a grunt? Maybe a sharp inhalation?

Hard to tell with the damn metal buildings bouncing the sound around. But it wasn't far. Just past the edge of the warehouse. He shuffled to the corner then popped out —ducking when a board swung toward his head.

A quick pivot and a step, and he had the fucker pinned...

CHAPTER TEN

"Christ."

Her skin was so pale. Nearly as white as her tee, except where it was red. Which was easily over half of it. She'd balled up her button-down shirt and cinched her jacket around the wad—slowed the bleeding. But it was already soaking through the ends—a few drops dripping onto the ground.

And yet, even barely standing, she'd tried to defend herself. Had dragged her ass across a few blocks. The girl was as tough as they came.

"Jericho."

Cannon holstered his gun, catching her when she slumped against him. God, it was like catching a dead body—boneless. She had just enough coordination to prevent her head from crashing against his chest, but that was it. She crumpled in his arms, her face curling against his shoulder.

"Easy, sweetheart. I've got you. But you need to stay awake, okay? Colt!"

Footsteps, then Colt was skidding in beside him. Kneeling at his level.

Cannon reached in his pocket. Handed Colt the keys. "Get the truck."

His buddy didn't say a word, just took off. There one second, disappearing around the building, the next. Cannon knew how fast the guy could run when needed, and damn—he needed it, now.

Cannon laid Jericho on the ground, performing a quick body scan—he needed to know if her obvious wounds were her only ones. A few cuts and bruises, most likely from the explosion, but nothing else looked nearly as bad as her side. Or her head.

Fuck, it appeared as if she'd smashed her head against a wall. Or maybe the dash. The window. All three. Either way, she definitely had a concussion. He just didn't know how bad.

He cupped her jaw, keeping his touch light. "Jericho. Come on, sweetheart, you gotta look at me. Open your eyes."

Her eyelids fluttered, but she didn't open them. Didn't do more than groan as her head lolled to one side.

"Jericho!"

He used his command voice. The one reserved for new members. That got them moving. Made them more afraid of him than whatever they were about to face. For Jericho, it got her eyes open. Glassy. Unfocused, but open.

He smiled. Wasn't that hard to muster one because, despite her current condition, she was alive. And that meant he could still save her. Still find a way to make all the dreams in his head a reality.

She managed to wrap one bloody hand around his wrist. "Cannon."

"Right here. Colt's getting the truck. Just hang on. I need to see how bad you're hurt. Okay?"

He clenched his jaw at her nod—god, it looked as if it took whatever strength she had left just to move her head an inch. He only pulled the edge of her makeshift bandage back, not wanting to start it bleeding or destroy what little clotting there was before he had more supplies. Before he could stop it. Laceration. Long. Smooth edges. A number of things could have caused it. "Do you remember what happened?"

Another inch of movement—side to side. Of course, she didn't remember. She was barely conscious. It was a miracle she was awake. Had remembered his name, let alone what had happened.

"It's okay. Gonna get you fixed up." He looked up when Colt roared to a stop beside him, jumping out of the truck with the first aid kit in hand. He tossed it on the ground next to Cannon then laid a blanket over her lower half.

Cannon muttered his thanks, opening the kit and grabbing what he needed. "I have to stop the bleeding. I've got some QuickClot. It'll plug whatever's leaking. Keep looking at me."

He removed the shirt, cursing at the slice on her side. Larger than he'd first thought. Deep. Knife wound. No doubt about it, now. Big one, too. Like his damn Ka-Bar. She watched him through half-lidded eyes, those eyes rolling back when he used his knee to apply pressure while he grabbed some gauze.

"I know. Hurts like hell, but...you've lost a lot of

blood. You can't afford another drop." He glanced at Colt. "Call Harborview. Tell them we'll be there in five minutes. They'll need a shit ton of blood."

"No. Cannon. No." Jericho tugged on his arm. Her grip much stronger than before.

He frowned. "You need medical attention. A transfusion. Stitches. Maybe surgery. I can't do that."

"No hospitals. I..." She swallowed, nearly blacked out until she wet her lips. Stared up at him, again. "Too dangerous."

"I'll protect you—"

"Not there. You can't..." She groaned, seemed to fade, then surged back. "Not from them."

"I'll call Art. He'll send a platoon of marshals—"

"No." She gulped in air, groaned in pain, then tried to grip him tighter. Failed, but he got the message. "Can't... can't be trusted."

Fuck. If someone in the service was behind this...

"I hate to agree with her, Cannon, but we both know how hard it'll be to isolate her at a hospital. Especially if she's worried about her office finding out. That's the first call they'll make once they discover who she is. The place will be crawling with marshals inside of thirty minutes. And, with the kind of attention she'll need, there'll be a ton of people in and out of her room. No way we can vet them all. Not that it'll matter if whoever did this wears a badge. Hell, we won't even be in charge." Colt speared one hand through his hair. "She'll be vulnerable."

"She'll be dead if she doesn't get help. Soon."

"Is there somewhere else we can take her? Maybe a veterinary clinic? Or a private doctor? Or one of those volunteer clinics where you don't need papers?"

"We don't have time to...wait. Open the back door. There might be another option, but if not, we're going to the hospital. I'll fucking handcuff myself to her side, if necessary."

Colt didn't argue, jumping up then opening the door. He was sliding into the driver's seat as Cannon cradled Jericho in his arms, his cell already in his other hand.

Cannon looked up at Colt. "There're GPS coordinates for a guy named Ice in the nav. Launch them and head there unless I tell you otherwise."

A rev of the engine, then they were moving. Fast but controlled. Cannon hit the contact number, praying his buddy was in town.

"Ya know, Cannon, if we're going to spend this much time on the phone, maybe we should define our relationship."

"Ice. Please tell me you're in Seattle and not still in Montana."

"Um, actually, yeah. Just got in. Harlequin's got a photo shoot scheduled."

"You at the loft?"

"As usual. Are you okay?"

"I'm fine, but Jericho... It's bad, Ice. Knife wound. She's lost a lot of blood."

"And you're not taking her to the hospital because?"

"She's a Deputy U.S. Marshal, and her prisoner transfer just got jumped. She's insisting it's too dangerous. Guy in the back was a mafia hitman. But there's a chance someone from the Marshal Service was involved. At least, that's what she hinted at."

"Fuck. All right. Bring her here. What's your ETA?"

"About five minutes."

"Roger. Lay it out for me. Is she responsive?"

"Barely. In and out. Wound's large. Lower left side. Thinking it was a tactical knife. Hit her head, too. She's pale. Pulse is weak. Skin clammy."

"Keep her warm. With a suspected head injury, try to keep her flat. Press on her nail bed. Does it pinken once you release it?"

He tried. Swallowed the resulting punch of fear. "Not even close."

"Do you know what blood type she is? Can you ask her?"

Cannon gave her a gentle shake in his arms. "Jericho. What blood type are you?" He tried, again, when she didn't stir. "Come on, sweetheart. Talk to me."

She blinked, managed to open one eye.

He leaned in close. "What's your blood type?"

"AB nega...."

"Good girl. You get that, Ice?"

"Yup. And it's good news. Means we have a lot more options than just O neg. Okay, I've got my bag ready. Supplies laid out. Harlequin will meet you downstairs. But, if your girl's too far gone, we're going to the hospital."

His girl. Hell yeah, she was. And he wasn't going to lose her. "Understood. Two minutes."

Cannon was accustomed to keeping a running clock in his head. He could scale a wall, infiltrate an insurgent cell and eliminate the threat in under two minutes. It felt like forever in the back of the truck. Watching Jericho slowly slip into unconsciousness, despite him constantly talking. Begging her to stay awake. Knowing there wasn't anything he could do he hadn't already done. That Ice was her only hope.

The guy was brilliant. Had been a Pararescue tech—PJ —for a dozen years. Was one of the best medics Cannon had ever served with. The guy had singlehandedly saved hundreds of Special Forces soldiers. Had literally carried some back from behind enemy lines. Never considering his own safety. Had been booted over some shitstorm that had saved a Marine's life.

Cannon prayed he could help Jericho because Colt was right. Cannon couldn't cover every possible threat at the hospital—not if there were marshals involved. And he didn't have the time to call in enough favors to have everyone who could be involved investigated. Not even if he called Jericho's uncle. Fact finding took time. Time they didn't have. Not right now.

Harlequin was standing outside an open warehouse door—much like the one where they'd found Jericho's car —waving them in. She had it closing behind them and was already punching in the code to the elevator up to their loft by the time Cannon had Jericho out of the truck and was heading for the lift. The other woman didn't talk, just deactivated all the security measures, ushering them into the space.

Ice had cleared a table and covered it with a sheet. He had what Cannon could only describe as a mini-trauma room set up. An IV stand. Bags. A bowl of water. Bandages. Instruments that gleamed in the overhead light. Ice waved them over then helped ease her onto the table.

In under sixty seconds, he had an IV started and had checked her vitals. Was assessing the damage to her side. "She'll need blood. I've called Midnight and Rigs. They'll be here shortly. But she can't wait. Any of you guys Rh negative?"

Cannon grunted. "A negative."

"Good. Sit. She'll need a pint or ten. What about you... I know I've seen you before. Delta, right? What's your name, again?"

"Brett Sievers. My friends call me Colt. And sorry. I'm O positive."

"That's fine. Midnight and Bridgette can help. Quinn, too. I'll hook myself up after I'm finished if she needs more. We should have enough. If not, I know where we can *acquire* some."

Colt straightened. "Give me the address. I'll go, now. Save you guessing later or having all of us weakened by multiple transfusions."

Ice glanced up. Grinned. Rattled off the address.

Colt nodded. "I saw a motorcycle downstairs. It'll be faster."

Ice chuckled. "Harlequin will have your ass if you scratch it. Keys are on the table next to the door."

The man nodded then left.

Cannon watched as Ice set up a direct transfusion—the red tube linking Cannon's arm to hers. "Does this mean you can treat her?"

Ice grunted then grabbed a case and removed some kind of probe. "That's the plan. Either way, she needs the blood. She'll never make it to a hospital without any, now."

Cannon frowned. "What the hell is that?"

"Portable ultrasound. I picked one up when it became apparent my medic days weren't behind me. I swear, my *brothers* keep me busier as a civilian than I was in the Air

Force. This will help determine if she needs more help than I can give her."

He had a portable ultrasound?

Cannon didn't question it. Didn't care where Ice had picked it up. If he'd bought it, stolen it or had it donated. All Cannon cared was whether he'd wasted what precious little time Jericho had by bringing her here instead of insisting on the hospital.

"Relax, Cannon. She's lost way more blood than I'd like, but she's not going to die. Doesn't look like the knife hit anything crucial. If it had…"

Yeah, she'd have been dead before Cannon had found her. Which didn't make him feel any better. Just staring at her pale skin. The bruised look beneath her eyes, and how her chest barely moved when she took a labored breath— it made the room heat. The air feel thin.

Ice sighed. "Breathe, buddy. It's going to be okay."

"So, she doesn't need to go to the hospital?"

"Should she? Absolutely. That's always the best call. I'm not a doctor. Don't pretend to be. But, under these circumstances—not worth the risk of having someone try to kill her, again. And no matter how hard we try, we can't guarantee her safety in a hospital. I can handle this. Looks like there's a small fragment in the wound. I'll give her some freezing. Remove it. Then, stitch her up. Once the infusion kicks in—gets her cell count back up—she'll feel and look a lot better. She'll need a round of antibiotics. I have a shot I can give her, today, and I can get her what she needs. Off-grid. I'll keep a close eye on her. If I suspect she's losing ground, we'll take her to the ER. I don't think that'll be necessary. She's insanely lucky. But she's gonna be sidelined for a week or two."

"Alive is all that matters. I can deal with the rest. I *will* deal with the rest."

Ice whistled, all the while working on saving Jericho. Christ, how did the guy do it? Not a hint of doubt or fear. Steady hands slipping the needle beneath her skin then probing the wound. Using some kind of tweezers to dig into the cut. "Sounds like someone just went to the top of your shit list. Bastard doesn't even know he's dead, yet. You got any leads?"

"She didn't say much. Said she didn't remember anything. Obviously, the fucker who was in the back is my prime suspect. But, when I told her I was taking her to the hospital... She perked up. Said it wasn't safe. That her office couldn't be trusted. Not sure what that means, but..." He looked up at Ice. "I think her partner was killed. There was a body in the car. Couldn't tell for sure. It was still burning."

He groaned. Fuck, he hadn't even called it in, yet. He'd been too focused on finding Jericho. After all, if it was Dave Faraday in the vehicle, he was already dead. Beyond help. But, considering there was a probable felon on the loose—a known hitman with mafia connections—Cannon should have called the second they found the car.

"I need to call it in. Should have, already. Not like me to let something like that slip."

"You had more important things to consider. Trust me. We've all been there. It's different when it's someone you love, and not like a brother." Ice glanced at him. "You do love her, don't you?"

"Ice—"

"Please. We all knew something was off when you were in Montana. Not like you to be the least bit distracted. And, if that wasn't enough of a clue, your hands are shaking. Never seen you shake, buddy. Ever. Me, either, until I met Harlequin." He snorted. "She does something to my brain. Can't explain it, but there's no sense denying it. I'd go to Hell and back for her."

"I've been to Hell. Got the blueprints. Whoever did this is gonna need to go somewhere worse if they want to try and hide. Not that they will for long. I promise you that."

He glanced at his hand—the one holding Jericho's. The one that was shaking ever so slightly. Just like Ice had said. He didn't want to let go, not even long enough to call the authorities. But... "I really should call this in."

"No need. I already called."

Cannon whipped his head around at the sound of Colt's voice. The guy was walking across the room, a cooler in his hand.

"I figured you had your hands full. Besides, if we need to keep Jericho's presence a secret for a while, it might be better if your voice wasn't on the nine-one-one tape." He placed the cooler beside Ice. "Got you five units. And your friends pulled up as I was getting in the elevator. They'll be up in a minute."

Ice nodded. "Good. We should have more than enough." He held up a small metal piece then placed it in a bowl. "Looks like the tip of a blade. It got wedged in her rib. Probably what saved her from more serious internal injury. Which means you were right. Someone stabbed her."

A dull roar sounded in Cannon's head, followed by white-hot rage. He'd see whoever had done this suffered. "The question is, did it happen before she got out of the car? After? Based on that bloody trail, I'd say she was stabbed while in the car. But how the hell did Brown get the jump on them if he was handcuffed in the back seat?"

"Hopefully, once she's recovered, she'll remember. Blood loss messes with memory. Give her a few days. She can probably fill in the blanks." Ice grabbed a needle—threaded it. "It does pose a concern."

Cannon arched a brow.

Ice started stitching the wound closed. "Once they discover she didn't die…"

"They'll come looking for her."

"They know about you?"

"Her boss does. The whole office, probably. There was an incident last night—long story. But, yeah. If nothing else, they'd know my name."

The door behind them opened. Cannon glanced back. Midnight, Rigs, Bridgette, and Addison came bustling in. Faces grim. They didn't speak, just took a seat—waited until they were needed.

Ice smiled. "Team's here. We'll set up surveillance. Keep watch in case they connect you to me. To Harlequin's place. We'll help keep Jericho safe until we get to the bottom of this. Then—"

"Then, we go hunting. And this is one trip where I won't be coming back empty handed."

CHAPTER ELEVEN

Did being dead hurt? Because that's all Jericho felt. Pain. Through her side. Her head. In her chest when she tried to breathe...

She was breathing. It took a while for her brain to process the thought. Confirm she wasn't dead. Which hit on more questions. Where was she? How had she gotten here, and what the hell had happened?

Jericho blinked. Opened her eyes, then closed them just as quickly. Seeing the scenery swim across her vision increased the throbbing in her temples. Made her nauseous.

She faded, coming back up from the dark feeling much the same. The pain was a bit better. A little less white-hot. Allowed her to open her eyes—get a look at the room. She didn't recognize it—obviously a bedroom. A dresser and some side tables. Closed door. A chair sat off to her right. Within arm's reach. Turned to face the bed as if someone had been watching her.

She glanced at her hand. It felt warmer than the rest of her. As if someone had been holding it. Anchoring her. She tried to remember—inhaled against the rush of pain— then gave up. Choosing to push onto her elbow. Took four tries just to sit up—lean against the headboard.

The room tilted a bit, then centered. She let her head rest against the wooden slats. Waited until she had the energy to do more than breathe. It was unnerving. Lying there. Her last coherent thought of getting into a car. Heading back to the office. She'd been with someone...

Another stab of pain, which wasn't worth the fleeting images she got as a result. Better to just accept something bad had happened and move forward. Decide what she was going to do next. If she was safe, and if not, how she'd take steps to get to safety.

Cannon.

His name formed inside her head. She had a vague recollection of asking him for help. Not directly. A discreet SOS she'd hoped he'd recognize. Act on. But... If he'd come to her aid, where was he, now?

It hurt too much to puzzle it out. Her limited energy would be better served taking stock of her current condition. First, body check. She was dressed in an oversized t-shirt, the spicy scent strangely familiar. She had bandages taped to her left side—what felt like stitches pulling against her skin. The stabbing pain in her ribs suggested she'd injured one or two. And there were a few butterfly closures along her forehead. But, other than that, she seemed okay. Could feel her feet, wiggle her toes.

She glanced around. No weapons. Nothing to suggest she was a prisoner. Though, she couldn't be sure, because she also didn't see her clothes. Her weapons. Hadn't she been wearing them when she'd gotten into that car? And, if she was hurt, why wasn't she at the hospital?

Panic gnawed at her consciousness. There was something about going to the hospital that scared her. Made her skin crawl. She couldn't place it, but she trusted her instincts. They'd never let her down, before.

So, the need to run...to find Cannon. She didn't question that, either. Grunted through the pain as she pulled the blanket to one side until she could swing her legs over the edge of the bed. The chair saved her from falling onto the floor—likely hurting herself more. Allowed her time to steady herself—get her feet under her properly. Not that she was convinced she'd make it to the door, but she'd try. Do whatever it took to get to Cannon, because he was the only clear thought in her head. The only image that wasn't foggy or disjointed.

Her legs shook as she shuffled across the room. Each step made her side burn, her breath stall, but it was worth it if it meant she'd be safe. If she could maybe get to a phone. Figure out how much trouble she was in.

The door handle rattled in her grip before she was able to twist it—sliver it open. A hallway. No armed men. No obvious traps. Nothing unusual. Soft murmurs echoed from somewhere in the distance—proof she wasn't alone. It also meant simply walking out of wherever she was probably wasn't an option. No doubt she'd have to walk past those voices, and she wasn't in any condition to fight. Hell, she wasn't sure she'd make it down the corridor before passing out.

She closed her eyes. Focused on breathing. On tempering the burn of every inhalation. Figuring out how to call Cannon. Hadn't they planned on dinner? Had she missed it? Was he looking for her?

"Jericho?"

She blinked, nearly fell when the door opened—tripping her against the frame. A guy lunged toward her, stopping when she flinched. Tried to back away, not that she was able to take more than a step before having to lean on the wall.

The guy straightened. Moved back a bit. He was large. Not as tall or as broad as Cannon, but huge, nonetheless. He was good looking, in a dangerous thug sort of way, with stunning green eyes and brown hair. He gave her a smile, keeping his hands turned palms forward. "Easy, honey. I'm not going to hurt you. Quite the opposite, actually. But...it's way too soon for you to be out of bed. You're going to pull out your stitches. Give yourself another concussion. Let me help you back to the bedroom."

"Who..." God, it hurt to talk.

"The name's Russel Foster. My buddies call me Ice. I'm a friend of Cannon's—"

"Cannon?" She sagged against the wall, shaking her head when the man—Ice, she thought he'd said—stepped toward her. "Where..."

Christ. Two words? That's all she could manage?

He sighed. "He hasn't left your side for two days, but...he had to go down to your office. Talk to your boss. Art Collins."

"No. No, it's... It's not safe. He..." Images flashed through her mind, making her inhale. She palmed her head. Tried to stop if from simply exploding. "He... I... It's not safe."

"Easy. You're still suffering from blood loss. The trauma. A concussion. You need to rest. Give your body time to heal. You'll remember once you're feeling better."

She shook her head, again, wondering how long she could stand there before she slid down the wall. Passed out. "Cannon…"

"Shit, Jericho. What the hell are you doing up?"

That voice. It was *his* voice. She managed to turn, see him standing in the hallway before her legs completely buckled. Slid her onto her ass. He was there in a heartbeat, scooping her up, holding her against his chest. She let her head fall against the crook of his shoulder as everything started to fade.

She blinked to find him hovering over her, tucking some of her hair behind her ear. She reached for his hand —was able to wrap her fingers around his wrist. "Cannon."

He leaned in close. "I'm gone for all of an hour, and that's when you choose to wake up? You're making me look bad, sweetheart."

"I…" She wanted to say she'd been searching for him. That he was the only person she trusted. That she needed him. But her tongue felt overly large. Didn't form the words.

He smiled. One of those devastating ones that warmed her all the way to her toes. "Shhh. Ice is right. You need to rest."

"No. Danger…"

"I know. But not here. You're safe."

"Nowhere's safe."

"I've got four ex-Special Forces buddies that are determined to prove otherwise. Another on the way. I'm not going to let anyone get to you. Not while I'm still breathing. Sleep."

She tightened her grip on his arm. At least, she thought she did. Either way, it worked—had him dipping a bit closer. "Stay."

"Damn straight. Wouldn't have left if it hadn't been necessary. But I needed to buy you more time before they find out where you are."

"No. I mean, stay. With me."

He chuckled. "Are you trying to seduce me?"

"I..." Her throat thickened, the panic from before crawling along her nerves. "I'm sc..."

His expression softened, those hard lines fading from around his eyes and mouth. "I know. But I'm here. And I'm staying."

He glanced behind him, mumbled something she couldn't make out. She was fading, her vision slowly disappearing around the edges. It felt wrong. Lying there. Alone.

The bed dipped, then he was lifting her. Placing her head on his chest, his arm around her back. She smiled. Didn't fight the pull of the darkness around her. Not as long as he was holding her.

Soft lips against her forehead. "Sleep. We'll talk when you're stronger."

I knew you'd find out... This is much kinder... It'll all be over soon...

"No."

Jericho jolted awake, the echoed voice spiking her heart rate. She needed to escape. Find Cannon. Get help.

Strong hands wrapped around her, stilling her movements just as pain flared through her side. "Easy, sweetheart. It's just a dream."

She froze, that deep gravelly voice soothing the panicky feeling beneath her skin. She glanced up. He was staring down at her, those copper eyes narrowed. One hand lifted to rest on her face, his thumb softly stroking her chin.

She relaxed, sinking into his embrace. "Cannon. I..." She hissed out her next breath. "Where am I? What happened?"

He grunted, shuffling until his back was against the headboard with her body cradled against him. "You're at a friend's place. You met him earlier. When you woke up. His name's Ice. Do you remember?"

Scattered memories shuffled through her mind, most of them too fragmented to make sense of. "Not really. Everything's pretty fuzzy."

"Expected. Ice says you lost two liters of blood. A less stubborn soul would have died."

There was an edge to his voice. One she hadn't heard before. One she swore was fear. But... She couldn't imagine him being afraid of anything. He was too imposing. Too much the warrior.

A few of the memories slotted into place. "You came for me, didn't you?"

His hand slid back until he was holding her head. "Was there any doubt? I'll always come for you. I'm just sorry I didn't get there sooner. Couldn't stop you from getting hurt. Whoever did this to you..."

That look. She recognized it. He'd had the same expression when she'd first made eye contact with him in the restaurant. Fear for her mixed with cold steel determination. No one had ever looked at her like that.

She managed to raise her hand—brush her thumb along his cheek. It was rough. Shadowed with stubble. Not quite a beard but close. "Thank you."

His eye twitched before he leaned down—rested his forehead on hers. He released a shaky breath, the heat from his skin warming hers. "Don't ever scare me like that, again. God, Jericho..." Another raspy exhalation. "When I saw your car on fire—thought I'd lost you..."

"Not gonna let you get away that easily... Wait. The car was on fire? What..."

She inhaled as images slammed into her head. Driving along the interstate. A black Suburban behind them. A bloody knife glinting in the light. There had been beeping and an explosion. She just didn't remember why. How all the events were connected.

"Jericho? Talk to me, sweetheart. Ice!"

Footsteps. The door crashing open. Then, fingers on her jaw, twisting her head slightly. A light flashed in her eyes as a man's face blinked into view.

The guy was touching the sore spot on her head, then snapping his fingers in front of her. "Jericho? Can you hear me?"

She grimaced, a jolt of pain pulsing through her. "Of course, I can hear you. I'm not deaf."

He chuckled. "Girl's as charming as you, Cannon. Okay, honey. Are you feeling dizzy? Seeing double?"

"No. Not anymore. I'm just...confused. Cannon mentioned the car being on fire, and all these images just shot into my head. But…I don't know how to make sense of them."

The guy—Ice, she thought Cannon had yelled—sighed, shoving a tiny flashlight back in his shirt pocket. "It's only been a few days. And the fact you remember anything is encouraging. Give it a bit more time—"

"A few days?" She turned to look at Cannon. "How long have I been here?"

"Five days."

"What? But—"

"Breathe, honey." Ice was back, fingers on her pulse. "Trust me, five days is nothing. Between the stabbing, the concussion and the blood loss…" He snorted. "You're lucky it hasn't been double that. And that's ignoring the fact you tried to walk out of here after only a couple. We've had to take turns watching you before Cannon agreed to even leave the bed." He winked. "Though, I don't think he needs an excuse to want to stay in it with you."

"Jackass." Cannon gave her hand a squeeze. "But he's right about you needing more time to recover. Christ, when we brought you in…" He swallowed. It sounded rough. Thick. As if he'd had to fight to get it down. "I've never seen someone that pale still breathing."

She sighed, relaxing against Cannon. "So, now what?"

He smiled, and she wondered if this was the kind of dizzy feeling Ice had been asking her about. "Now, you focus on getting better, while we continue gathering as much intel as we can without drawing too much attention. As far as the Marshal Service is concerned, you're missing. We'd like to keep it that way until we know why you were attacked. Who's targeting you."

"Missing? Why wouldn't you tell..." She inhaled, more images rearranging inside her head. "What happened to Dave?"

Cannon's jaw clenched, and he looked around the room then back at her. "Jericho."

"What? What aren't you telling me? Did he get hurt? Is he missing?"

He reached up, tucked some of her hair behind her ear. "I'm sorry, sweetheart. He didn't make it."

"What do you mean?" She looked around at Ice and the other men standing in the doorway then back to Cannon. "He's...dead?"

Cannon's hand covered hers, his grip around her waist tightening. "He was killed in the explosion. They checked the DNA against what they had on file. It was a confirmed match."

She shook her head. "No, no, that's not right. He's not dead."

"Jericho..."

"No. I mean he was dead. Next to me, but..." She palmed her head. "Crap."

"Stop trying to force it." Ice, again. Eye level. "You need to rest. I know this is a lot to take in, but if you push too hard, you could relapse. Suffer side effects from the concussion. Please, just...rest."

"You're standing here telling me my partner's dead. I can't just lie in bed. God..."

But the tears she'd expected didn't fall. Instead, anger burned beneath her skin as a sour feeling settled in her stomach. Something didn't feel right, and she couldn't shake the unnerving sensation that they'd gotten the story wrong. That there was a much greater threat than they suspected.

Cannon turned her then wrapped his arms around her. "I know this has got to be tearing you up, but you're in no condition to fight. Not, yet. Christ, you're lucky you're alive. If you hadn't shared your location—if I'd gotten there five minutes later..."

His chest heaved against hers, and she knew. Knew he was using every tactic he'd learned in the military to keep his emotions in check. That a piece of the man he'd been before the Army had beaten any form of softness out of him was bleeding through.

He drew a deep breath against her back, then his lips brushed over her cheek. "It's not very often I get a chance to take care of my girl. In fact, I've never really had one, so this is a first. Close your eyes. I'll get you something to eat in a bit. Okay? And I promise you, we'll get whoever did this. Just not today."

"But..."

"Strategy, Jericho. You can't help us if you put yourself in the hospital."

"No hospitals." She inhaled then looked at him. "I...I don't know why I said that."

"Doesn't matter. I'm keeping you safe, and that means right here. With us."

She glanced at the other men, again. They had the same steely determination in their eyes. Her resistance fled, bone-weary exhaustion taking its place. "A day. That's all I can promise."

"Then, we'll start with that."

Ice straightened. "You two stay put. I'll get you both

something to eat. Drink. And, tomorrow, we'll talk. Okay?"

She nodded, relaxing into Cannon's embrace as the others left, closing the door behind them.

Cannon sighed, dropping a kiss on her cheek. "I know this is killing you. I just need you to trust me—trust my team."

She looked up at him, his expression a mix of lethal bruiser and sexy secret agent. "You've had that since the night in the bar. I knew you were going to change my opinion of men."

He chuckled. "Seems only fair since you've changed the way I picture the future playing out. You're dangerous, sweetheart."

"I like the sound of that." She stifled a yawn. How could she be tired when she'd done nothing but sleep for five days?

Another laugh. "Stubborn. Come on. Rest until Ice brings you some food. Then, you can eat and sleep some more."

"All I do is sleep."

"And that's all you're gonna keep doing until you don't look like death warmed over." He dropped another kiss on her earlobe, making her shiver. "I'll stay with you."

"Just my luck. I finally get you into bed, and all we do is sleep. Doesn't seem fair."

"Don't worry. As soon as you're up for more, you won't be getting any sleep. Take advantage of it while you can. Because having you nearly die on me…" He sighed. "It's put a lot of things in perspective. And, once we take care of the trouble you're in, we're going to have a long chat. The kind that ends with you agreeing to move in with me—where I can keep an eye on you."

She inhaled, unable to get her mouth to close. Had he really just asked her to live with him?

"Not now. First, you get better. Just know this... I don't do anything half-assed, and I never back down." He looked up when Ice walked in carrying a tray of food. "Eat. Rest. Then, we go hunting, because I have big plans for the future, and we can't make them a reality until we've eliminated the men threatening you."

CHAPTER TWELVE

Jericho Nash was going to be the death of Cannon, and there wasn't a damn thing he could do about it. *Wanted* to do about it. But...he wouldn't argue if she agreed to be a bit less stubborn.

Not even twenty-four hours since she'd woken up— truly woken—and she was sitting at the table, watching the rest of his team take their seats. A bit of color had returned to her cheeks, but she still looked weak. Had needed to stop halfway to her chair to catch her breath. He'd offered to carry her, but she'd stuck out that adorable chin of hers and had insisted she needed to do it herself. That she couldn't waste any more time lying in bed, doing nothing.

She seemed to forget the part where she'd nearly died. Had required five units of blood just to keep from coding. That her body was still healing, even if, outwardly, her wound looked better.

She hadn't reacted when Ice had changed her bandage —shown her the line of stitches across her lower ribs.

Cannon had wanted to punch his fist through the wall. He wasn't sure even killing the fucker who'd stabbed her would be enough. Would tame the rage at the thought of her being hurt. Being targeted. But it would be a start.

Of course, finding the people responsible wasn't as easy as he'd hoped. Ty Brown had vanished. Simply disappeared—no doubt hidden with the help of the Macmillans' resources. If Brown was smart, he'd be long gone. Off to some remote country with no extradition laws.

Damn good thing guys like him weren't that smart. That they seemed to think they were untouchable. The bastard was still in town. Still on the payroll. Cannon knew it. Sensed it in the soldier part of his brain that hadn't shut off since Jericho had sent him that SOS. That was determined to stay on high alert until he'd eliminated everyone remotely connected to her attack. Which meant he could still hunt the creep down. Show Brown what happened when he messed with the people Cannon loved.

There was no point in denying that fact, any longer. He was in love with Jericho Nash. From her untamed mass of auburn hair all the way to her dainty toes. The woman had him tied around her finger. And not with slip knots he could easy undo. Unbreakable chains guaranteed to rip out his heart if he tried to remove them. The heart she'd resurrected that night in the bar.

The only saving grace was that he wasn't the only one. Though she hadn't said anything, Cannon knew Jericho was feeling just as conflicted—just as invested—as he was. It had been evident in the way she'd looked at him whenever he'd woken her to check her condition—the dreamy gaze. The need mirrored in her eyes. Even with her skin still deathly white, a slight blush had colored her cheeks whenever he'd touched her or pulled her against him. Not to mention the fact she'd called out his name. Repeatedly. Even now, all he had to do was glance at her—smile—and her face lit up. Literally glowed. As if he'd flicked some hidden switch.

His buddies hadn't missed any opportunity to mention it, either, the fuckers. Seemed to derive extreme pleasure from the hold she had over him. He'd have knocked them on their asses if they hadn't put theirs on the line to keep her safe. Were willing to do anything to protect her. He just wished he didn't feel so out of control. He had zero experience dealing with these emotions.

Danger? Not a problem. He'd faced a lifetime's worth of that. Was intimately connected to it. There wasn't a threat he wouldn't face, a challenge he couldn't overcome.

Dying? He'd made peace with that during Ranger training. When anything soft had been beaten out of him. Turned to stone then forged into steel. After going through Delta Force selection... Yeah, he'd walked out stone cold and focused. Had mastered locking away his feelings—his fears—and losing the key.

And now...

In a matter of weeks, Jericho had managed to open that box and expose everything. Reduce him to a shadow of his former self. Sure, he could tackle anything her enemies might throw his way. Could face a room—a squad—full of hitmen and thugs and come out the other side intact. He hadn't lost an ounce of skill or determination. But when those plans involved her—when she was in the room, with him. At risk?

He lost it. Narrowed his focus to her, and only her.

Tunnel vision got good men killed. Got their teammates killed. When it came to guys like him... It made them more than dangerous. Or deadly. It made him unpredictable. And his buddies, his damn brothers, needed him to be steady. To carry out his objective as planned, not alter it because he got it inside his head she was in trouble. That he needed to take out her targets, first. Abandon everything in order to see to her safety.

At least, he wasn't completely alone in that, either. Ice, Midnight, Rigs... They all suffered from a similar fate where their partners were concerned. Appeared just as single-minded toward the women they loved. It didn't solve his issue—how to freaking deal with it—but there was solace in knowing they shared his insanity.

Ice stood next to Jericho, giving everyone a stern look before nodding at her. "Okay. Despite the fact you still need more time to heal, I'd be lying if I said we didn't need more intel. Answers only you have. But..." He pointed a finger at her. "If I think you're pushing too hard, or you're draining yourself, I'm stopping this. And don't even bother trying to give me the puppy-dog eyes. Unlike Cannon, I'm immune."

Jericho glanced at Cannon and bam—that inner light that gleamed out of every pore lit up. Made him blink because... Fuck. She was too damn beautiful when she looked at him like that. As if he was the center of her world.

She smiled then focused back on Ice. "Unless it's Harlequin. And she doesn't have to do anything other than smile."

Ice chuckled, gazing at the woman in question. "Didn't take you long to figure that out."

Jericho shrugged. "I'd be a pretty lousy marshal if I didn't notice. And I doubt the puppy-eyes would actually work on Cannon."

"You're right." Ice winked at her. "All you have to do is breathe."

She looked at him, again. Studied his face. Cannon tried to appear unaffected. He'd been doing it for years. But damn... Her face. Beyond the beauty, beyond the light, there was lust and heat, and something else. Something deeper that tugged at him. Made him reach for her hand—take it in his. It was small and cold and perfect.

He sighed, raking his other hand through his hair. "Everyone has a weakness, sweetheart. But I can be stone cold if it involves your safety. No compromising there, so... Don't think I'll challenge Ice's decision if he thinks you're endangering your well-being."

She snorted. "You guys do realize I've been taking care of myself for years, now, right?"

"And you've done an excellent job. But, I'm betting you didn't have hitmen and mafia money trying to take you down. You do, now. Which brings us to why we're here." Cannon took a deep breath, slowly blowing it out. As much as he wanted answers, a part of him still worried she'd remember something she shouldn't. That the amnesia was her brain's way of protecting her from damaging events. The kind you didn't bounce back from.

He motioned to the others. "I've given everyone a basic rundown. That, coupled with what you've been able to tell us so far, has painted a decent picture of what went down, but..."

"There're holes." She relaxed back in the chair. "Things are still fuzzy."

"That's to be expected." Ice gave her other hand a pat. "I'm hoping that, if we walk through the last of the trip, it might jog a few of those more stubborn memories. If you're up for it?"

"Just tell me where you want to start."

Ice smiled. "All right. We understand you were transporting a prisoner—a guy named Ty Brown. Mafia hitman. That everything seemed to be going all right until you got back to Seattle. So, let's jump to there. You're in the car, turning onto I-5, but then, you ended up in the industrial district. What happened? I can't imagine that was the intended route."

"It was Dave. He was convinced we were being followed by a black Suburban. He damn near crashed the car swerving into the off-ramp."

"Did it follow you?"

"No." She eased her hand free then speared her fingers through her hair, wincing when it obviously pulled against the lump still visible on her forehead. "I've been doing this job long enough to know when I'm being followed. I'd been watching. There wasn't anything suspicious about the Suburban."

"Did you tell Dave?"

"Of course, but he said something about me being preoccupied with the text Cannon had sent. I wasn't but... I guess it hit a nerve, so I went along with it."

Rigs leaned forward. The man still seemed surprised that Jericho hadn't made a scene when she'd first met him. That she'd taken his visible scars in stride and brushed them off as if they weren't there. "Is that when you sent Cannon your location?"

Jericho groaned, palming her face as she braced her

elbows on the table. "It's against protocol. I know, but... Dave didn't call to update our route. Was acting like a complete ass. And I got this feeling..." She looked up. "I knew it was breaking the rules, but I also knew I could trust Cannon. That, if I was wrong, he'd keep it between us."

"Damn fucking straight." Cannon reclaimed her hand, sandwiching it between his. "You always, and I mean always, trust your instincts. If you think something's off, it's because it is. And everyone at this table would rather you call in backup and be wrong, than toe the line and get yourself killed."

"Cannon's right." Rigs straightened. "If you hadn't trusted those instincts—"

"I'd be dead, too."

Cannon grunted. "Over my dead body."

Jericho turned to him. Smiled.

Rigs chuckled. "I'd hate to be the other guys. They don't have a clue the caliber of enemy they've made. So, what happened next? How did it all fall apart?"

She stared at the table. "That's where it gets fuzzy. I remember Dave saying something about the Suburban, again. He thought it was waiting for us."

"But it wasn't?" Rigs hedged.

"I swear there was nothing there. No parked cars, no people standing on the corner. Walking along the street. I searched the intersection then..."

They waited, but she just sat there, staring off.

Cannon shifted closer. "Jericho? You okay?"

She looked up, face pale, chest heaving. Her fingers clenched around his, the tremble in them impossible to miss. "He stabbed me."

"Who?" Cannon scoffed. "Dave?"

She surged to her feet, stumbling back. Ice was at her side, looking as if he planned on catching her if she fell, but he wouldn't need to. Cannon wasn't about to let her get so much as another scratch.

He shouldered in beside her. "Easy, sweetheart. Slow your breathing. Everything's going to be okay."

"Okay?" Her voice was strained. A full octave higher than usual. "My partner—my friend—just tried to kill me. Left me for dead in a car set to explode. How is that going to be okay?"

"Breathe. Slower."

She closed her eyes, swayed, but he had her. Wrapped her in his arms while Ice checked her pulse. The guy frowned but backed away.

Cannon brushed his mouth across her ear. "We'll figure it out."

She took a few shuddering breaths. "I don't understand. Why?"

"Sweetheart. I'm not saying I don't believe you, but is it possible it might have been Brown who stabbed you? Maybe he incapacitated Dave while you were looking the other way then attacked you."

Another fierce shake of her head. "It was Dave. I remember staring down, seeing him wipe the blade off on his pants before he grabbed my hair and smashed me against the dash. Then, the window. After that... I can't be sure what happened, other than you showing up." She glanced back at him, eyes glassy. "I remember that. You saving me."

Fuck, his damn chest constricted at the look in her eyes—the love staring him in the face. All he'd done was show up. Track her down. And he'd had help. If he'd been on the ball, he'd have left his damn office the second she'd pinged him. Worried about the reasons and ramifications later. Those precious minutes he'd wasted...

"Thought I told you I'd always have your back. And the asshole's lucky he's dead."

"Which makes no sense. Why try to kill me if he didn't have a plan? If freeing Brown was setting Dave up to be killed?"

"We're talking about a hitman with mafia connections. I don't think anything Brown does has to make sense or seem justified."

"No." Her hair bounced wildly around her shoulders. "I heard voices. Footsteps. Something about them meeting up. Are you sure it was Dave in the car?"

Cannon motioned to Bridgette.

She pursed her lips together. "I had Jeremy double check the file for me. The ME said the DNA matched to what the Marshal Service had on file. But...that's all they really had to go on. I'm afraid there wasn't much left."

Jericho made a strangled moaning sound then nodded. "I don't have a clue what's going on."

"We'll get to the bottom of this. Promise." Cannon drew her a bit closer. "It explains why you were worried about a hospital, though. If you didn't realize Dave was dead, you probably thought he could track you down if he discovered you hadn't died in the explosion."

"I guess, but..."

"But it doesn't feel right."

"Not even a little. There's something else—something I'm missing. Or forgetting." She finally relaxed against him. "Maybe we'll get more answers once I go back. Can scour through the files."

"Not until you're stronger. Until I know you'll be safe there."

"I hardly think anyone's going to target the Marshal Office."

"Not risking it." Cannon shook his head at the look she flashed him. "Stubborn. Just...let me call in a few favors. Have the rest of your office checked out. If Dave was dirty..."

"Art's clean. I'd bet my life on it."

"I'm not as trusting as you are."

"He's clean."

"Okay. We'll call him—soon. Maybe arrange for a time for you to go in when only he's there. When a few of us can shadow you without having to answer a bunch of questions. But this isn't over until Ty Brown is either back in custody or dead—preferably the latter. Until we're sure there aren't more people gunning for you—possibly people you work with."

"There will always be people gunning for me. It comes with the job."

"Calculated risks, sweetheart. This isn't random, and it isn't isolated. Maybe it was just a prison break. Maybe Dave made a one-time deal, and this was Brown or the Macmillans tying up loose ends, and you got caught in the crossfire. I just want to make sure that's the case before you put a giant bullseye on your back. Okay?"

"Okay."

"Good. Now, how about we sit down? Get something to eat, and we can go through it in more detail."

"Who knew you were such a worrier?"

"Don't let it get out. I can't have everyone knowing I've gone soft."

"It'll be our secret."

"Right. Okay...the beginning, again. And, this time, let's slow it all down. I want you to tell us everything. Every small, seemingly insignificant detail. From what you were listening to on the radio to what Dave ate. I want to know what you felt, smelled and saw throughout the trip. If he left you alone with Brown, even just to go to the bathroom. And then, we'll plan."

CHAPTER THIRTEEN

It was midnight. Again.

Two days since she'd sat at the table and walked through the incident, and she still hadn't done much more than sleep and rest. Cannon had gotten her a laptop—used his new status to gain access to the Marshal Service database. But, even after scouring through a bunch of files—the ones she could access and not raise suspicions—they weren't any closer to figuring out why Dave had attacked her. If he'd made a deal with Brown, the Macmillans, or if her memories were skewed. If it hadn't been Dave, after all. Just her messed up mind playing tricks on her. A by-product of the trauma, shock, and blood loss. Not to mention the concussion. It was to the point even she was questioning herself.

No one had come out and told her she was nuts. Not with Cannon standing over her like a damn watchdog. The other men might have been his teammates—his brothers—but there was no denying she came first. That he'd defend her, period. Whether it was right or not.

She wasn't sure what she'd done to deserve that level of devotion. Hell, they hadn't even had sex. One panty-melting kiss in his truck, and a month's worth of coffee and texting. Oh, and he'd saved her life. Three times, now. The bar might have turned out okay, but she counted it, just the same. He'd come to her aid, then, and it had only escalated since. Armed thugs. Attempted murder... It didn't matter that they were dealing with a hitman. With the mafia. He treated them all the same. Waved it off as nothing compared to what he'd dealt with in the service. The years he'd spent undercover.

He'd shared a bit about his past, seeing as she had fairly high-level security clearance. Though, she knew it barely touched on everything he'd done. That he couldn't tell her any in-depth details. But the fact he'd opened up, at all, had shocked her. Made her realize just how much he trusted her.

It also made her realize how far she'd fallen. How much he meant to her. Thirty-odd years of avoiding any kind of meaningful commitment, and Cannon had stolen her heart in only a month.

No, not stolen. That seemed inadequate in terms of what he'd done. Stolen implied there was a chance she might get it back. That she could give it to someone else. He'd possessed it. Claimed it as his. Had trapped it, and hidden it away in some kind of impenetrable fortress. *That* was more along the lines of what he'd done.

But what scared her more was that she didn't even care. How could she when everything she learned about him only made her love him more? Want him in her life more. Just...more.

She groaned as she pushed up, leaning against the

headboard. She'd never really been the romantic type. Hadn't fantasized about finding that special someone. Getting married. Having kids. Fate. Soul Mates. They'd never factored in. Until now. Until he'd surpassed her expectations that very first night. Since then…

It had been a slow slide into utter madness. Even now, knowing he was out…investigating, made her edgy. Because she knew he was hunting. Trying to track down Ty Brown. Make her world safe, again.

She should be with him. Guarding his back. Keeping his ass intact. Not that he was alone. She'd seen Rigs and Colt walk out with him, so…he didn't lack for backup. And with men whose skills far surpassed hers.

Still… Hadn't she heard that love rarely made sense?

"Shouldn't you be sleeping?"

She startled, hand flying to her chest as her focus swung to the door. Cannon was leaning against the frame, silhouette just visible by a muted light in the hallway. It struck her how massive he was. How utterly unyielding.

"Jesus, Cannon. Make a little noise before you simply appear in a doorway."

"Didn't want to wake you."

"You saw me leaning against the headboard."

"Noise gets you caught. And caught gets you dead. Old habits, sweetheart." He walked into the room, moving smoothly across the floor. He didn't make a sound. Not a step, not a whisper of cloth across the weapons she was sure were hidden beneath his jacket.

He stopped beside a chair, laying some items on it before continuing to the bed. It dipped against his weight as he sat on the edge, toeing off his boots before turning to look at her.

Moonlight illuminated half of his face, accentuating the hard angles. He was still in warrior mode. Lips pressed firmly together. Eyes wary. He'd shaved a few days ago, but a healthy scruff had already grown back, shadowing his jaw in a deep gray.

Even looking every inch the lethal soldier he was, he was stunning. Handsome in a way that transcended symmetry and pretty features. He was rugged. Masculine. A man who'd seen the worst sides of humanity without losing his.

She reached for his jaw, enjoying the way the stubble caught on her fingers. "Find anything?"

A huff accompanied by his furrowed brow answered for him. But he shook his head once, anyway. "Found a few fledglings. But nothing that would lead us to Brown. Asshole's good at hiding. I'll grant him that. But we're equally good at hunting, so…"

So, it was only a matter of time. That he'd search until he'd obtained his prize. Then, his gaze swept the length of her, and she knew he'd have that same hard determination where she was concerned. That he wouldn't stop until she'd surrendered, either.

But in a completely different way.

The thought ignited a billow of heat low in her core. She'd been at his side, night and day, for a week. Granted, she only really remembered the last couple days, but her body remembered all of it. Had grown accustomed to sleeping with him—his shoulder as her pillow. One muscular arm wrapped around her back. His hand resting either above or below her wound. The feeling of being completely safe. And she wasn't sure she could go back to how it was before. Texts goodnight then sleeping, alone.

She didn't want to be alone. Not anymore.

Which meant, it was time.

Cannon's eyes narrowed. She couldn't quite make out the copper color in the moonlight, but the way he tilted his head. Stared. She knew he was trying to puzzle her out. She'd spent the past few minutes sitting there just staring at him. Lost in the thoughts of his body pressed against hers. Every inch touching.

A chuckle, then he was placing his hand over hers on his face. "Something tells me those thoughts of yours aren't on Brown or whether or not it's safe for you out in the world, yet."

She shrugged. Most of the stitches had fallen out, already, and it was nice not to feel them tugging against her skin. Even her ribs felt better. Not without pain, but definitely manageable. "It's kind of hard to focus on that when you're this close."

"While I love where you're heading with this, sweetheart, you're—"

"Fine, Cannon. I'm fine."

"You're better. Not going to die on me if I look away for a second. Go out on a scouting mission. But your ribs—"

"Are healing. Sure, I won't be going for a run or asking you to spar with me for a while. But touching, kissing..." She shuffled closer, sliding her other hand along the opposite side of his jaw. "I could definitely muscle through that."

"I'd rather you didn't have to muscle—"

She kissed him. Used her grip to tug his head down as she simply slid the last foot separating them on the bed. He inhaled against her lips, then he was kissing her back. Threading his fingers through her hair, digging the other into the top of her ass as he pulled her flush against him. His tongue traced the edge of her mouth then delved inside.

Heat. Spice. A heady mix that was just him. He moaned as their tongues tangled, lifting off to nip his way along her throat before repositioning and launching another attack. The hand in her hair flexed, tugged a bit, then released.

His rapid breath caressed her chin when he eased back, resting his forehead on hers. "Christ."

She smiled. "And that was just a kiss. Imagine what it could be like without any clothes on."

His muscles tensed beneath her fingers. "While I'd love nothing more than to finally make love to you..."

She laughed. "I'm not going to break."

Another flex of his fingers. Of them fisting around her hair, somehow bringing her even closer as he shifted a bit to grab more of her ass. "Jericho..."

"God, the way you say my name. Consider me seduced."

"Sweetheart. You're still weak."

"Not that weak." She huffed at the clench of his jaw. The way he closed his eyes as if in pain. "Cannon. Rick."

He snapped his gaze up—eyes wide. As if he'd never heard his name before.

She released one hand from behind his neck—cupped his jaw. "We can take it slow. Trust me. I've had plenty of sleep."

"But that's the problem." He untangled his fingers from her hair, lifted his hand from her ass, then stood, moving over to the door. He closed it then turned and leaned against it.

The warrior was back, not that he'd ever truly left. But there was no denying the hard line of his jaw, the way his nostrils flared in the dull light. He took what appeared to be a calming breath, fisting his hands at his side.

"Since I joined the service, my life has been all about control. Allowing your emotions to rule your actions is the fastest way to get yourself killed. So, we train—long. Hard. Until every movement, every action is planned."

She braced some of her weight on one arm, tilting her head off to one side. "Still not seeing how this equates to us making love being a problem. If you're saying you like to be in control in the bedroom—"

"That's the problem! I look at you, and fuck...that control vanishes. Poof. Just gone. It's like you short circuit my brain. None of the signals get through. I have to rely only on my instincts. My senses. My damn feelings."

He pushed off. Took a step closer. "This is uncharted territory for me. You're still hurt. You need gentle. To be cherished. And all I can think about is how desperate I am to touch you. How my damn skin itches to rub against yours. I want to take you in my arms and thrust inside. Pound you for hours." He released a strangled breath. Rough. Painful. "I don't want to hurt you, and I don't know if I can give you the kind of loving you deserve. That you need. Not when you put my control to the test with nothing more than your smile."

The tightness in her chest that had taken root since he'd walked into her life eased. And, finally, she could breathe. Because it all made sense.

Jericho eased off the bed. At least, standing, walking—

it didn't hurt like it had before. Just a slight ache. Nothing she couldn't live with. And she knew, once he'd taken her in his arms—removed the shirt she'd borrowed from him and put his lips on her skin...

She wouldn't feel anything but burning need.

Cannon didn't move, didn't breathe, as she stepped over to him. Not until she drew her finger along his shoulder then down his chest, settling it over his heart. It pounded against her palm, the rhythm nearly as fast as hers.

She smiled. "First of all, you're not the only one who's running blind. I've never felt like this before, either. Never been this far gone. I feel like I've jumped off a cliff but haven't hit the ground. That I just keep falling. It's unnerving, if I'm being honest."

"Jericho—"

She placed her finger over his mouth. "It's still my turn, Master Sergeant. Second, you're assuming I want gentle. That I need you to hold back. I've told you I'm not fragile, and you loving me—however that has to happen— isn't going to break me. But, more importantly... You said I test your control, right?"

He nodded, eyes wary, his chest rising and falling rapidly beneath her other hand.

She tapped his lips with her finger. "Seems to me, you also said there isn't a test you've failed, yet."

He grunted, gently removing her finger from in front of his mouth. "This is different."

"Is it?"

"We're talking about your well-being."

"Which will be compromised by never-ending frustration if you don't pick me up and carry me over to that bed. Followed by a night of making me see stars." She drew a pattern along his chest. "You *can* go all night, can't you?"

A twitch of the muscle in his temple. "You're not helping me, sweetheart."

"Is this better?" She reached her other hand down—cupped his shaft through his pants.

He shuddered, grabbed her arms—hard—then forcefully gentled his touch. "Dangerous."

"Good. If I were looking for safe, I'd be dating a banker. Or an accountant. And I'd be dead. So, stop worrying about control or if you're gonna break me, and kiss me, already."

Cannon stood there, staring, for nearly a minute before closing his eyes, then leaning forward. She let him lead, knowing it had to be his choice. That, if he was convinced having sex was going to set her healing back, there wouldn't be anything she could say or do to change his mind. How had he put it before? She was his weakness—had far too much power over his decisions—except where her safety was concerned. He'd claimed he couldn't be swayed, and she knew he hadn't been joking.

So, she waited, her hands palming his chest, her heart beating so fast she heard it strumming inside her head. She wet her lips as he moved in closer, hovering a breath away. God, the heat pouring off of him. She didn't know how he wasn't sweating.

She was. Sweating and breathing and praying for him to do…something. Forget about the sex hurting her. Standing there—almost touching—was going to kill her. Make her heart explode or maybe she'd simply die from anticipation.

"Rick…"

Cannon opened his eyes, that wonderful copper color lost in the ebony pupils. "There's just something about the way you say my name."

"Make love to me, and I'll scream it." She chuckled. "Well, maybe not scream since we're not alone. Not really. I mean, I'm sure one of your buddies is up guarding—"

He covered her mouth with his, swallowing any last words. She stepped into him. It wasn't more than a few inches, but it felt as if she'd bridged a canyon. A huge divide separating his body from hers. All that thick firm muscle pressing against her—his erection hard and thick nudging her hip. She swore it lengthened as the kiss drew on, nearly taking her to her knees when he finally eased back.

He tsked, gently pulled her shirt over her head then scooped her into his arms, careful not to jostle her ribs as he headed for the bed. "I knew I'd never win an argument with you. The only question left is… How are we going to start this off?"

CHAPTER FOURTEEN

Cannon was going to die. Right there in the bedroom. Jericho in his arms, her body snugged against his. She seemed completely at ease, while his damn heart pounded against his ribs, his dick so long and hard, he expected it to explode at any second. And take him with it because the way she was looking at him...

He'd been in complete control. After four hours spent casing a bar Ty Brown was rumored to frequent only to come up empty handed, Cannon had used the ride home to calm his nerves. The ones that were getting antsy with the utter lack of progress. Over a week since Jericho had nearly died, and he'd gotten nowhere. Not one concrete lead.

So, he'd used some breathing techniques—gone over a bunch of old army strategies—just to rid himself of the excess adrenaline coursing through his veins. The twitchy feeling that usually required a pitcher of beer or a few rounds of sex to quiet. But since he hadn't thought either was on the table...

Sure, he wanted Jericho. Was certain he'd used up every reserve ounce of restraint the past few days resisting the urge to do more than hold her. But, she was hurt. Had stitches. And he knew how to shut down his needs. Lock them in a box and tuck them away until the timing was right. Until she didn't look as if she was about to pass out. Didn't grimace every time she moved.

He'd been doing just fine—had prepared himself for the instant infusion of her scent. The cute snuffling noises she made when she slept. How she'd curl into him the moment he got into bed with her—stay that way until she woke the next morning. Then, he'd walked into their room and spotted her leaning against the headboard, seemingly lost in thought.

He'd adapted. Put more of his energy into staying loose. A quick conversation, and he'd continue with his plan—tamp down the burning ache in his groin. The one giving him permanent blue balls. He'd strip down to his boxers, pray his dick didn't rip through the fabric, then take pleasure in holding her all night.

Everything had been going according to plan, until she'd stared at him with all the heat he was feeling inside. He'd tried to talk his way out of it. Remind her she was still healing. Still weak. But she'd trumped his hand and kissed him.

His brain had fried. All rational thought just burned away, with nothing left but raging desire. Arousal so damn strong he wasn't even sure he'd get his pants off before shooting his load. Not that he'd be done. He was sure he could go several rounds and not come close to quenching his need. Easing the ache in his balls. But that was the problem.

Despite being better than when he'd found her, she still wasn't a hundred percent. Her mouth still twitched when she walked. And just thinking that he could hurt her—would hurt her because, damn it, gentle wasn't on the table. Wasn't even close to being viable. Not when he was jumping into the abyss.

Sure, he'd had his fair share of lovers. Had even casually dated an admin clerk at one of the bases until he'd been sent undercover two years ago. But all of his previous encounters had been nothing more than a release. Mutual pleasure. If he needed it hard, fast, the women he'd bedded hadn't minded. Had known going in what to expect. He made sure they enjoyed themselves, but in the end, it was all about getting whatever else was bothering him out of his system.

He'd lost a couple of teammates? A night of sex helped push away those traitorous emotions. Had been the ultimate distraction. Until now.

He didn't want a distraction. Didn't need to escape. In fact, all he could think about was how he could make her see those stars she'd mentioned. He wanted to taste her skin until the flavor was seared into his memory. Savor the way her body molded around his. Expose the heart she'd resurrected.

Cannon just wanted to feel. Everything. With her.

Which meant not losing control. Not pushing her onto the bed and jumping on top. Shoving his jeans down just enough to free his dick then sliding into her. Thrusting his hips until he'd ground her into the mattress.

The exact opposite of what he was accustomed to. What his body was demanding, right now. And he wasn't sure how to get from holding Jericho in his arms to making love to her without causing her more pain.

He couldn't stomach the thought of that. Of his touch bringing her anything but pleasure. Sure, she seemed confident it wouldn't, but he was easily double her weight. A thousand times stronger. He could bruise her without meaning to by just holding her. And with his brain already blasted by lust...

Jericho laughed, pressing her hands on his chest once he'd managed to place her on her feet without shoving her onto the bed. "You really are a worrier. Relax, Rick. You're not going to hurt me."

Fuck, the way she said his name. No one called him Rick unless he was either being introduced or bitched out. Neither of which happened all that often. But, damn, he liked the way her voice formed the word. Made it sound natural.

He smiled, palming his hands over hers. "You keep saying that, and I keep wondering if we're both talking about the same thing. Because the way I feel..." He sighed. "It's gonna be years before I'm remotely calm around you. Before I can look at you, touch you, kiss you without it blindsiding me. Taking me to the brink the second you get close."

Her gaze softened, and he swore there was love staring back at him. "Then, how about we expend some of that energy before we get to the main event? Blow off some steam, so to speak."

"And how are we going to do that? You're not up for running a marathon. And that's what it would take for me to feel any form of control."

"You asked before how we were going to start this off.

I have a solution." She placed her hands on his waist, released his belt, his button and zipper, then slowly dragged them down, going to her knees in order to pull them off.

She stayed there, her hands fingering the top of his briefs, her face lit up into a smile as she arched one brow. "I was hoping you could paint your first release across my chest. Ease just a bit of that ache. Then, we can move to the bed."

Fuck.

Fuck, fuck, fuck.

Her mouth? She wanted to take him in her mouth? He was barely hanging on, had very little blood left in his head—the one he needed to use, right now, to think his way into another option. One that wouldn't have him gagging her when he started jamming his dick between her lips—and she wanted to suck him off? Christ, the girl was nuts because just one pass of her mouth was going to set him off.

He gathered her hair—fisted it around his fingers—intent on tugging her to her feet. Making this all about her, but she looked up at him. All big green eyes, with that light shining through, and he froze. Just stood there, mesmerized.

She smiled, nearly blinding him with the light, now, then removed his boxers. His dick bobbed out. Thick. Heavy. Like a damn pipe. He couldn't remember ever being this hard. This excited.

Jericho hummed. "I'll go out on a limb and suggest you haven't been completely focused on the mission, lately, either. Because...damn."

"Jericho—"

"Shhh. Do you know how long I've been imagining this? Been waiting for you to make a move? Just...stand there and enjoy."

He grunted when she fisted his shaft—ran her closed hand along his length. "Sweetheart. I'm on the edge. Another pass like that, and—"

"And what?" She stared up at him, again. "You'll come? Because that's kind of the point."

Cannon sighed in defeat, using the last of his neural functions to remind himself not to yank on her hair. Thrust into her mouth, because he wanted to do both. Wanted to watch her swallow him, feel all those silky strands bite into his hands.

Instead, he focused on breathing. On clenching his jaw. On tensing his muscles. Anything to prevent him from finishing after only sixty seconds. He made it exactly five times that before he was done. No longer able to hold back the searing pleasure burning along his spine. Shattering that fragile hold he'd been clinging to.

Jericho paused for one blinding heartbeat, her gaze rising to his before she closed her eyes and let him lead. He started moving. Short little jabs that increased the pressure in his sac. It gathered strength, coiling tight until the dam broke. He had the good sense to pull back, free himself before he was coming. Long white jets splashing across her chest as he emptied on her skin, finally curling over her to brace a hand on the bed behind her.

He wasn't sure how he remained on his feet. Didn't know if he was pulling on her hair or squishing her against the bed because nothing was working. His mouth, his lungs, his fingers, his brain. He was lost in a white haze where all that registered was that he was such a goner.

A few minutes—or was it hours—later, he managed to blink. Open his eyes. He was still braced against the bed, but Jericho had wedged herself between his arms—when had he released her hair? She was just sitting there, watching him. A huge smile lifting her lips. She'd cleaned herself off. Hell, maybe she'd showered. He'd completely lost track of time. Didn't know if he'd spent half the night trying to catch his breath. A feat he doubted would ever happen as long as she was close. Was anywhere in the same room. Maybe just being on the same planet.

Then, she touched him. Wrapped her small fingers around his arms, and bam. He was back. Desire, once again, red-hot inside him. More blood filling his dick. He had a moment's thought about not hurting her. About controlling his movements, then he was shifting forward, sinking one hand back into her hair. Cupping her head as he leaned her down on the mattress, using his other hand to wrap one thigh around his ass.

He placed that hand on her injured side, below the closed wound—a mental note not to touch her anywhere else—as he positioned himself above her. She encircled his hips, her hands smoothing up his arms then behind his neck.

He braced his weight on his elbows, staring into her eyes. "God, you're beautiful."

Another smile that tightened his chest. Made it hard to breathe. "Make love to me."

Hell yeah. He angled his hips. Pushed into her then stopped, cursing inwardly when he realized he'd forgotten the damn condom. He grunted, went to move when she tightened her grip, waiting until he met her gaze.

She shook her head. Levered up until her mouth was beside his ear. "You've already saved my life by giving me blood. I hardly think we need a barrier between us. I don't want a barrier between us. And I'm on birth control, so..."

He started moving. Thrusting. Claiming her as the words settled inside his mind. She didn't want him to wear protection? True, he had given her a direct transfusion. Had shared so much more with her, but still... Bareback implied trust. While she'd told him, repeatedly, that he had hers, having her show him...

Jericho moaned, eating at his mouth as he upped the pace. She matched his movements, lifting her hips, begging him not to stop. He couldn't stop. Colt could have picked that moment to barge in, tell Cannon that Ty Brown was walking down the street. That it was their one chance to capture the guy, and Cannon wouldn't have been able to pull himself away. Not when he felt whole for the first time in years. Hell, in his adult life.

She did that to him. Filled all the spaces he hadn't realized were empty.

Cannon lowered his head, kissing her neck, her shoulder. Any inch of skin he could reach because it wasn't enough. Bodies joined, her legs wrapped around his back, fingers digging into his flesh, and it wasn't enough contact. Not enough of them touching.

Jericho shifted. Grabbed him around his ribs as she tried to lift against him. He lowered more. No way he'd have her hurt herself. Twist her ribs. She inhaled when he allowed his weight to push her slightly into the bed, brushing her lips against his cheek.

"God, Rick."

He came. Exploded. Died in her arms. Hips grinding, body shuddering. He was gasping for air, trying to breathe through the heat—intimately aware he hadn't come close to getting her off. That he'd completely screwed their first time together.

He clenched his jaw, willing enough blood back to his brain to take stock, when she started pulsing around him. Moaning his name as her body convulsed beneath him. He didn't deserve her orgasm. Hadn't earned it. Had been too caught up in his own release. The rush of fire through his groin, but fuck, he'd take it. Take the way she writhed in his arms, head thrown back. How she contracted around his shaft, drawing out another few spurts. Her eyes were squeezed shut, her skin flushed pink. Her breasts pressed against his pecs with every frantic breath, her nipples like tiny brands against his flesh.

Crap. He hadn't even tasted them. Hadn't touched her. Kissed her. Worshipped her the way he'd pictured in his mind. He'd just climbed on top and started thrusting. Zero foreplay. Exactly the opposite of what he'd sworn he'd do.

He'd make it up to her. He had to because he needed more of this. Of sinking inside her, hearing her breath pant against his cheek. Feeling her unravel in his arms. So, he'd beg. Plead. Whatever it took to convince her he could do it right. That he wasn't using her just to get off. That her pleasure, her happiness, meant more to him than his own.

Jericho breathed heavily beneath him, holding him tight. "Christ, Cannon, that…"

Here it came. The part where he'd been selfish. Had only been focused on his own release. He hadn't meant to be that way. Had planned on spending hours touching and tasting her skin. But…god. He was way out of his element. Couldn't seem to keep enough blood in his brain to focus on how to make her feel special. Because she was. More than she realized.

Another raspy breath. "That was incredible."

It was?

"I've never come that hard, that fast."

She hadn't?

"Promise me we'll do that, again. Just the same."

Just the same?

He frowned as he pushed up higher on his elbows. "Did you hit your head, again? Because that was all wrong."

She laughed. "Then, don't do it right, because… damn."

"You deserve to be pampered, sweetheart. Not have me rut like a damn grizzly."

"I've always been partial to bears." Another laugh. "Rick…"

He closed his eyes at his name. When his dick surged back to life just from her voice.

"Do I want all that other stuff? Sure. But, baby…that doesn't mean anything else is wrong."

Christ. He *really* didn't deserve her.

"Still, I was thinking we could give it another go. Unless you're tired. Or sore."

Shit. He'd forgotten her ribs were still healing. That he

was supposed to be keeping things light. Gentle. Here he was, crushing her into the bed after claiming her as if it had been a mission sent down from heaven.

He went to shuffle off her when she slid her hands behind his neck and pulled him down, pressing her lips to his. And, just like that, all thoughts of moving, of giving her a chance to catch her breath just vanished. Burned from his brain as he focused on kissing her. Tangling his tongue with hers. Tasting the sweet essence that was uniquely her.

Jericho held his forehead against hers when he pulled back. "God, you take my breath away."

"That's because you make me breathe through you." He smiled, staring down at her. And he knew, right then, he was going to spend the rest of his life with her. No questions. No doubts. Whatever it took. He'd told her before that he didn't back down, and now, it was time to prove exactly what that meant.

"Then, I suggest you take a deep breath because I definitely want to give this another go."

CHAPTER FIFTEEN

"Do you have a death wish? Because it's certainly starting to look that way from where I'm standing."

Jericho sighed as she focused on Cannon. There was no missing the hard tone, the pinched lips and narrowed eyes. He'd been edgy as soon as she'd suggested they talk about her going back to the office. Hearing her say she wanted to head in *today*...

He'd gotten that look, again. The one that was a mix of pride and fear. That she'd caught a glimpse of in the restaurant, as well as when she'd been hurt. And she'd bet her ass that his last statement was his way of dealing with the fear part. Something she assumed he hadn't experienced much of. No doubt, fear had been beaten out of him during his initial Ranger training. If not then, it had definitely been buried after making it into Delta Force.

He hadn't talked too much about his time in the Teams, but she knew what it took to make it through selection into Special Forces. It wasn't that he didn't have any form of self-preservation. It's just that everyone else came first. And she had a nagging suspicion she'd sky rocketed to the top of his list.

Sex changes everything.

It's what her mother had told her, time and again. But, after sleeping her way through a handful of lovers, Jericho hadn't really understood what it meant. Until this morning.

Until Cannon.

He hadn't just rocked her world, he'd unhinged it. Sent it spinning off on some weird orbit. The kind that never quite recovered. Never resumed its original path. That was her. Still reeling, trying to adjust to a different form of gravity. One that pulled her toward him then refused to let go. Even now, standing there, looking him in the eyes, it was all she could do not to cave—ease the tight lines around his eyes.

That's when it hit her. It wasn't the sex that had changed her. It was the emotions that one act had brought to the surface that had shifted her equilibrium. Left her feeling off-kilter. The kind of feelings she suspected involved one tiny word.

She wouldn't say it. Not, yet. Because, as soon as she admitted she loved him, there would be no going back. And she knew she'd have to start looking at every decision—every risk—not just by how it affected her, but how it affected him. Affected *them.*

That's what love was. A constant compromise. A dance between doing what she *wanted* to do and what she knew Cannon *needed* her to do in order for him to remain sane. She had no idea how to juggle that. How to be a Deputy

Marshal and be Jericho Nash—the woman in love with Rick Sloan. Warrior.

And the man who'd saved her life.

She groaned inwardly. Maybe if they'd stopped after the first time, she'd have had a remote hope of staying distant. Pushing down her feelings until she could examine them rationally, later. But, for some crazy reason, Cannon had gotten the impression that he'd ruined their first encounter. How had he phrased it? That he'd done it wrong?

She hadn't understood what he'd been referring to. She'd been hanging on the edge after the first thrust, and feeling him empty inside her had been her undoing. It had taken her minutes, maybe hours, to breathe, again. The only saving grace had been that he'd been equally affected. Had stayed poised on top of her the entire time before finally easing off.

That's when he'd muttered something about not loving her right. As if he could find a wrong way. She'd still been seeing the stars she'd mentioned when he'd asked if they could try, again. Give him a chance to do it right. She hadn't thought it was possible for him to make her come any harder than she already had. In fact, she wasn't sure she *could* orgasm, again.

God, had he proved her wrong. On all accounts. After finally finding the strength to move, he'd carried her to the shower. She vaguely recalled Colt glancing their way before disappearing into the shadows. She'd been about ready to slap Cannon up the side of the head for carrying her into the bathroom—naked—until he'd stepped under the spray and simply held her.

They'd stood there for five minutes before he seemed

willing to move. To release her long enough to grab some soap—wash her. She'd casually suggested she give him another blow job when he'd grunted, the firm line of his mouth suggesting he'd made some sort of decision.

He'd been unrelenting after that. Against the shower wall. Then, the door. Again, in the bed. That time, he'd teased her forever before finally sending her over. There wasn't an inch of skin he hadn't tasted, a spot he hadn't licked and kissed. He'd been overly gentle all morning, as if he was afraid he'd hurt her, despite her assurances to the contrary. Never straying more than a few steps apart.

And now, he was standing four feet away looking as if she'd dealt him a physical blow.

Cannon shifted on his feet, obviously still waiting for her answer. But how could she say anything without either alienating him or crucifying herself?

Instead, she took a calming breath, resisting the urge to grimace when her ribs burned. Cannon might not have hurt her, but a few rounds of rambunctious sex had definitely irritated her side.

Another frown. "Okay, if you don't want to answer that, then how about telling me how sore your ribs are? Because I saw your mouth twitch when you inhaled, just now. You're hurting, again, sweetheart."

"My ribs are fine. I'm fine. Everything's..." She would not say *fine* one more time.

Fatigue weighed on her shoulders, and she took a moment to drag out the chair from the table—sit back down.

Cannon tsked then marched over to the counter. He turned his back for a few moments, then returned to her side, a steaming cup in his hands. He placed it between hers. "Drink."

More tea. The man seemed to have an endless supply today. Every time she'd turned around he'd shoved a cup in her hands, giving her the same single-word order. She was starting to wonder if he was some kind of wizard. Making the damn mugs just materialize out of thin air. But, the liquid was warm, and after a week of mostly water and crackers, it was nice to have something different.

She took a sip, using the pause to gather her thoughts, waiting until Cannon reclaimed his seat next to her. She glanced around at his buddies—brothers. Teammates. Hers, now, too. They'd sat quietly during the discussion, then allowed Cannon to voice his objections, without interrupting. Though, they looked more than a bit amused by her and Cannon's bickering.

Jericho focused back on Cannon, fully aware he was the one she needed to convince. "To answer your first question, no, I don't have a death wish. I just need answers. And the only place I'm going to find those are at the office. I can't access enough files, here. Not everything is available remotely. I need my computer. The records' room. Hell, to talk to Art."

"You still think you're missing something."

"I *know* I'm missing something. I just can't figure out what's bothering me. Every time I get close to placing it, my memories get hazy."

"That's because you're still recovering."

Damn. She should have seen that one coming. Though, he had a point. While the wound had closed and most of the stitches had dissolved, she wasn't a hundred percent. Maybe not even seventy-five. Her reflexes were bound to be slower. And, if she were being honest, her ribs did hurt. Sure, all the endorphins last night had blocked out any discomfort. But now that they weren't making love—the pain had bled through.

All of which Cannon was obviously aware of because he was looking at her as if he could read every thought. Track the progression of her ideas by the way she tilted her head or furrowed her brow. Lying wasn't going to win her any arguments. And, whether she wanted to admit it or not, she wanted him to be on board. Needed him to be. He and his buddies were the only people she could truly trust. And the last thing she wanted was to brow-beat them into helping her.

Because she knew Cannon would insist on shadowing her. Whether he agreed to the plan or not, and if she wasn't smart about her decisions, she could get him hurt, next time. Or, god, killed.

She couldn't think about that. Him dead. Especially from a bullet meant for her. It made it hard to breathe. To think about what needed to be done in order to put Ty Brown, and whoever else was involved in the incident, behind bars.

So, she took the only course of action left. "You're right. I am still recovering. While I feel better, I know I'm slow. There's no way I could outrun anyone, or chase them down, and having to fire my gun would probably drop me to the ground from the resulting pain. But, despite all of that, I need to go back."

She held up her hand, stopping him from interrupting. "I know. But...they killed my partner, Cannon. My partner. Whether he was the one who stabbed me or not, it doesn't erase all those years when he had my back. When he kept my ass alive by eliminating the threats I couldn't see. If nothing else, I owe it to him to uncover who set that bomb. Killed him and left me for dead. Surely, you can understand that."

A twitch beneath his left eye. "Now, you're just fighting dirty. You know I understand, but..." He huffed. "Damn it, Jericho, the moment you step foot outside this loft, you'll be a target. And not like before. This won't just be the usual risks you're accustomed to because of your job. If Ty Brown knows you're alive, and we all know he does. Art couldn't outright lie and say you'd been killed, so Brown is going to know that *missing* means alive. He's going to be gunning for you. He'll assume you remember everything that went down, which means you're a loose end he can't afford to have flapping in the breeze."

She tilted her head, studying the way he glanced around the table then back at her. He was hiding something. "You think he's put a contract out on me, don't you?"

Cannon's expression never faltered. "Brown. The Macmillans. Not sure who."

"But you're sure *someone* has a contract out on me."

Another glance around the table. "Yeah. I'm sure."

"How?"

"Excuse me?"

"I said, how? How do you know there's a hit out on me? You said none of your investigations have paid off, so why are you so sure—"

"Because we got confirmation from one of the local gangs this morning."

She blinked. "What..."

Cannon looked over at Addison—an ex-detective and Rigs' wife. "Addison still has some connections from when she worked narcotics. She pulled in a few favors and heard it from a very reliable source that someone associated with the Macmillans put out a hit on you. Two-hundred and fifty thousand to whoever can prove you're dead."

Jericho stared at him while the words sank in. "Well, crap." She pushed to her feet, pacing away before turning back to face the table. "That's...unexpected. And a bit insulting. I would have thought I at least warranted double that."

"Not funny. But, do you see why I'm concerned? I can shadow your ass until we're pushing eighty. Drop anyone who comes hunting for you, sweetheart. But, once you go back to work..." He sighed. "You'll be limiting my resources, even with the new status your uncle got me."

"I can't hide forever. And I can't quit. Being a marshal isn't something I do. It's me, Cannon. The biggest part of me. You know I'd do anything for you, but please don't ask me to do that."

His eyes softened, and he stood, walking over to her before taking one of her hands in his. "I'd never ask you to quit. All I'm suggesting is that you wait until we eliminate Brown. If he's dead or back in custody, there's really no reason to continue chasing you. Whatever else you might have on him, at that point, will be pretty moot, because they already have enough evidence to lock up his ass for life. He'll be forced to accept either a life in jail or start talking and swing a deal. In fact, I wouldn't be surprised if the hit got switched to his head, instead of yours."

"But that's part of what I don't understand. Why is he

gunning for me, anyway? He's already a felon. Already has every Deputy Marshal in the state hunting him. Why would killing me change anything?"

Rigs cleared his throat, gaining their attention. "If you ask me, something must have happened inside that car that puts a whole new spin on things. This something that's bugging you that you can't remember... I'm betting you heard or saw something that could completely alter either the case against Brown or his employers. Something even worse than what they have, now, so... If they kill you, nothing else will change."

Jericho snorted. "It would be great if I could remember this apparent game changer."

Rigs shrugged. "They don't know you have amnesia. Regardless, like Cannon said, you're a loose end, and we all know those have a way of biting you in the ass. I'd be trying to kill you if I were in Brown's shoes. Guy might not be Einstein, but every warrior knows an enemy left alive today is one that can kill you tomorrow."

She let her head tilt back. Christ, this was so much more than she'd planned on.

Cannon leaned in close. "Just a few more days. Then, if we still can't find him, we'll go in and talk to Art. Or go visit Admiral Hastings. Maybe one of them can swing some temporary arrangements so Colt, Rigs and Midnight can team up. Surround you with the best mini JSOG unit we can."

Ice grunted. "Thanks for including me in your little joint special operations group, Cannon. I appreciate your faith and support."

"You know damn well the medic stays put unless

someone's down. I need you healthy in case we run into another emergency."

"Still, it'd be nice to be included. Just once."

"You'll get over it." Cannon looked at her. "Well?"

She glanced around at the men then focused on Cannon. On anything other than the tug of her heart to make him happy. "So, what you're saying is that, if we eliminate Ty Brown, we eliminate the threat against me."

He frowned. That obviously wasn't how he'd been expecting her to answer. "In a nutshell—yeah. That's the hope, anyway."

"Well, if Ty Brown is the problem, then there's one way to fix it."

"What's that?"

"We take the war to him. I tracked his ass down once, I can do it, again."

"Jericho…"

"I didn't mean by myself. And I'm not asking to go to the office. You're right. It'll be too hard for you to have my back, especially if your team is sidelined."

Cannon furrowed his brow. "What, exactly, are you suggesting, then?"

"Simple. We do what we both do best. We go hunting."

CHAPTER SIXTEEN

Cannon had lost his mind. Why else would he have agreed to accompany Jericho on a hunt for Ty Brown? The guy who'd nearly killed her. Who'd most likely killed her partner. And who had put a hefty bounty on her head.

Insanity. Plain and simple. That, or he was so damn in love with the woman, he couldn't see straight. Couldn't tell a good plan from a bad one because he was too focused on her. On bending to her wishes. Keeping that blinding smile on her face.

Because seeing her lost, afraid that he wouldn't—no, couldn't—love her if she returned to her life as a Deputy Marshal had changed him. Made him view the situation from an entirely new perspective.

And he didn't like it. Not when it meant taking her feelings into consideration instead of just doing what was safest. What kept her out of the line of fire. Because that's where she was. In the crosshairs of any asshole who thought he could take her down—collect the hit money. Cannon was good. Exceptional, in fact, at protecting his teammates. Had pulled off some impressive feats to keep his brothers alive. Ensure they all made it back alive. And he was fast.

But he wasn't faster than a bullet. And, with her sitting in the chair across from him, he couldn't cover every possible angle. No one man could.

Of course, he had his team along. Rigs and Midnight had arrived at the bar a few minutes before them. Had remained visible long enough to give Cannon a curt nod when he'd walked through the door with Jericho and Colt. Then, they'd vanished.

Cannon knew they were still there. Spaced out in order to give Jericho the most protection. Cover as many targets as humanly possible. Ready to take out any threat or die trying. Along with Colt, sitting on Jericho's other side, they'd made a virtual wall around her.

But nothing was absolute. And knowing he could lose her—here. Now. If he wasn't fast enough. Smart enough. Good enough—it messed with his head.

He was accustomed to being laser focused. Emotions safely tucked away. Fear, a distant blur in his rearview mirror. So, sitting there, a cold sweat beading his skin, his stomach turning endless summersaults…

It was foreign. Took him back to the first few days after joining the Army. Before he'd become cold. Removed. Lethal. When he'd been so sure that he'd live and die in the Teams. That he'd never fall in love.

Jericho had torched those plans. Burned the fuckers into ashes then buried them under a few feet of concrete. Sure, he'd made the decision to retire before he'd even met her, but if she hadn't fallen into his life—if that night at the bar had gone differently—Cannon might have returned.

Re-enlisted, because civilian life hadn't made sense. Hadn't seemed worth the constant pull between doing what he'd been trained to do, but remaining inside the law. He'd been the law in the field. Had been given an objective then told to execute it. Whatever it took to get the job done.

Out here... Men like him either learned to toe the line or they ended up in jail. Or dead.

But she'd changed that. Had made adapting worth it. Made him a far better man without even trying. Which meant, it was time to end this mission. And, if he needed to use deadly force—he wasn't going to hesitate or lose sleep over the casualties. Brown had started a war Cannon planned on finishing.

Her hand covered his, drawing his focus to her face. Fuck, she was beautiful. Those green eyes. Full pink lips. Her soft, thick hair pulled into a ponytail. Just staring at her eased the tight feeling in his chest. The edgy gnawing sensation in his gut. He'd do anything for her.

She smiled, and it felt as if the sun had exploded in front of him. "It's going to be okay. Promise."

He snorted, forcing himself to resume his scan of the bar—watch for any sign she'd been targeted. "That's supposed to be my line."

"But I'm not the one about to crawl out of my own skin. I'm actually surprised you're not frothing at the mouth." Her lips quirked. "Or working your way through every guy in here—wrestling them to the floor until they prove they aren't a threat."

"Don't need to get close to tell that. I can see it the

moment they walk in. Or look this way." He glanced at her, again. "But, I'm not taking any chances. Someone could sneak in through the back. Hide in the shadows. And let's not forget Brown's made a living out of killing people and *not* getting caught."

"I caught him."

Cannon laughed. Fuck, he loved her. "Yeah, you did. So... Any ideas on where else he might be? We've been here for hours, and he's still a ghost."

She glanced at the new phone he'd given her then tucked it back in her pocket. "Nothing interesting happens before midnight. We've still got a bit of time. And trust me... If he's going to show, it'll be here. Guaranteed."

Cannon merely nodded. He'd been casing a different bar every night for a week. Had gone over Brown's previous moves and anticipated where the bastard would most likely come out of hiding. This place...

It hadn't made the list. It was too—country, for one. As soon as he'd walked through the door, he'd had to stop himself from turning to Jericho and asking her if she'd taken them to the wrong place. Nothing but a sea of Stetsons and kicks, with some cover band singing Alabama songs on a raised stage. Knowing every cowboy in here was most likely armed hadn't eased his tension, any, either.

Also, it was outside Brown's territory. If he got into trouble in here, he'd be facing another gang, along with whoever was chasing him.

But Jericho hadn't seemed fazed. In fact, she'd smiled and headed for a table in the corner. The one *he* would have picked—a feat that had made him smile. She really did have good instincts. Which shouldn't surprise him. She was one hell of a marshal.

Cannon gave her fingers a squeeze. "What makes you so sure he'll come...here?"

She laughed. "First, with the kind of heat Brown has chasing him, he can't go to his usual places, but he can't venture completely outside his safe zone, either. And this place is pushing the boundaries of the Macmillan's turf. The perfect compromise. Second, it's in one of the nastiest parts of the city. Even I wouldn't come here without your team as backup. And third..." She glanced around. "It has everything he hates. A country band. Redneck boys. Overly priced beer. It's the last place anyone would look. So, it's the first place he'll go."

"You think he'll venture that outside his norm? Humans are still animals, sweetheart. Prone to habits."

"That's true. But he's suspected of killing a federal marshal. That enforces a lot of restrictions. He knows he's on the top of our most wanted list. That they'll probably call in more marshals from out of state. Have the SOG team on permanent stand-by. It's been nearly two weeks. He'll be getting cabin fever, by now. Guys like him aren't used to living in hiding. And, after his stint in prison... He'll be itching to taste freedom. Even if it means coming to a dump like this."

"That's very intuitive. I'm impressed. Is that how you caught him the first time?"

Her smile faded. As if that light inside her had just burned out. "I'd tracked his ass to three different bars on three separate nights, just like this one. But he always managed to slip away before we could arrest him. I swore someone tipped him off. Then, Dave got a call from one of his informants. Said they'd seen Brown at this club downtown, which was odd. It was too obvious. But Dave insisted, and Brown practically fell into our hands."

"I'll trust your instincts over luck, any day. We'll give it until one. If he's not here by then, we'll head home. Try somewhere else, tomorrow. Or we can come back here, if you want."

She nodded. Though she didn't show it, Cannon sensed her tension. But not at being in the bar. Or having to face Brown. It was failure that had her on edge. She knew Cannon hated the idea of putting her safety at risk, and she probably felt as if she had to prove herself to him.

She didn't. Whether Brown made an appearance or not wouldn't change the pride filling Cannon's chest. Jericho was tough, and strong, and incredibly shrewd. He wouldn't have chosen a bar like this. The men he'd hunted had been more animal than human. Always relying on their instincts. When shit went sideways, their decisions had been predictable. It might have taken Cannon a few attempts to unearth their location, but it had never been a surprise. Going this far outside the norm...

He'd have to alter his way of thinking. Adapt to this new kind of urban predator. Just another reason to keep Jericho close. She challenged him. Made him a better warrior. A better man. Of course, once Brown showed... That's when Cannon would be in his element. Eliminating the threat. It didn't matter, then, that Brown's thought processes were slightly skewed to what Cannon was accustomed to. There wasn't a fight he couldn't handle. A combat scenario he couldn't adapt to. And that's what this was. War.

He shifted slightly closer to Jericho, resisting the urge to hold her hand or lay his arm along the back of her seat —brush her shoulder. Give her a physical show of his support. Instead, he maintained his vigilance, studying every face that entered the pub. A couple of guys piqued his interest, their gazes lingering a bit too long on Jericho. He watched the way they moved, noting the bulges beneath their armpits. The occasional bead of sweat across their foreheads.

Nervous and packing. Definitely threats.

Cannon glanced over toward the far end of the counter, grinning when Rigs stepped out of the shadows. He winked—the bastard—then headed for where the men were leaning against the bar. Rigs stopped a couple of chairs over, ordering a beer as he kept an eye on the newcomers. The men glanced Rigs' way, visibly winced, then looked away.

Rigs had claimed his scars made him invisible in a weird sort of way, and damn if he hadn't been right. People were quick to pretend he wasn't there, and that would be their mistake.

Damn. Cannon would have to see if he could lure the other men back—have them stay in Seattle and work for him. He could really use the extra help, and having men he trusted was invaluable. Guys like Colt. And his buddy Six—who was getting into town in the morning. Ready to jump in and do whatever was necessary without even knowing the risks. He'd told Cannon that. Which hadn't surprised Cannon in the least. These were men he could trust without question. Men he'd die for.

He glanced at Colt. He knew his buddy had already identified the new threat. Colt had tapped the table three times then moved his chair in order to block more of Jericho from the men's sight line. Colt hadn't been obvious about it. Had looked as if he was angling his seat better to talk to them. But the end result was the same.

Shit. Cannon really hoped he didn't get any of his teammates shot. Or worse. Knowing they'd give their lives for him—for the woman he loved, even if he hadn't said it out loud, yet—was one thing. Having them actually have to step in front of a bullet...

He'd hoped he'd left that kind of sacrifice behind. Just his dumb luck that civilian life wasn't any safer than his life in the Teams. Not that he should have expected anything different with the line of work he'd chosen to pursue. But like it or not, a part of him thrived on the thrill of the hunt. On putting his life at risk. Wouldn't have been a very good soldier if he wasn't hard-wired that way. No sense questioning it, now. Of course, falling for a woman who was just like him...not his wisest choice. Not if he had any hope of maintaining his sanity.

Jericho nudged his arm, arching a brow when he focused on her. "You've obviously noticed the two men at the bar, seeing as Rigs popped into view. I was thinking that maybe, now, would be a good time to visit the ladies' room. See if they follow. Pretty sure you and Rigs could have them both unconscious inside of five seconds, if they do."

Cannon chuckled. "You're encouraging me to fight? Are you sure you don't still have a concussion?"

"It won't be a fight." She stood. "Give me a minute or two lead."

Cannon shook his head, watching her walk across the room then down the hallway. More than a few of the men tracked her progression, though most were likely just drawn to the sexy sway of her hips. Christ, the woman was sin in denim, and she didn't even seem to notice.

He waited a minute then stood, acknowledging Colt with a curt nod before trailing behind Jericho. He made his way to the bar, first, ordering another round to be sent to their table. The bartender grumbled something as he took Cannon's money, not wasting any time standing there. Cannon glanced at Rigs then headed for the hallway to the bathroom before stepping into a shadowed doorway. If the men were going to make a move, it would be when she was on her way back.

Music from the band echoed down the corridor, every beat from the drum vibrating through the floor. He waited, wondering if he'd read the situation wrong, when footsteps headed his way. Two. Heavy. They stopped then started, again, as if they were checking behind them.

Cannon remained hidden until they were just off to his right before stepping out. A quick scan, and he confirmed it was the men from the bar. They each had a hand beneath their armpit, attention centered on the ladies' room door. They were mid-step when Cannon moved out, both men tripping sideways in order to avoid colliding with him. He didn't waste the distraction, grabbing the bigger guy's arm as he stepped into him. Cannon kept the bastard's hand pinned to his side, preventing him from drawing the pistol tucked in his holster. A firm elbow to the jaw and Cannon had the man reeling backwards. A shift of his leg and a quick lunge, and the creep was down —head connecting hard with the floor. It cracked against the old wood, rolling the man's eyes back as his head lolled to one side.

His buddy barely had time to blink before Rigs was on him. Rigs was probably twenty pounds lighter and three inches shorter than the other man, but it wasn't even a contest. Rigs hit him with two strikes to the chest and throat, then dropped him with a firm kick to the knee. The guy wobbled for a few seconds, falling beside his partner with a boot to the head.

Cannon stepped beside Rigs when Jericho peeked out of the washroom, gaze settling on the two men laid out on the floor. She grinned then joined them, crossing her arms on her chest.

"See, I knew it wouldn't be a fight." She crouched beside the men, checking their pockets. "Looks like they both have wallets, which means they aren't professionals. Probably more of Macmillian's crew. There's a closet at the end of the hallway on the left. Might be wise to leave them in there."

Cannon sighed but grabbed his guy and dragged him down the corridor, dropping him inside the closet. Then, he helped Rigs with the other, closing the door behind them. Jericho was staring into the bar when they returned.

She glanced over her shoulder at Cannon. "Answer me something?"

"What's that?"

"Do you trust me?"

Cannon frowned. "What the hell kind of question is that? Of course, I trust you."

"And Colt? You trust him with my life, too, right?"

"I wouldn't have men with me I didn't trust with both our lives." He moved in beside her. "What's going on, Jericho?"

She motioned to the door. "Looks like we won't need to come back tomorrow."

Cannon followed her gaze, clenching his jaw when he spotted a man in jeans and a leather jacket—nothing the way he'd pictured Brown to dress. But there was no denying it was him. The shape of his jaw, the slicked back hair. Even dressed to fit in, he owned his space. Every movement broadcasted that he was dangerous. A man intimately connected to death.

But so was Cannon. And not from the safety of a scope.

Jericho snagged his arm when he went to push past her. "Down, boy."

"Screw that. He's mine."

"Cannon." She huffed when he went to pull his arm free. "Rick. While I'd love nothing more than to watch you take him out, I have an idea."

"Better than me choking the life out of him?"

She smiled, and damn, his traitorous heart sped up. "The fact he showed up *after* these two guys obviously spotted me suggests that I might have gotten it wrong. I don't think Brown was planning on coming here, tonight. I think he sent a bunch of men out to places I'd case to see if *I'd* come out of hiding. And once they reported I was here…"

"He came hunting for you. Which means he'll have additional forces either on the way or positioned outside."

"Even Brown isn't stupid enough to kill a federal marshal inside a crowded bar. This might be a rough part of town, but the folks here still have phones. Cameras. And the owner probably has some kind of video surveillance. He'll try to spook me then have me killed once I leave. While he's still in here. Not that a wanted man needs an alibi, but if we can't prove he killed Dave, and he has witnesses to prove he didn't kill me... That could go a long way to swinging a deal should he ever get caught, again."

"So, what's your plan, sweetheart? Because you definitely have a plan if you're asking me if I trust you and Colt."

"I go sit down, wait for him to approach me—"

"Fuck that. You're just assuming he won't pull a gun and shoot you. I'm not that trusting of a professional hitman."

"Cannon. I promise you, he's not going to try to shoot me. Besides, I'll have Colt with me. And you can leave Rigs or Midnight in here, as well. Take the other with you."

He snorted. "You want me and Rigs to take out the men he has coming. The ones positioned outside."

"That's the true risk."

He grunted, glancing at Brown as the man sauntered to the bar. Midnight appeared behind him, giving Cannon a quick nod before disappearing into the crowd. But the guy was watching. No doubts about it.

Cannon rolled his shoulders. Fuck, he hated this. Hated having to trust her life to his buddies. Not because he didn't have faith in them. Or her. But because it was *his* job. *His* duty. Deputy Marshal or not, Jericho was his to protect. To love. And he took that job seriously.

Jericho squeezed his forearm. "I'll be fine. You're the one who'll be taking all the risks. Do you think it's easy for me to ask you to do this? To put your life on the line for me? I might not be a Black Ops soldier like you, but I still took an oath. Still have a job to do. And knowing you could take a bullet meant for me... I don't like it. But I'm not too proud to say you're, by far, the more skilled warrior in this type of situation. And with my side still sore..."

"Fine. I'll head outside. But I'm leaving everyone else in here." He held up his hand. "Please, I can take care of a few men on my own. But, if there are more in here, and they don't share Brown's reservations about killing a fed, then I want you as protected as you can be. Like you just said. You're still healing. The last thing you need is to get caught in some kind of shootout where you'll go sacrificing yourself for the greater good."

He moved in close, lowering his face until it hovered an inch above hers, their lips nearly touching. "Do *not* go and get yourself hurt."

"As long as you do the same."

"They might think they're killers, sweetheart. But they're about to meet the real thing."

CHAPTER SEVENTEEN

He was serious.

Jericho knew it. From the glint in his eyes to the grim line of his mouth. Cannon actually considered himself a killer. And, hell, she knew he had been. Had eliminated an undisclosed number of tangoes during his time in the Army. Probably more than Brown and all his men put together. Definitely more than she'd ever face throughout her career.

But that didn't make him a killer. It made him a warrior. Cannon seemed to forget that he'd acted in defense of his country. On orders from men like her uncle. Sure, Cannon had pulled the trigger, or used his knife—shit, probably his bare hands. But it hadn't been for profit or sport. Or like some of the creeps she'd faced—for pleasure. And it had taken a hefty toll on him.

She could see that, too. From the shadows on his face, to the way his jaw muscle twitched just before he steeled his resolve. Pushed down any kind of emotion. He was deadly, but every encounter cost him. Ate away more of the man beneath the soldier—more of Rick.

But that part of him was the reason she was alive. Hadn't died in the restaurant or after being stabbed. She'd have to work harder to make him see that she loved both sides of him. That he could be lethal and loving. That he didn't have to lose Rick in order to be Cannon.

Of course, telling him she loved him would be a good start. And, despite being nervous, she needed to just grow a set and trust him. Right, because she had so much experience in relationships. In being in love.

She sighed. They'd just have to learn together because she was pretty damn sure he wasn't any more skilled in that arena than she was. Just her luck, she finally found equal footing with the man, and it involved risking her heart.

Jericho gave herself a mental shake, watching as Cannon mumbled something to Rigs then headed into the main section the bar, promptly disappearing from sight. She didn't know how he did it. There one second, then just gone. Vanished. As if he'd fallen into a hole. Or been beamed away like *Star Trek*. The guy was huge. Massive in a way she'd never experienced before. And, still, he moved like a shadow.

Rigs stepped up beside her. "I'll follow behind you to the table, but I won't stop. Won't give anyone any reason to think we're together. You won't have to say anything to Colt. I'll make sure he gets the message. Just don't do anything crazy. And, if bullets start flying, get down."

He snorted at her glare. "I know. Addison is just like you. Noble to a fault. All about the badge. The oath. But… Ice will kill me if he has to patch you up, again. Especially

196 | KRIS NORRIS

with your side still injured. Not to mention what Cannon
would do. And I'm not ashamed to say, the guy isn't
someone I'd want to fight. Clear?"

"I said I wouldn't take any unnecessary risks. That's all
I can promise anyone."

"Had a feeling you'd see it that way. Just be careful."

He waved her out, and she headed for the table. Rigs
trailed behind her and off to her left, shielding her from
Brown's view as she walked back to Colt. She slid into her
chair as Rigs reached them. He flashed some kind of hand
signal at Colt then kept moving—disappearing just like
Cannon had done. Damn, were they all that stealthy?

Of course, they were. Cannon had said he wouldn't
have men with him he didn't trust with both their lives,
which meant they were equally skilled. Equally lethal.

Colt shifted his chair, again, this time angling it so he
could tackle her out of her seat if the situation called for
it. At least, that's what she assumed. The guy was as
paranoid as Cannon. But she stood by her assumptions.
She knew Brown. Had studied his file until the words had
all bled together. And she was certain he wouldn't try to
kill her, himself. Not when he could have someone else
take the fall.

Colt grabbed a drink and slid it over to her, leaning in
close as he placed one in front of him and another on the
floor beside him. He obviously wanted to hide the fact
Cannon had been sitting there, previously. Make Brown
think there was only the two of them.

Colt smiled, and for the first time, she noticed how
handsome the guy was. Dirty blond hair—longer than
Cannon's—and rugged good looks that she was sure had
charmed him into a steady supply of beds. But where

Cannon came across as dangerous, Colt seemed almost surfer-like. Pretty features that were a direct contrast to the skill she was sure he possessed. Cannon had told her that Colt had been part of his Delta unit for seven years, which meant the other man was also lethal. He just didn't look it.

Which was probably part of the reason he was good at infiltrating different groups. He didn't appear like the kind of man who could disarm you or kill you before you could blink. That made him a different kind of deadly.

He chuckled. "Do I want to know what you're thinking because..." He whistled faintly. "The look you're giving me. It's like you just realized the dogs at your feet were wild, all along."

She laughed, keeping part of her focus on Brown, but if he'd noticed her presence, he wasn't showing it, yet. "I was just thinking that you don't look like the kind of guy I'd peg as being a threat."

"That's because I'm not."

"Not to me. But to Brown or any of his men..."

Colt shrugged. "Being underestimated can come in handy. I'm sure you're familiar with that. I'd assume most men don't see you as a viable threat, either. But I've heard what you're capable of. Saw, firsthand, how badass you are. Very few people would have had the resolve to escape that car—walk all that way in your condition. You're as dangerous as any of the men Cannon has working for him, Jericho. Maybe more so because you're the perfect distraction." He winked at her. "Those were Cannon's words, by the way. 'The perfect distraction.' He told me that after he'd met you. That he bet you could bag any felon you wanted because you blinded them with your beauty."

She snorted. "Cannon said that?"

"I may have…paraphrased a bit."

"He doesn't tend to use that many descriptive words. Though, it's nice to see not all soldiers are plagued by his shortcomings."

"Actually, I think it's just you. He's never had any issues barking out orders. Expressing himself. But with you… The man's a goner, and he doesn't even realize it. Or maybe the real problem is—he does."

Colt's eyes shifted, and he leaned even closer. "Tango on the move. Stay close. And, if he looks as if he's going to hurt you…"

Colt didn't finish, but he didn't have to. Jericho knew what would happen. *He'd* either take Brown out or get between her and whatever Brown was planning to do.

"Deputy Marshal, Colt. If the man's going down. I should be the one to pull the trigger, badge and all." Except for the part where she wasn't sure if she could without her ribs affecting her aim. Her draw. Though, chances were he'd be so close, she couldn't miss.

But then, neither could he.

Colt merely shrugged, again, saying everything without speaking, at all.

Jericho focused on Brown, instead. On the way he walked around the bar then zeroed in on them. She maintained eye contact, pushing her jacket back to expose her badge and weapon—let Brown know she wasn't here for the booze or music.

Brown stopped next to the table, eyeing Colt before

dragging out a chair and sitting on it. "Deputy Marshal Nash. What a surprise. Rumor had it you'd been killed."

Jericho smiled. "Lord knows you gave it your best shot. Guess you should have stuck around."

"I wasn't the one who tried to kill you. I merely took advantage of the situation."

"Oh, so this is you turning yourself in?"

He laughed, placing his elbows on the table. "I have to admit, I'm surprised you came here, tonight. Even with your new guard dog in tow." He looked over at Colt. "Cannon, isn't it? Funny, I'd heard you were overly large. I mean, you're big, but..."

Colt matched Brown's positioning. "Guess it's a matter of perspective. I believe the lady asked you a question. Are you going to come peacefully, or do we have to insist?"

Brown glanced around the bar. "I wouldn't suggest drawing your guns. You wouldn't want this to turn into a bloodbath, would you?" He focused back on her. "I didn't come alone."

She straightened. "Neither did I."

"You've got, what? Two or three men in here. Maybe four. I've got over a dozen outside. More in here. Even if you managed to cuff me, reach the door without any resistance, you'll never make it to your car alive if you try to take me in. Though, you weren't living through this, anyway, so..."

A dozen men? Just outside? And Cannon was on his own. Shit. She should have insisted he take Rigs with him. Hell, Midnight, too. Cannon was the one who needed backup. Instead, his team was stationed around the bar, babysitting her.

She swallowed the sick feeling clogging her throat.

"Who said I wanted to take you in? You're a wanted man, Ty. Dead or alive, as the saying goes."

"You? Open fire inside a crowded bar? Don't make threats you're not willing to see through. We both know you'd never risk it. Too many possible casualties. You might want me dead, Nash, but you're still the law. Still bound by that badge on your hip."

He leaned back in his chair. "Maybe that's why you brought the Army guy with you. Maybe you're hoping he won't have any issues in killing me. Still, I can't help but think that, if anyone starts firing, it'll snowball. You and your friend might have restraint, but I'm betting others in here won't. My men see me go down..." He sighed. "There's no telling how they're react."

"Is that why you came over? Thought you could scare me into letting you go?"

"Just wanted to clear the air. Get the situation out in the open. You tried to play it smart at that restaurant, but Wilson was too damn stupid to take your offer. I don't suffer from his lack of forethought. I'm betting you'll make the right decision tonight, as well. After all, I'm not the one in danger." He looked up when the bartender stopped at the table, handing each of them a drink. "Have a round on me. Calm your nerves. I'll be here the rest of the night, in case you were wondering."

Brown pushed away then stood, grinning as he turned then walked over to the bar. Colt laid his arm across the back of her seat. To most, it would look like a romantic gesture. Comforting. But she knew he was making it easier for him to grab her—take her to the ground if things turned ugly.

She balked at him. "What the hell, Colt? I don't need

protecting. You heard him. He's got a dozen men outside. Maybe more on the way. Go help Cannon."

Colt merely glanced her way for a moment. "Cannon'll be just fine. Though, you have a point. We should hold out for a bit. Give him time to eliminate the men who haven't arrived, yet. He'll let me know when it's safe for us to make our move."

"You want to give him *more* time? But—"

"Trust me, Jericho. Brown's the one who should be worried. He may be considered a pro in the civilian world, but he's got nothing on Cannon. By the time Cannon gets in here... Brown won't know what hit him."

Ten men. Shit, make that twelve. Two more getting out of a sedan. Sneaking into the shadows. Chances were, there'd be close to twenty by the time midnight came and went.

Cannon moved in behind some dumpsters. The bar was on a corner lot, backed by a couple of vacant stores. There was a sorry excuse for a park across the street. Mostly just a swing set and some benches surrounded by unkept bushes and trees. A small patch of grass in the center that looked more weed than anything else. Run-down apartment buildings towered over the area on the other side, a dilapidated church on the next corner over.

The perfect place to launch an assault. Even if Jericho managed to apprehend Brown, she'd be cut down before she'd taken more than a couple of steps out the door.

Not tonight.

He patted down his vest. One last check of his

equipment. He'd gone back to his truck—retrieved it. Somehow, he'd known it would come down to this. Him slinking through the alleys and buildings. Taking out Brown's men one-by-one. And he'd be lying if he said he was disappointed. Though, he'd try not to kill all of the bastards Brown had hiding in the shadows, taking them out—leaving them for the cops to 'round up—soothed the part of him that longed for revenge. That wanted to even the score. They'd made this personal. Hurt Jericho. He wouldn't truly feel at peace until he'd given it back tenfold. Knowing he was taking armed and dangerous thugs off the streets didn't hurt any, either. Gave him just a hint of moral high ground.

He headed down the alley backing the bar, making his way to the next street. He crossed the road then carefully picked his way back amidst the shadows. He'd tackle any forces holed up in the park, first. Those were the dangerous ones. The men who most likely had rifles. Even if they weren't overly skilled, they could still hit Jericho when she left. It wasn't that far.

It only took him a couple of minutes to get into position—scope out the terrain. Three men. One on top of a dumpster beside the apartments. Two in the trees. All of them had rifles. Scopes. He couldn't tell the make, but it didn't matter. They weren't going to get a chance to use them.

He headed for the apartments, first. Then, he'd work his way forward. A quick sprint along the side of the building, a jump and a push up, and he was crouched on the metal surface—the sniper stretched out on his stomach in front of him. The asshole didn't have a clue Cannon was there until he was unconscious at Cannon's feet. A couple of zip ties and some duct tape, and the guy wouldn't be going anywhere until the cops rescued him.

Cannon rolled the guy to the side, taking up his position. A small pile of cigarette butts suggested the creep had been waiting a while. Not that it surprised Cannon. Picking a vantage point—setting up a nest, regardless of how amateur it was—took time. Which meant these were likely the only snipers Brown had. The rest of his men would be thugs. Guys who planned on using brawn or firepower to get results.

Cannon readied the rifle, sighting the men through his scope. He couldn't risk climbing the trees in order to subdue them. Too many ways it could go south—alert Brown's forces that someone was on to them. And, with the numbers Brown had enlisted, Cannon couldn't afford to take any chances—to leave any threat unanswered.

Two shots, and the men were down. One caught up in the branches. The other buried inside some bushes. Remote enough they wouldn't likely be spotted by civilians, not that any were out. This place was like a dead zone. Though, that was probably a nightly occurrence. Even Jericho had admitted it wasn't the sort of place anyone ventured alone.

Except for Brown's thugs. The ones next on Cannon's list.

He vaulted down then headed for the alley, working in a circle around the bar. The first couple of encounters were quick. A few punches followed by some strategic kicks, and the guys were down. Bound and gagged. The next set were more skilled. Some martial arts knowledge. Knives and guns. Took him a full minute to drop them—a non-lethal knife wound taking out the last guy. But, it *had* been the bastard's own knife.

There were four men waiting in cars. Spread out around the lot. They thought they were being stealthy, extending their coverage, but it only made it easier for Cannon to pick them off.

Thirty minutes since he'd left the bar, and he'd eliminated thirteen men. One had arrived late. Bastard hadn't made it two steps out of his truck.

But it wasn't over. Not, yet. Not until Cannon was sure the stream of tangoes was done. Which meant lingering a bit longer. He could down two dozen men, but it wouldn't matter if he missed one. If some asshole arrived after Cannon had ventured back inside—told Jericho it was safe. Every soldier knew he could die just as easily from the last bullet as he could from the first. And he wasn't putting Jericho's life on the line.

The rain picked up, blanketing the area in a foggy haze. Cannon make a few more circuits of the park and alley until he was confident Brown was out of men. Then, he headed inside, still keeping to the shadows. He stayed hidden, constantly scanning the bar. But the odd guy he thought might be a threat was quickly dealt with by either Midnight or Rigs. His buddies were impressive. Never drawing attention to themselves. Moving seamlessly through the crowd.

Midnight crossed in front of him—gave him the "all clear" sign then positioned himself at the end of the bar. Rigs appeared at the other side, leaning against the counter. Relaxed but primed.

Cannon glanced at Colt. The other man had known he was there from the moment he'd walked back into the bar, but he'd stayed at the table. Their gazes met, held, then Colt was talking to Jericho. Nodding and motioning toward Brown.

She smiled, and damn Cannon's heart kicked. Hard. Left an ache in the middle of his chest. Fuck, she was beautiful. The way she rose from her seat. If he didn't know, firsthand, how badly she'd been injured. Knew that her ribs were still bugging her. He wouldn't have been able to tell she'd nearly died several days ago.

When she started walking toward Brown, Cannon had to drag his focus off of her. Scan the room then slowly shift over toward them. But it was hard. Not watching the way her hips swayed—the confident line of her silhouette —required all his training. He made sure he was only a reach away when she stopped in front of Brown, one hand palming her pistol. The other resting by her belt. Ready, but calm. Detached.

Brown arched a brow, leaning against the counter. "Something on your mind, Marshal Nash?"

"It's Deputy Marshal Nash." She didn't flinch. Didn't so much as blink. "Ty Brown. There's a warrant out for your arrest. Please turn around and put your hands behind your back."

He chuckled. "Going to test my bluff, are you? Betting Cannon can keep you safe?"

"I don't have to bet. It's a sure thing."

"Do you really want his blood on your hands, too? Isn't Faraday's enough?"

A small twitch of her jaw muscle. "I asked you to turn around."

"And if I refuse?"

In one fluid motion, she stepped back, drew her gun,

and aimed it at his head. She grimaced slightly—most likely from the pull on her ribs, but it wasn't stopping her. Slowing her down. Her arms were trembling a bit. Though, Cannon was probably the only one who noticed. Who was that intimately aware of her.

She held firm. "Then, I'll be forced to shoot you."

Brown stood there, his smile slowly fading when no one made a move toward her. He glanced around the bar, the lines on his mouth deepening.

Jericho inched closer. "Turn. Around."

Brown reached toward the gun Cannon knew was holstered inside his jacket, but he didn't even make it to his side before Colt had the man twisted and pinned to the bar, arm wrenched behind his back, a bloody cut across his forehead.

Colt leaned down close. "The lady asked you to turn around."

Brown grunted as Jericho slipped the handcuffs around his wrists. "You won't make it out of here alive. I promise you that. Your boyfriend can't save you."

Jericho grabbed his elbows, hoisting him upright. "See, that was your first mistake." She nodded toward Colt. "*He's* not Cannon."

Cannon waited until Brown made eye contact, the man's face paling. "I am."

CHAPTER EIGHTEEN

She'd done it. Jericho had dragged Ty Brown's ass into the Marshal Office and locked the door on his temporary detention cell. Caught the man who had killed her partner —perhaps stabbed her, if her memories weren't reliable. In all accounts, she'd won.

So, why did it still feel as if she'd lost? Was merely a pawn in some grander game? While she hadn't expected to feel better about what had happened—getting blindsided. Losing Dave—she had hoped it would give her a small measure of closure. Instead, the feeling that she was missing a vital piece of evidence had increased until it suffocated the very air around her.

"Hey."

What the hell wasn't she seeing? What couldn't she remember?

"Jericho?"

It was after she'd hit her head—had it smashed into the dash and the window. Something about other prospects? Had it been Dave talking or Brown?

"Jericho!"

She blinked, glancing over at Cannon as he wove through the streets. A passing car flashed light across his face, highlighting the furrow between his brows before it fell into the shadows, again.

"I'm sorry. Did you say something?"

He snorted, shaking his head as he placed one large hand over hers. "Where'd you go? Because you haven't been here, with me, since we left the office. Something wrong?"

"Not wrong. It's just…"

How did she voice her concerns without sounding ungrateful? He'd taken out over a dozen men on his own. All for her. So she could arrest Brown without risking her life. And he'd done it without asking her for anything in return. The guy never ceased to amaze her. Never seemed to consider his own well-being in place of hers.

And she was still doubting everything. Still dwelling on missing pieces that might be nothing more than her imagination. Snippets from another moment intruding on the present.

He squeezed her hand. "You haven't remembered that game-changing piece of information, yet, have you?"

"I don't even know that there is something. Just this gut feeling. Ghostly memories that never quite take shape. We got Brown, thanks to you. Your teammates. That should be enough."

"No one said those two items had to be exclusive of each other, sweetheart. If your gut's telling you there's more to this than what we know, then you should trust it. Capturing Brown was a good first step—one that might allow you to investigate this further without having to look over your shoulder every second you're on the job. But digging deeper doesn't negate all we've done."

"Then, why do I feel as if I'm being ungrateful?"

He glanced at her. Smiled. And the sexy secret agent was back, stealing her breath, and her heart, with that easy tilt of his lips. "Because you're stubborn. Hate having other people take risks for you. A trait I'm determined to break because we all need a team, Jericho. People we trust. It's about time you realized you're not alone. Not anymore."

"I wasn't alone, before. I had Dave. He…"

He'd ditched her. Lied to her. In fact, she couldn't help but wonder if anything had been real between them since she'd joined the Marshal Service. Or if it had all been a ruse from the start. If he'd been playing her the entire time. Questions she'd never answer if she couldn't remember those precious few minutes in the car.

Cannon sighed as he eased his truck to a stop. "Sorry. I shouldn't have dredged this all up, again. I just… Whatever you're missing, it can wait until morning. I think we've earned the rest of the night off. And Art said they'd be holding Brown until the marshals had a chance to question him, and the feds decided where they wanted him. That he'd be there at least until tomorrow night. We can go back in. Question him, ourselves. Maybe he'll be in a better mood to talk once he realizes just how much shit he's in. That there might be a contract on his head, now. But, until then, we recoup. Rest. Give those ribs of yours more time to heal."

Jericho gazed up at him. His copper eyes had darkened to more of a burnished bronze. The skin along his cheekbones taut. While he still had the suave air about him, she didn't miss the fierceness in his expression. The new-found tension gathering around them. A quick glance at his groin, and she knew why. The man was more than a bit aroused.

She ran one hand along his arm. "Christ, you're built like a damn tank. Is that why they call you Cannon? Because of your size?"

"Mostly because I hit twice as hard. Punch my way through anything."

"Mmm, I like the sound of that. Which brings me to the point where I don't think we'll be doing much sleeping. At least, not initially." She lowered her hand—squeezed him through the denim.

His nostrils flared as his eyes closed slightly. "Jericho."

"I love the way you say my name. Say it, again."

"Jericho." He chuckled at the shiver that wove down her spine. "The last time I indulged you, your ribs were twice as bad the next morning. And don't even try to tell me they aren't hurting, now. I saw you wince back at the bar."

Did the guy see everything?

He exhaled. "I think—"

"That's the problem. You think too much. Trust me, any bit of discomfort I might feel later will be more than worth it." She reached for his face—brushed her thumb along his chin. "You wouldn't make a lady beg, would you?"

His jaw clenched, twitching the muscle next to his left eye. "You're determined to fight dirty, aren't you? No..." He placed a finger over her lips. "Don't answer that. I already know what you're going to say. So, how about a compromise? We'll sleep for a couple of hours, and if you still want to make love once you wake up, then I'll make all those fantasies inside your head come true."

She laughed. "You act as if there's going to be a time I *won't* want to make love to you. Not going to happen, but if *you* need to rest, first..."

He kissed her. His lips molding to hers, one hand lifting to sink into her hair—hold her head. His fingers flexed against her scalp, tightened around some strands, then tipped her head back as he tugged her against him with his other hand. Deepened the kiss.

She moaned into his mouth. He tasted like heat and man—a hint of soda from the bar. She tried to wrap her fingers around his shoulders, but he was too large. Too much muscle for her to do more than dig the tips in slightly.

Cannon grunted, lifting his mouth, breathing, then kissing her, again. Harder. More desperate. Each advance and retreat lengthened, until she wasn't sure how long they'd sat in his truck, locked in a never-ending embrace.

Good. She didn't want it to end. Didn't want him to let her go—lose the feel of his arms banded around her. His heat seeping through her clothes—warming her skin. It felt right. Felt safe. As long as he was holding her, nothing could harm her. He was impenetrable. A massive wall of flesh and bone and muscles. Of heat and desire and, damn it, love. Because that's what she felt for him. Love.

It was there in the way she was willing to pass out from the lack of oxygen rather than worry about taking a breath. How her heart thundered in her chest, matching his frantic rhythm. How the rest of the world faded. Just disappeared. Nothing left but his mouth on hers, his body shielding her.

Harsh breaths. His. Hers. They mixed until the windshield started to fog. The night air cooling her skin. Cannon finally eased back but didn't move more than an inch away.

He nuzzled her cheek and neck, his fingers fisting around her hair. "Shit, sweetheart. All it takes is a look. A smile. A kiss, and I'm lost. Forget what I was doing. My mission. My training. My damn sanity. I just focus on you. What you're feeling, if you're safe. How I can put another smile on your face."

She grinned, brushing a kiss across his jaw. "So, you're saying I turn you into a *loose* cannon?"

"Very funny. Except…" He pulled back enough she could look him in the eyes. "It's true. Knowing there were men actively gunning for you… It made me reckless."

"Like challenging all those men on your own?" She scoffed at his narrowed eyes. "We both know you should have taken Rigs with you. Or Midnight. Both. I was safe with Colt. The man's as paranoid as you are. As damn protective, too. You were the one in danger."

He stared at her, gazes locked. Mouth pursed tight, before he sighed. "Can't help it. Already had to cope with nearly losing you, once. That…"

"Do you think it would be any easier for me to lose you? That I don't feel the same? Having to sit there, knowing what you were facing, alone. Damn near lost my mind."

He chuckled. "We're quite the pair. Just…give me some time. I'll see what I can do to lose this junkyard dog mentality where you're concerned. Try to ease up on my protectiveness. And, before you remind me you're a federal marshal, it's not because I doubt your skill. It's built in. Etched in my DNA. I know how it sounds, but whenever something or someone challenges you, all I can think is—fuck that, she's mine."

Damn, how could she argue with that? With him wanting to protect her, not because he thought she was weak or couldn't handle herself, but because he cared. He hadn't said he loved her, either, but that's what he meant. What he was trying to convey without putting it out in the open. Making it real. Concrete.

She shook her head. "That's incredibly Neanderthal. And perfectly romantic. Fine. I'll give you some adjusting time. But don't make me have to kick your ass to prove myself."

"Wouldn't dream of it. Now, I think we need to renegotiate our next steps. Because if I don't get a taste of your skin soon..." He tucked his keys in his pocket then opened the door. "Stay right there."

"But..." She frowned as he jumped out of the truck, scanning the area before making his way to her side. She gasped as he opened the door then lifted her into his arms, slamming the door shut behind them then heading for the main entrance to his office.

"Um, Cannon? This is your office."

"Yup."

"Aren't we heading to the loft?"

"Sure are. But my loft. Not Ice's. Spent the last month upgrading a part of the upstairs. Thought it made sense to combine the two spaces. I have a pretty extensive security system. Would have brought you here before, but we needed to go somewhere no one suspected. Where they wouldn't track you down. And, since your office knew about me, it made sense to stay at Ice's. Now that the main threat is over, I figure we can let Ice and Harlequin have some alone time. The others, too. Except Colt. He's crashing in the spare room. And Six will be here in the morning."

"Six?"

"You'll see. Just, relax. You're in good hands."

He winked at her, the overly confident bastard, then headed inside. He hadn't been joking about the security measures. Alarm systems. Fingerprint readers. What she swore was a damn retinal scan. All sorts of boxes and codes, but Cannon managed to handle them all without putting her down.

Then, he was climbing the steps—opening another door, with yet another code box. By the time they were inside his apartment, her pulse was thrumming, a needy ache throbbing between her thighs. She'd never been carried—not like this. Not as an adult. Feeling his muscles move, knowing he wasn't even breathing hard, that he was primed and ready to take her—it registered in the same part of her brain that had swooned when he'd said she was his. That ancient section of her DNA that relished an alpha male in full rut.

That was insanely in love with Rick Sloan.

Cannon walked through the apartment. Lights off. Nothing to guide him but either memory or the kind of night vision she only achieved with googles, taking them directly to his bedroom. She'd only noticed one other door —most likely a washroom—the rest of the area was open. She couldn't tell what kind of furniture he had or if he'd done any decorating, but she got a good view of the bed. Big. What looked like a thick duvet and full pillows.

He placed her on her feet at the foot, his hands falling

to rest on her hips. He gave her a sloppy half-smile. "What's with the look?

"What look?"

"The one that suggests you're not too sure if agreeing to come up here was a good idea?"

She swatted him in the chest, biting back a moan when her hand just bounced off. "I'm just surprised. I didn't picture your bedroom being this…"

"Neat?"

"Comfy looking. I mean, you spent fifteen years in the service."

He laughed. Rich. Deep. The kind that made her melt inside. "What did you think I'd want to sleep on? A cot?"

"Or a mattress on the floor. Maybe just the floor."

Cannon made a point of scanning the room before staring down at her, and damn, the look on *his* face. It meant more than the answer because *he* was the answer. To all the questions rattling around in her head. Whether she ever discovered the truth behind Ty Brown's escape. If she could truly go back to the office after everything that had happened. If she'd ever trust another partner other than the man standing in front of her, fingers lightly digging into her flesh. His gaze fixed on her.

He lifted one hand—tucked some hair behind her ear. "Honestly, if I hadn't met you that night in the bar. If you hadn't asked me to join you for coffee. If I hadn't hoped that one day, I'd carry you through that door—I might be sleeping in a bag on the floor. But that night changed everything."

He traced his thumb along her jaw line. "*You* changed everything. No way I could have ever asked you here and not had you comfortable. You…"

He leaned down until his forehead was resting on hers. Close. Intimate. Just the two of them, their increased breath sounding around them.

Jericho wrapped her arms around his neck, kissing his chin until he met her gaze. "For the record, I would have stayed even if it had been a sleeping bag on the floor because I'm here for *you*. To be with *you*. And you're worth any sacrifice."

She laughed at his wide eyes then nodded toward the bed. "But I'm really glad there's a bed because we're going to be spending a lot of time rolling around on it. Starting now."

CHAPTER NINETEEN

He was worth any sacrifice?

Had she really said that?

Cannon stared into Jericho's eyes and damn near died. Right there. At the foot of his bed, his woman pressed against him, her arms around his neck—his fingers gripping her hips. If it wasn't for his painful hard-on—the way his damn heart was thrashing inside his chest. The clammy feel of his skin—he would have sworn he was dreaming. Still lying in Ice's spare room with Jericho in his arms, wishing he could be right where he was. Home. With her.

He hadn't had a home in, what? Ever? He'd grown up poor to a single mom. Had worked whatever job he could find to help with bills. That's why he'd joined the Army. To escape. Alleviate the burden on his mother to care for another human being. His thoughts, not hers. She'd always made sure he knew she loved him. Was proud of him. That he was wanted. That she'd gladly go without if it meant he'd have enough. But he'd seen the hardship.

Experienced it. Known that she'd be better off without him. That he could send some of his pay home to her without having to live on the streets.

But despite everything—her obvious love—he'd never really felt as if he'd been living in a home. A dwelling, sure. A roof with four walls. But that feeling of coming through the door and being at peace? Like stepping into a private oasis? He'd never had that...

Until just now when he'd crossed the threshold with Jericho in his arms.

He needed to tell her he loved her. Pray she felt the same. But, while he didn't enjoy being patient, he could be, when called upon. And, if she needed more time to get to where he was—if everything she'd experienced over the past couple of weeks was too much for her to process. Was clouding her judgement—he'd wait. As long as it took because *she* was worth it. Worth the risk of getting hurt.

Jericho went to her toes, palming his face with both hands as she lightly touched her lips to his. "Rick."

That was it. A breathy sighed version of his name, and he was lost. Closed that fraction of distance—consumed her lips. It wasn't a kiss. It was a full scale attack. A maneuver designed to break any of her remaining walls. The ones she'd erected after losing her dad so young.

Cannon had learned a bit about her past. Growing up in the shadow of her father's ghost. His sacrifice. Hastings had told Cannon a few details about the mission—how Mason Hastings had died. Heroically. Saving the lives of three other men. Cannon didn't need to know the rest. That was enough to confirm his thoughts—that Jericho's need to prove herself stemmed from a sense of duty. As if she had to be worthy of living.

She didn't. That's not how it worked. Men like him, like her father, her uncle—they didn't want others to acknowledge their sacrifice. It was for the men they served with. So their families could continue living in relative safety. Cliché as it was, it was for freedom.

But Jericho hadn't gotten that memo. It hadn't made it over her damn walls. But it didn't matter. Cannon could scale walls. Jump right over the fuckers, and if that failed, he'd simply blast right through. He hadn't been joking. That's why his buddies had nicknamed him Cannon. Because he just busted his way through anything that defied a softer approach. Anything that stood in his way of accomplishing his mission.

And Jericho was his new mission. His lifelong one. Whether she knew it, yet, or not didn't matter. He'd find a way to tell her when the time was right. Like after he'd kept his promise—made all her fantasies come true.

He didn't know what they were. Hell, they'd only shared one night together. Sure, they'd made love a number of times. In the bed, the shower. Hadn't he taken her against a door? All the ways *he'd* envisioned. So, now, it was her turn. Whatever she wanted. He'd find a way to make it happen.

Jericho gasped in a breath when he finally released her. "Christ. I might not make it to the bed before I come if you kiss me like that, again."

"Oh, sweetheart. Never issue a challenge to a Delta Force soldier."

"It wasn't—"

Like hell, it wasn't. And, it wasn't one he could leave

unchecked. Which meant cutting her off with another kiss. One that made the first one appear tame. That left her writhing in his arms as he swept his hands down her body. A few swipes and twists, and he had her weapon tucked on the side table, her jacket and shirt off. Her bra hanging by one wrist. A quick breath, a crouch and a strategic lift, and her pants and underwear were gone. History. Forgotten somewhere on the floor behind him.

He didn't care where. Didn't care if they ever found them, again. Just another reason to keep her naked and in his bed for the foreseeable future. He was sure he could somehow get Colt or Six to leave some food at the door. Bribe them. Cannon would owe them, but he didn't care. Not if it meant staying there with Jericho.

In his new home. What he hoped would become *their* home.

Hell, he liked the sound of that. Loved it, in fact. Just like he loved the brush of her smooth skin beneath his hands. The way it beaded as he skimmed his fingertips over her sensitive areas—the back of her knees. Her hips. Along her ribs. The soft curve of her breast. The pulse point on her neck.

It was like drawing a map of what turned her on the most. What made her sigh, pant, claw at his back. Cannon didn't just want her aroused. He wanted her desperate. Clinging to her control with the same hair trigger he was.

When he slipped a finger between her folds—dipped inside her then rubbed the tip around her clit—she exploded. Drenched his hand as she rode it through her orgasm, falling limp in his arms after damn near taking him over with her.

He'd held on. Barely. And only by clenching every

muscle. Thinking through a few complicated strategies he'd faced in the Teams. He just hoped he'd last more than a few strokes once he got inside her. Had all that warm, wet release sliding across his dick.

Shit, he had to stop thinking about that. About what it was like to be inside her, because it was the best damn feeling he'd ever had. Hot. Tight. So fucking wet.

Jericho clung to him, finally managing to make eye contact. "How did you…" She panted through a small tremor. "I've never…"

Good. He wanted to be all the firsts he could manage. The first man to get her off like that. To go bareback. To gain her love. Then, all the rest that followed.

He smiled, lifting her in his arms then taking her down on the bed. "God, I love watching you come. Let's do it, again."

There was just one problem. He wasn't naked—yet. And getting that way involved letting her go. Actually lifting his hands from her skin. That soft, smooth flesh beneath his palms. Exactly what he didn't want to do.

But, just when he thought he'd finally convinced his fingers to let go, she did it for him. Yanked his shirt over his head. Sure he had to release her for a second, but not nearly as long as if he'd had to remove his own shirt. And his pants? Gone. He'd felt a tug on his waist, then they were off his hips—falling onto the floor. Thank god he'd disarmed all but one pistol before getting in his truck. And that he'd had the sense to place it and her Beretta and holster on the side table before stripping her down. At least, he thought he'd done that. He couldn't quite remember what had happened between her saying his name, then her coming in his arms. But they were both there. A quick glance confirmed each weapon was within reach should he need it.

He wouldn't need it. Colt was bound to be in the spare room, by now. The man would stand watch until Six arrived closer to sunrise. Cannon could afford to let his guard down a bit. Could trust his brothers to have his back.

Which meant he could focus on Jericho. On increasing the pink flush of her skin as he moved over her—slid home. On making her chant his name as he started up a steady rhythm. In, pause, then out. Each thrust gained strength, each retreat slightly shorter until his hips didn't stop moving. Until he was pounding her into the mattress. Making the headboard bang against the wall.

She had her fingers digging into his back. Scratching his skin. Urging him to go harder as her legs squeezed his hips, her heels pressing into the small of his back. She levered up. Met each stroke. Then, she was coming, again. Shouting his name, trying to pull him closer. He kept going. Drew it out until the fire in his sac exploded. Had him emptying into her in long, steady pulses.

Dark spots edged his vision as he stayed poised above her. His arms beneath her with his fingers locked around her shoulders. He was probably squishing her into the bed, at least from the waist down because he couldn't move. Couldn't do anything other than lay there breathing.

Air in, air out. Repeat. Until his vision finally cleared. Some of the blood returned to his brain. But the clarity only made him realize he'd done it, again. Jumped on top of her and pumped away until they'd both finished. Hadn't he promised to make her fantasies a reality? To do whatever it took to ensure her pleasure above everything else?

Fuck. Why was he so bad at this? Where the hell had his control gone? He never lost control. Never deviated from a plan once he'd committed. Especially when it was a damn good plan. One guaranteed to keep her coming back for more. And it had been so freaking simple.

Find out what she wanted. If she had any secret desires. Handcuffs. Blindfolds. Maybe a light spanking or him talking with an accent—he wasn't sure he could, but fuck, he'd try. Anything for Jericho. But, so far, he hadn't even let her ride him.

She was right. She *did* make him into a loose cannon, and not in a good way. Which meant he'd have to beg for forgiveness. Again. Not exactly the kind of record he wanted to keep going. Him, screwing up their love making. Over and over.

Cannon took a deep breath—cursed when he realized he was probably squishing her more—then pushed up higher on his elbows. He braced himself for any kind of reaction from her, only to freeze when he noticed the tears dotted along her cheeks.

Actual fucking tears.

It was dark. Nothing but some moonlight filtering in the window on the far side of the room. Through the skylight overhead. But there was no hiding the moisture on her face. The way her eyes were squeezed shut. Nothing to drown out her shuddering breaths she sucked in as if simply breathing hurt.

Cannon opened his mouth, tried to talk. To say her name. Ask her if she was okay, but nothing came out. Not a word, a sound. All he could do was look down at her, at those tears on her cheeks. At her obvious discomfort. At what *he'd* done, and silently curse.

She made the first sound. A raspy exhalation that ripped at his heart. Made his damn chest hurt. Right in the center. Jericho opened her eyes, saw him and cringed.

Shit, buggering, fuck.

He didn't know what to do. Had absolutely no experience to draw on. Sure, he'd had a few women get weepy on him from drinking. From being physically hurt on a mission. But this… Emotional pain? Pain he'd caused from making love?

Obviously, it hadn't been making love for her. Not if she was crying. Should he sit up? Pull out? Leave?

He should definitely pull out. Fuck, what was wrong with him?

Jericho stopped him from moving, her tiny fingers holding him captive as she tugged against his shoulders. He could break her grip easily. Just a push against the mattress, and he'd be up and away. Like Superman. High above her, making his escape. But he couldn't. Couldn't break whatever power she had over him. Instead, he lowered until most of their bodies were touching. Until he was really crushing her into the bed, again.

She smiled. Fuck, it was breathtaking. All pretty pink lips and white teeth that shined in the pale moonlight. Her lips were wet, but he didn't know if she'd licked them or if it was from the tears. If she'd cried that much while he'd been seeing stars. Lost in his own pleasure.

Her fingers slid off his shoulders to rest on his biceps, a frown shaping her pretty lips. She tilted her head to the side. "What's wrong? You're…shaking?"

He never shook. Not under fire. When he was

outnumber. Outgunned. Out of options. But there was no denying the tremors in his arms. The slow slide of fear down his spine. He could try to pass it off as his muscles being fatigued, but lying wouldn't change the fact that they both knew it was her. Only she affected him like this. Reduced him to the man beneath the fatigues.

Cannon clenched his jaw. "What's wrong? You're crying, that's what's wrong. Christ, Jericho. Whatever I did, I..."

What could he possibly say to make it right? That he was sorry? That he wouldn't be an insensitive prick, again? Because he didn't even know what he'd done. Couldn't remember anything after she'd rasped his name, other than the feel of her skin beneath his. The warmth of her body surrounding him.

Jericho's gaze softened, and she smiled, again. As if everything was okay. As if he hadn't just fucked up their second night.

He shook his head. "I don't know why you're smiling. There's nothing I can say to make this right."

"Are you always going to jump to the worst possible conclusion? And is that an Army thing, a Delta thing, or just a guy thing?"

"Not funny. You're crying. There are tears on your cheeks. It doesn't take a genius to know that's not a good thing."

"Oh, baby, they really should teach you guys more about how to understand women. I'm crying because you made me see more than just stars. Because I've never felt this...this...complete. Like I'm part of something bigger than just myself. A part of you. I'm not sad. I'm happy."

"You're...happy?"

"Exceedingly so. The tears mean you did everything right. More than right. That…"

Christ. The first time he'd messed up, she'd told him he was incredible. Now, she said he'd made her happy. Complete. He really should have paid more attention to his mother. Asked her the important things like how to understand women, because nothing made sense, other than the fact he wasn't in the doghouse. Hadn't scared her away. In fact, now that his initial fear had eased, he sensed that they'd grown even closer.

Jericho cupped his jaw, waited until he was looking her in the eyes, completely focused on her. "There's something I need to tell you, but… I want to wait until after we sleep. When we're not riding this sexual high. So, you know I'm sincere. Okay?"

Hell no. He would *not* let her be the first one to say the words, *I love you*. He knew that's what she wanted to tell him. It was there in the dreamy look in her eyes. In the way her fingers flexed against his muscles. After everything she'd given him, he needed to be first. To take that risk.

Cannon eased off to one side, still maintaining eye contact. But the fear he thought would surface, didn't. Instead, he felt light. Confident. Free.

He touched her cheek, wiping at the moisture still clinging to her creamy skin. "So, telling you that I'm crazy about you. That I can't picture my life without you in it. That I'm so damn in love with you, I can't focus on anything else but making you smile. Admitting that when we're still entwined like this means it's not sincere? Is that a Deputy Marshal thing, a woman thing, or just a Jericho thing? Because it means *everything* to me, sweetheart. Regardless of where we are, what we're doing. And it's not going to change come morning, other than getting even stronger. You... You undo me."

Damn it. More tears. Streaming down the sides of her face. Had he misread everything? Again?

That small hand on his jaw squeezed tight. "It means everything to me, too. I just didn't want you to think it was just the sex talking. That I'd regret telling you I love you in the morning. I won't, but..." She gave him a watery laugh. "I love you."

Relief. Swift and sure through his chest. Loosening the tight feeling there. Making everything—perfect. "Hell yeah, you do." He dropped a quick kiss on her lips. "Hold all those thoughts."

Cannon slipped off the bed, quickly darting to the bathroom. He cleaned up then brought a warm wet cloth in for her. She watched him as he wiped away their combined releases, her gaze following him over to the small ensuite then back.

He tsked as he climbed beneath the blankets, taking her in his arms then tossing the covers over both of them. "I know that look, but...sleep, first. Let your ribs rest a bit. I promise I'll be pounding into you, again, in the morning."

Jericho laughed, easing her head onto his shoulder, her leg across his. "Not so fast, soldier. Next time, I'm on top."

"Challenge accepted. As long as you realize we'll be finishing with you plastered against the headboard as I claim you from behind."

"Always a counteroffer with you. Fine, I accept. Just, don't let go, tonight, okay?"

He cinched his arms around her. "Wouldn't dream of it. Sleep. We'll talk about moving your stuff here, in the morning."

She stiffened, pushing up onto one elbow. "Moving all my stuff here?"

"Unless you hate this place. We could—"

She silenced him with a dainty finger across his mouth. "Again, with the worst case. This place is perfect. And I really don't have that much I need, so... We can start fresh. Together."

Damn straight, they would. And he'd make sure this thing with Ty Brown was over. That they hadn't missed anything. That she was as safe as she could be. That she stayed that way because this was only the beginning.

He dropped another kiss on her mouth. "Together."

CHAPTER TWENTY

The truth is, Jericho, you were always a better marshal. A better friend. I knew you'd eventually find out...

That voice. Jericho knew that voice playing inside her head.

If the damn Marshal Service doesn't think I'm dead, we're all fucked. And, since I'm not your only source, you might want to consider that before you decide to make any changes in our agreement... What? No, there won't be any issues. We're off the route, and she's out cold. No, I can't kill her outright... I know what I'm doing. I have a car waiting. We'll meet in thirty minutes... Don't be late.

"No!" She bolted upright, fighting against the covers, her chest heaving. The icy slide of panic clawing at her throat, leaving goosebumps across her skin. Sun streamed in through a window on the far wall—from a skylight overhead—casting long shadows across the wooden floor. By the looks of it, she'd slept late. Well past noon.

The lingering echoes of the dream sounded in her mind, quickly fading into nothing more than ghosted words that didn't make sense. It had been important—the dream. She felt it. As if she'd been on the verge of remembering everything. Why the whole situation still felt wrong. Why she couldn't move forward. Why she was still chasing the truth when everyone else had already filed it away.

Trust your gut. That's what Cannon had told her. And she owed it to herself—to Dave—to keep searching until the doubts faded like the dream had.

Which meant she needed to get back to work. No more hiding. If Cannon was still worried, the man could shadow her ass. Though, she had a feeling he'd be doing that regardless. That he'd find a way to be available and present during any future risky endeavors. Not that she really blamed him, seeing as he'd had to back her up— save her butt—more than once.

She mulled the thought around as she finally took in the room, but nothing looked familiar. Just a huge bed. A dresser. A photo on one of the walls. Had they gone to a hotel last night? She threw back the covers and stood on shaky legs before remembering where she was—the loft. Cannon's place.

Soon to be *their* place.

It all came rushing back, now. The takedown at the bar. Locking Ty Brown's ass up at her office. Cannon carrying her into his room. Making love.

Then, he'd said he loved her. And she'd answered in kind.

Jericho fell back onto the bed. She'd actually told Cannon she loved him. Out loud. Not that she regretted it. She didn't. But it made everything so...real. And he wanted her to move in with him. Live in his loft. *Their* loft.

The idea shouldn't make her so damn excited. While she didn't dislike her apartment, it had never been home. More of a place to hang her jacket. Kick off her boots. She hadn't even taken the time to decorate it. Not really. Other than a photo of her dad in uniform alongside of one of her and her parents taken just before he'd died, she didn't have anything on the walls. Any kind of personal items scattered around the place. Anything remotely important to her was stored away in a couple of boxes. Ones she'd planned on unpacking but never had.

She'd been waiting. She realized that, now. That there was some hidden part inside her that had been hoping to find Cannon. That she'd been searching all this time without even knowing what she was looking for until he'd smiled at her in that bar—dared her to see life from a new perspective.

Theirs.

And, now that she'd removed the blinders she'd been wearing—the ones that only saw her as a Deputy Marshal. Fighting alone—she knew she couldn't go back to that life. To being nothing more than a gun and a shiny star on her hip. She needed...

Cannon.

Hopefully, the fact she'd woken alone wasn't an indication he regretted what he'd said. That he'd been wrong, and it was just the afterglow of sex that had spurred him to confess his love. Asked her to move in with him. That the sunlight hadn't burned those feelings and thoughts away.

Of course, he was probably just making some coffee. She smelled the faint scent of it from beyond the door. Motivation to get her back on her feet and into the shower. It wasn't a huge ensuite, but tidy and clean, with a decent-sized glass shower at one end. Large enough she could fit in with Cannon—barely. But, the guy was larger than most people, so... They'd have to find a way to make it work. Because she definitely wanted more showers with him. Have him hold her under the spray. Rub soap across her skin. Deflect the water when she went to her knees to give him the best damn blowjob of his life. Let him see his release painted across her chest.

Oh, yeah. She could easily picture them sharing this space. It already looked as if they had similar tastes. Or, maybe, just the same lack of decorating skills. Either way, she was up for the challenge. And she really didn't have much she needed from her place. Some clothes, her computer. Those two boxes, and the couple of photos on her wall. Done.

Jericho made a mental list as she had a quick shower, fought to get a comb through her hair, then dressed. That coffee scent grew heavier as she opened the door to a short hallway. She took a few steps, stopping at the door she remembered seeing the previous night. It was another bathroom, but there was also another bedroom next to it.

Hadn't Cannon said something about Colt staying in his spare room? Had the other man been in there when they'd stumbled in? Had he heard them making love? She hadn't been exactly quiet. Hadn't thought there was anyone else in the loft. And hadn't the headboard clunked against the wall at some point?

God, she hoped Cannon had more spare rooms downstairs. It was bad enough Colt had already gotten a glimpse of her naked in Cannon's arms. Adding this to the list just tipped her embarrassment over the edge. How was she supposed to look the other man in the eyes and not blush? And, seeing as he was Cannon's only co-worker at the moment, they were destined to spend a lot of time together.

She cringed inwardly as she made for the room in front of her. It opened up into a large communal area. Part kitchen, living room and dining room, with tall ceilings and beautiful brick work along a couple of the outer walls. Everything was done in gray tones with industrial piping running across the wooden beams. The only splash of color was a blue throw rug and matching pillows.

Very masculine but appealing. Soothing, almost, which seemed a bit odd considering Cannon's past. His present career. When his personality default was set to extreme overdrive. But, maybe the place helped him unwind. She already felt a thousand times more relaxed than she had in a long time.

Though, the mind-blowing sex probably had more to do with that than the furnishings and paint scheme, but she'd give it all the benefit of the doubt. And, like his room, the place was neat. Very little to clutter the area, other than the essentials. All oversized, she noticed. Probably in order to accommodate his size. No sense investing in a couch you'd fall off of if you fell asleep.

Jericho took in her surroundings as she padded over to the coffee maker. Damn pot was empty, though it had recently been brewed. Which meant she'd have to wait several minutes for the infusion of caffeine she desperately needed.

"Here."

She screamed as a bag of coffee beans appeared over her right shoulder, spinning deftly to her right as she grabbed a pan out of the sink and brandished it in front of her. A tall man with dark hair and matching dark eyes stood off to her left, amusement tilting his full lips into a killer smile. He looked around the same age as Cannon, maybe a couple of years younger, with just a few faint lines around his eyes and mouth. He was large, muscular, but not nearly as massive as Cannon. Though, she guessed he was just as deadly.

The guy was obviously ex-military. She recognized the look, now. Ice, Midnight, Rigs—they'd all had the same haunted shadows in their eyes. Men who had faced the impossible and had somehow managed to come out the other side intact. Scarred, but intact.

Damn, hadn't Cannon mentioned something about another buddy of his showing up today? What the hell had he said his name was?

The guy raised his other hand, keeping them both shoulder height. "Easy. I surrender. No need to get violent."

She groaned, placing the pan back in the sink. "You really shouldn't sneak up on folks like that. What if I'd grabbed my gun?" Which she shouldn't have left sitting on the bedside table, but she hadn't thought she'd need it in the loft. Had wanted to save time disposing of it in case Cannon was up for a quickie.

The guy shrugged. "I would have taken counter measures if necessary."

"Are all you Spec Op guys so damn cocky? And calm? Seriously... I'm not exactly your typical civilian."

"Nope. You're Deputy U.S. Marshal Jericho Nash. You joined the Marshal Service eight years ago after an exemplary five years of service on the Seattle police force.

You have an extremely impressive success record and have brought in an unusually high number of felons considering you aren't part of the dedicated unit that hunts them down. You seem to have a knack for being in the right place at the right time."

She blinked. How the hell did he know so much about her?

He chuckled, extending his hand. "The name's Casey O'Reilly. But my friends all call me Six."

Six. That was it. The name Cannon had said a few times. Why hadn't she remembered it? Maybe because she'd been too focused on Cannon. On the way his muscles moved. How his lips twitched. The deep bronze of his eyes, not to mention the gravelly tone of his voice. The one that sent shivers racing along her nerve endings. Made her stomach scatter into a thousand butterflies as heat settled in her core.

Another chuckle.

Damn, she'd drifted off into thought while standing there, staring at Six. "Seems you already know all about me."

"Only what Cannon's mentioned." Six's smile widened. "Guy's pretty focused on you. Has a way of bringing you up into any conversation. Poor bastard doesn't seem to realize how far he's fallen..." He paused, narrowing his eyes before shaking his head. "I stand corrected. I guess he knows exactly how far he's fallen. About time, too. I knew he was yours as soon as he called me after that night at the bar. Glad he's finally admitted it. Colt and I thought we'd have to beat it out of him." Six leaned in closer. "A guy can only pretend for so long before he has to acknowledge the truth. Even if it is scarier than any other mission he's faced."

"You knew after that first night? I didn't even know. And how do you know he's admitted his feelings?"

Six shrugged. "I'm not wrong, am I."

It wasn't a question, the cocky bastard.

Jericho crossed her arms. "Since you didn't ask, I'll refrain from answering." She motioned to the coffee beans. "Were you the one who drank *all* the coffee?"

"It's been a long trip. Besides, Cannon went out to get you some caramel latte drink and some bagels. Apparently, you live on the stuff. He should be back soon. But, I'll make another pot if you'd like. Tide you over until he arrives. From what I've heard, you could use the pick-me-up. Sounds like it was a long night last night."

Shit. Had Six heard them, as well? Had they kept the other two men up?

Six moved in beside her, readying the machine. "Colt says you brought in that guy who escaped—Ty Brown. The one who hurt you. Killed your partner. Sounds like the loss of sleep was worth it."

Oh, he meant they'd had a long night at the bar, collaring Brown. Not that he'd heard her and Cannon getting it on. Christ, she really needed to get her mind out of the bedroom and back on the job.

She gave herself a mental pep talk, turning to lean against the counter as Six flipped on the coffee maker. "Cannon's the one who was busy. Who took all the risks. I just waited until he'd cleared out Brown's men then arrested the jackass." She sighed. "He seems to forget I'm armed, as well."

"Cannon's always been protective of his team. When

he made unit leader, he took the position very seriously. Wouldn't think of getting to safety until all of his men were accounted for. And his last stint undercover…" Six whistled. "It was hard. Being on his own. Then, having to break ranks in order to save a fellow serviceman. The guy would have sacrificed himself for strangers, let alone a soldier. Thankfully, it didn't come to that." Six glanced over at her. "For you… I bet he'd fight the devil, himself."

"I would. No question."

Jericho jumped as Cannon's voice sounded directly behind her, nearly knocking into him when she spun to face him. She placed a hand on her chest, willing her heart to stop pounding out of her rib cage. "Jesus. Don't any of you make a noise when you enter a room? Damn near scared me half to death."

Cannon smiled, and damn, it did that butterfly thing to her stomach, again. "Sorry, sweetheart. Old habits. Noise—"

"Gets you killed. Yeah, you've mentioned it before. Sneaking up on an armed federal marshal could get you killed, too."

Cannon merely shrugged.

She huffed. "Like I was telling Six, you Spec Op guys are all just a bit too cocky for your own good."

"I'll take my chances. Besides, you're not wearing your holster, which means your weapon's still on the nightstand." He laughed at her. "Don't pout. I brought you caffeine and sugar. Your favorite combination. And bagels."

Jericho inhaled as he handed her the latte. "You're forgiven."

Cannon shouldered in beside her, lightly pressing his

side against hers. "I'd hoped to surprise you in bed. Thought you'd sleep later. You were pretty wiped out after last night."

Six chuckled until Cannon swatted the man up the backside of the head. Six made a point of schooling his features, though she knew he was still smiling on the inside.

Cannon sighed. "Ignore him. He hasn't been around regular people for a while."

Six snickered. "As if you're the embodiment of social interaction. Outside of Jericho, how many non-military people do you associate with?" Six nodded at Cannon's glare. "That's what I thought. And, for the record, I let you swat me. Don't think I wasn't aware it was coming."

Cannon took a swig of his coffee before handing Six one then placing a variety of bagels on a plate he grabbed out of the cupboard. "And to think I asked you to join me voluntarily. I must be losing my mind." He glanced at Jericho. "How are your ribs?"

Had he seriously just asked how her ribs were? When their tumble in the sheets would have been the reason she might be sore? Was he trying to make her blush?

She smiled. "I'm fine."

"And if you had to draw down? Chase a felon through an alley? Tackle them? Would you still be fine?"

"Cannon...Rick. I think we both know it'll be another week or two before I'm a hundred percent. But that doesn't mean I'm not fit for duty. I'm sure Art will have me riding a desk until he's satisfied I can do a weapon check without dropping to my knees. You don't have to worry all the time."

"Of course, I do. I love you, which means, it's my job to worry."

Jericho knew her mouth gaped open. He'd just said he loved her. Again. In front of Six. And he'd said it as if he was asking her if she wanted butter on her bagel. Or if she was warm enough. As if it was easy. Natural.

She turned to face him, with every intention of returning the sentiment, when Colt's hand appeared beside her head, her phone in his grasp.

She jumped—again, damn it—this time making an unflattering shrieking sound. "Christ. Can you all please stop scaring me? Learn to scuff the floor or something when we're in the loft. I doubt there are any tangos, as you call them, hiding in the showers."

She frowned at Colt. "And when did you come in?"

"I was with Cannon, but it appears you only have eyes for him."

Jericho groaned, palming her face. "Maybe I should have slept longer. Is it too late to change my mind? Start this day over?"

Colt laughed. "Don't worry. Cannon's just as focused on you. And you wouldn't have gotten much sleep. Your phone's been going off for a couple of minutes. You had it on silent, so I didn't hear the first few vibrations. Looks like your office wants you."

"Art's been calling? But I'm not officially back, yet." She took the phone, scrolling through the missed calls. "Shit, three times. It must be important."

She unlocked the screen when a blast of music filled the room.

Cannon reached into his back pocket. "Looks like Art's

trying another route. He's calling the burner number I gave him."

"You gave him a burner number?"

"I told you. I don't give out my personal cell to anyone —other than you and my brothers. I'm keeping this one just for Art." He hit the button. "Sloan."

A pause as his eyes darted to either side. "She's fine, Art. Was just getting something to eat. Left her phone in the bedroom." He chuckled. "Do you really want me to tell her you said that? Didn't think so. What's up?"

Another pause. Longer than before until she found herself shifting from one foot to the other. She hated not knowing what was being said, especially when she knew it involved her.

Cannon straightened. "He did what? That's... unexpected. Of course." He looked at his watch. "We'll be there at eighteen-hundred."

Jericho stared at him after he ended the call, trying to be patient, but the brute just stood there. Silent. "What? What's unexpected? Why was he trying to call?"

"Easy, sweetheart. You'll pop a blood vessel."

"Cannon..."

"It seems that Ty Brown wants to swing a deal. Says he'll give the feds everything they need to bring down the Macmillan enterprise if they put him in Wit Sec."

She blinked. Obviously, she'd misheard him. "You said Brown wants to give up his employers? The same ones he refused to move on for months? That he wasted time in a federal penitentiary for? But he wants to talk, now?"

"That's what Art said. The feds are there, now. Art said to meet him at the office at six. Guess we'll get all the details, then."

"But...the man is wanted in connection with the murder of a federal marshal. Attempted murder of another. Why the hell would the feds cut him a deal when we gave him back to them practically gift wrapped?"

"I—"

"So, that's it? They're just going to let the bastard waltz into Wit Sec? I mean, I know how the game's played, but... I thought they might reconsider due to the severity of Brown's latest charges."

"Jericho." Cannon gently grabbed her shoulders, waiting for her to look at him. "Those are all great questions, but I don't know the answers. And worrying about it before we can get them will only give you an ulcer. Sit. Eat. We'll go through everything. Make a list of what you want answered, then head over when it's time. Okay?"

She blew out a raspy breath. She *hated* waiting. "Fine."

He tossed Colt his truck keys. "Colt. Six. You guys will take my truck. Go ahead of us. Circle around the office. Keep an eye out. When you're sure it's clear, one of you come up. The other can keep watch. You'll need the code on the off chance you'll have to get inside. If Brown really is going to cut a deal, that makes him one hell of a liability. And I don't want Jericho caught in the crossfire, again."

She swatted his shoulder. "I can handle myself."

"Never said you couldn't. But we have no idea what kind of firepower we could be up against. No sense getting shot because we were stupid."

"You realize you're describing pretty much every day on the job for me, right? I rarely know exactly what I'm up against. There's never enough information, and things rarely go as planned."

"Which is why we're taking Colt and Six along. I'm calling Rigs, too. Just to be safe."

"If this is you working on your protective instincts, you're going to give yourself a heart attack." She sighed. "But, I suppose we can't be too careful, considering Brown's history. The resources that could be used both for and against him. Just...try not to kill everyone who looks my way."

"No promises, but I'll be on my best behavior."

CHAPTER TWENTY-ONE

Well, shit.

That was all Cannon could think as he stood there, shaking his head as Art laid out the plans involving Ty Brown. Plans that dashed any hopes of Jericho getting her answers, but succeeded in putting Cannon right in the middle. The one place he didn't want to be. Not when he knew his proposed involvement was like a slap in the face to her. After all she'd sacrificed—nearly dying. Losing her partner. Busting her ass to apprehend Brown. Return him to custody—she was being benched. Put on medical leave until she could pass her firearm's practical, again.

Not that Cannon disagreed. After all, she *was* still healing. Despite her incredible strides forward—how well the wound had healed. Her unshakable resolve—she wasn't quite ready to return to the field. And she knew it. But she seemed determined to ignore the signs. Refused to admit she'd been in pain just drawing her weapon on Brown.

Which made Art's decision sting even more. She was

proud. And not seeing this situation through to the end obviously ate at her. It was evident in the purse of her lips. The narrowing of her eyes. Even the way she replied with curt one-word answers. The girl was pissed.

Add in the fact Brown had specifically requested that Cannon be part of his temporary security detail until the out-of-town agents arrived in a few hours, and Jericho's mood had turned nuclear.

Except when she looked at him. Even angry and frustrated, her gaze softened, and the tentative smile she flashed him lit up her face. Made him want to hike her up on his shoulder and carry her off. Back to his loft so they could spend the next few days discovering every inch of each other's body. Though, he had a pretty good road map of hers, already, the thought of putting every tiny freckle and mole into memory was too damn hot to resist.

But that wasn't in the cards. Not unless he refused Brown's request. Cannon studied Jericho, trying to determine which course of action would ease the tension straining her shoulders. Take the scowl off her pretty mouth.

Art cleared his throat, gaining their attention. "Look, Jericho, I know how frustrating this must be for you, but it's standard protocol."

Her jaw clenched. "I'm fine, Art. Brought the creep in last night without incident."

Art glanced at Cannon then back to her. "All right. Then, let's go run through the firearm's course."

Her face paled a bit. Not enough Art might notice, but Cannon saw the slightly whiter hue. The way she sucked in her bottom lip for a moment before flicking it free. "You really are a bastard, you know that?"

"A bastard who cares. Hell, until a couple of days ago, I thought you were dead. Cut me some slack, okay? I promise to give you the next mass murderer we have to track down. But...let Cannon see this one through on your behalf. He can ask Brown whatever questions you have rattling around inside your head."

The man chuckled at her wide eyes. "Please, I know you far better than you think. And I'll do what I can to see you get some kind of closure. But, after all that's happened—with our reputation at stake due to Faraday's possible, albeit unsubstantiated, involvement, both with the Macmillans and your injuries—we need to tread very carefully. The fact Brown requested Cannon is curious, too. I'd like to figure out why, and maybe riding with him to the safehouse and spending a few hours waiting for his detail to arrive will shed some light into it. I'll also give me a chance to get to know Cannon, better."

Jericho crossed her arms over her chest. "I still say I could sit in a car and watch Brown sweat. I'd be safe with Cannon." She held up her hand when Art looked about to argue. "Fine. But I'd like a few hours to go through some files I couldn't access before. Figure out if I really am going crazy."

"No one else is in today. So, you can stay until we get back. Then, you're taking a couple more weeks off."

She stuck her tongue out at him before turning and heading for her desk.

Art snorted. "Well, at least she didn't flip me off. I guess that's something." He twisted to fully face Cannon. "You on board?"

Cannon glanced at Jericho, again, but she was already

at her seat, punching on the keyboard. "You're putting me in a tough spot, you know that, right?"

"Thought you Delta guys thrived at being in the line of fire."

"With tangos, sure. With the woman they love…"

Christ, he'd said it, again. Out loud, and to Jericho's boss. As if it was nothing. Just a fact, no different from him admitting he was packing a suppressed M9 or that he'd parked in the garage.

Art paused, looked over at Jericho then sighed. "Guess even the best of the best have to fall sooner or later. I'm glad she found someone who won't let her down, because she's had enough of that to last a lifetime." Art made direct eye contact. "You *won't* let her down, right?" He nodded at Cannon's death stare. "Didn't think so. Okay, we leave in ten. The feds will rendezvous with us at the safehouse in a couple of hours and take over security. I've got a team of marshals flying in from out of state to help. Pray there isn't another leak out there I haven't plugged."

Art shook his head. "Do you think Dave really was involved? There was something going on with him. That's a given. But actually being involved with organized crime…" He whistled. "That's an entirely different level."

Cannon shrugged. "Jericho's memory is still foggy, not that I'm surprised. The amount of blood she lost, and that concussion. But she swears it was Dave who stabbed her. My gut tells me something's off. Him dying doesn't make sense if he was their inside man. You'd think having a federal marshal on the take was worth more than freeing a hitman. Guys like Brown are replaceable."

"Agreed. But, if there's even a chance Jericho's account is right, if Dave was involved and did try to kill her, I'll have to play my cards very close to my vest. Which is why I didn't argue when Brown requested you. And why I'm bringing in personnel from out of state. Why the Bureau is assigning agents the same way. The less chance there is that the Macmillan family has any influence over them, the better." He nudged Cannon. "Go make peace with her, and I'll grab you as soon as we're ready." He turned then glanced back. "Oh, and thanks, Cannon. I appreciate your help."

Christ, how could Cannon argue with that? He nodded at Art then made his way over to Jericho's desk, leaning his hip against the edge as she stared at her monitor. Her shoulders hunched before she focused on him.

Shit. She wasn't just upset. She was hurt. But he had a feeling it wasn't because she'd been sidelined. Being back here... It had to dredge up some conflicting feelings. He'd caught her glancing over at Dave's desk and bet his ass her ex-partner weighed heavily on her mind.

He placed a comforting hand on her shoulder. "You okay?"

She looked over at Dave's desk, again, then huffed. "Not sure. I didn't think it would feel like this."

"Angry?"

"More like empty. Numb. He had my back for eight years. To have it end like this..." She stared at her desk for a few moments. "Maybe everyone is right. Maybe my memories are skewed from the injuries, and it was Brown who did everything. Maybe Dave was just another victim like me."

"Always err on the side of caution, sweetheart." He motioned to her computer. "Find what you were looking for?"

"Not, yet. I pulled up the coroner's report. I can't place it, but something's wrong. Or missing. Every time I read it, I get the sensation that I'm being lied to. Not by the ME, but by something she said. I just can't figure out which fact is bothering me." She raked her fingers through her hair then slumped on her desk. "I'm really starting to question my sanity."

"Just...don't push it too hard, yet, okay? I know you don't want to admit it, but Art's right. You're still recovering. And that includes your head. Ice warned you that too much pressure could aggravate that concussion you got."

Jericho swiveled in her seat—made eye contact. "How can I be pushing too hard when all I can do is sit here? And that's only until you come back."

Cannon reached for her hand—took it in his. Christ, it was so small compared to his. Delicate bone structure. Smooth skin. Yet, he knew she could hold her own against any opponent.

He smiled, hoping it might ease some of the tension. And damn if the smile she returned didn't calm him. The woman was dangerous, and she didn't even seem to realize how much control she had over him. How far he'd go to see her happy. See that smile lift her pretty lips.

He gave her hand a squeeze. "If my involvement is going to affect us—affect our relationship—I'll bow out."

Her eyes widened, and an adorable flush colored her cheeks. "Just when I think you can't make me love you any more than I already do, you pull a stunt like this."

Jericho pushed to her feet then circled until she was standing beside him. Close. So close, no one would miss that they were a couple. Intimately involved.

Good. He wanted everyone to know. Wanted to shout it from the rooftops. Tattoo it across his arm. Jericho was his. And he'd do everything in his power to make that a permanent arrangement. Too damn bad there wasn't anyone else in the office.

She brushed a finger along his jaw. "Go. Keep Art safe. See if Brown will talk to you. There must be a reason he asked for you specifically. Just, take Six or Colt with you. Have them follow."

"Isn't that against protocol?"

"Fuck protocol. Safety first, especially since Brown has already executed an escape. For all we know, this is just a ploy to repeat that. Has been their plan all along. Place doubt on the Marshal Service so Brown could ask for alternate arrangements. Ensure Art was involved to make it all look above board. Whatever the reason, you're the best marshal for the job. Just come back in one piece, okay?"

"Always. And I'm leaving Six and Colt here." He silenced her with a firm finger over her mouth. "Like you said. There's no telling what Brown's motivation is or if this is all part of a grander scheme. One that could have you in the crosshairs. I want you protected. Still healing, remember?"

"But—"

"I'll have Rigs shadow me. Addison's riding along since she knows these streets and the local gangs extremely well. I'll be fine. Promise."

"This isn't an argument I'll win, is it? And don't answer. It was a rhetorical question."

"Your safety will always come first. Sorry, sweetheart, but even if I manage to tame the junkyard dog side of me, that's not going to waver. I love you. That changes things for me."

"And you just did it, again."

Damn, he was such a goner.

He stood, watching her closely as he leaned in. "You sure?"

"Positive. I hate being sidelined, but that's because I know I'm not fit to be out there, yet. I do need more time. I just…"

"You're not a quitter. I get it. But being part of a team means knowing when you have to let your teammates finish a job for you."

"Teammates, huh? I can live with that. But I want details. All of them. I'll keep looking through the files. See if I can unearth what's bothering me until you get back."

"Then, we'll go home and pick up where we left off last night."

"You've got yourself a deal, soldier. Just remember. I'm on top, this time."

"Do you two need some alone time or are you ready to go, Cannon?"

Cannon glanced over Jericho's shoulder, chuckling at Art's expression. "Ready."

He looked past Art to the man standing in the doorway, hands cuffed. A cruel smile twisting his lips. Cannon headed for the guy, stopping inside his personal space and making him take a couple of hurried steps backward.

Cannon moved in even closer, hoping that death vibe Addison had claimed surrounded him was in full force. "Understand this. I don't care how important you are. What incriminating evidence you have stored inside your head. Who you can bring down. You so much as twitch, and I'll kill you. No hesitation. No regrets. I might not know exactly what happened inside that car. But the end result was someone I deeply care about got hurt. Nearly died. That's all the reason I need to make this personal."

Brown swallowed then coughed, glancing over at Art. "I thought you said he was deputized?"

Art shrugged. "He is. But the man spent fifteen years eliminating threats. That's a hard habit to break. And, frankly, I'm with Cannon. If this *is* a setup, you'll be the first person I shoot. Now, I suggest you tread very carefully if you want to live to testify."

Brown nodded, following Art out as Cannon walked behind them. Colt was standing just inside the doorway. Cannon made a few hand signals, grinning when Colt nodded then moved to the other side of the doorway. The man had his phone out and was talking before the elevator doors closed.

Good. He'd make sure Rigs knew the plan and was waiting to follow them. Not that Cannon wanted to intentionally break the rules on his first official assignment, but he couldn't chance this was an ambush. An elaborate plot to take him out of the equation—leave Jericho unprotected.

She wasn't. Colt and Six would have her back or die trying. No doubts. No reservations. Being teammates meant they protected what was important to each other. And the men knew exactly how precious Jericho was to him.

Art didn't say anything as they made their way downstairs, through the parking garage and over to a waiting SUV. Cannon arched his brow when Art handed him the keys, but the other man was already busy settling Brown in the back then climbing into the passenger seat.

Cannon scanned the area. Being part of the federal building, the garage was fairly protected, but only from the outside. If there were more moles inside the service, they'd have easy access to this level—could spring an attack on them before they'd even left the premises.

He glanced at his watch. He'd set it up to relay messages, but Six hadn't so much as texted him. Which meant his buddy hadn't spotted anything concerning, yet.

The SUV dipped against Cannon's weight as he eased behind the wheel, waiting for Art to give him the address. Art sat there for a few minutes then leaned forward and inputted the address into the GPS. It called out the first set of directions, the tinny voice echoing inside the cab.

Cannon huffed. "Your safehouse is in the warehouse district? That's...unexpected. And pretty damn close to where I found Jericho."

"I wanted to keep him away from populated areas."

"Agreed, but you're practically asking someone to ambush us. All the high vantage points. The adjoining streets. We'll be targets the entire ride."

"It's not far, and we'll only be staying there for a few hours."

"That's assuming we make it. And that's a pretty ballsy assumption."

"Isn't that why you'll have one or two of your men following us?" He chuckled at Cannon's narrowed eyes. "Spent several years in the military, myself. I wasn't Special Forces, and nowhere the extremist you are, but I'm familiar with how you boys think. And there's no way you're trusting me with your life when we hardly know each other. I'm actually surprised you called to let me know Jericho was alive. That seemed—uncharacteristic of you."

"Jericho insisted you were clean. Trusting her means supporting her judgement calls." And, fuck, he hoped that Jericho hadn't read her boss wrong. That the location of the safehouse was just a coincidence and not a clue to who else might be dirty. Who had helped arrange the first hijack.

"Glad to know someone still has faith in me. And, if things do go sideways, we don't want to be anywhere close to downtown. To places where civilians can get caught in the crossfire. And, once we're situated, we'll have the same advantages and disadvantages as anyone gunning for us or Brown."

"Like I said. Ballsy. But, you're the boss."

Cannon started the engine then headed for the exit. He held his breath while the large metal gate rolled open, mentally planning all the steps he'd take if some asshole was waiting on the other side of the door with assault rifles or RPGs. How he'd maneuver the vehicle, draw his weapon and shoot before they could fire. Or at the least, get Art safely out before anything exploded. Finding nothing but misty rain lit up by the streetlights was a pleasant surprise, especially when surprises generally involved bullets. Bloodshed. A full unit of tangoes trying to kill him.

He switched on the wipers as he pulled into the street, quickly joining the evening traffic. There weren't many cars on the road, not that he was surprised. With it being Sunday night, there weren't many reasons for people to visit the area. The courthouse was closed, as was the

Marshal Office. Sure, the odd deputy might work on a weekend, but most of that involved fieldwork. Not sitting around at a desk.

An uneasy feeling settled in Cannon's gut. The weekend also meant the building wasn't protected like it usually was. True, the only way to get in and out was through code-protected doors. But that wouldn't save Jericho if there was another leak. If someone she knew was dirty.

Despite his reassurances, he didn't buy Dave as a victim. There had been too many signs that the man had ventured into something dark. That, coupled with Jericho's memories, all made Cannon believe Dave was alive and actively involved in dealings much bigger than just Ty Brown. Cannon hadn't said all of that to Jericho, yet. He hadn't wanted to give her false hope that her partner wasn't dead. Regardless of how their relationship had ended, the man had been important to her. Eight years of partnership wasn't easy to erase. And Cannon wanted to spare her feelings as long as possible.

He glanced at his watch, again, pent-up energy making him tense. But there was no reason to feel so antsy. Six and Colt were watching over Jericho. Still…

Cannon looked in the rearview mirror, locking his gaze on Brown. "Why did you request me, personally?"

Brown's eyes widened then narrowed before he plastered on a fake grin. "I'm about to stab a very powerful enterprise in the back. Thought it would be wise to have the best possible protection."

"Bullshit. Unless you're admitting there's another leak in the Marshal Office or those agents from the Bureau, because no one else would know you'd swung a deal. Not this quickly. So, the chances your boss is onto you is pretty slim. Which means there're two options. One—this is all a scam, and you're setting us up. Probably a bit of payback involved, too. Or two—you're afraid of someone on the inside and figured I was your best chance at making it into Wit Sec in one piece."

Brown's gaze didn't falter. "You think you're so smart. That you have all the answers. You don't know shit."

"I know that you won't live to enjoy your victory if you don't answer my question."

"I know how it works. Make all the threats you want, but the information I have is bigger than you. Than any one marshal."

"Already warned you that I don't give a shit about that. I just want to know the truth."

"I told Nash the truth. I didn't stab her. It was all Faraday. I just took advantage of the situation—same way I'm doing here. Watching out for number one."

"All right. Let's say you're telling the truth. Why did you help the man fake his own death? Because there's no way he's dead. It doesn't add up."

Brown's grin slipped a bit, the muscle beside his left eye twitching, and fuck, Cannon knew. Right then. Jericho was right. Had been all along. Which meant...

"Shit." He swerved over to the curb, ignoring the couple of horns that blared behind him.

Art grabbed onto the handle by his head, twisting to stare at Cannon. "What the hell, Sloan?"

"This isn't just an ambush. It's a distraction. They wanted us gone so they could go after their real target. Damn it..."

He was on his phone—hitting Six's number.

"We're in the middle of a transfer. Christ, get off—"

Cannon cut him off with a raise of his finger. "Shit. Six isn't picking up. They must be jamming the cell service." He hit another number. "Rigs. Change of plans. We're heading to the office. Do me a favor and call Ice and Sam. Have them meet us there. They'll have to stay with Art— keep Brown alive. I'm betting on snipers. Skilled, so everyone needs to stay sharp. But their resources will be divided—half on Brown, half focused on Jericho."

"Damn it, Cannon. What the hell is going on? We can't just change plans. This isn't one of your missions. You're acting on behalf of the Marshal Service." When Cannon hung up then turned the wheel, preparing to spin the damn SUV around, Art pulled his gun—aimed it at Cannon's head. "Keep to the schedule. Get this damn Chevy moving. We can discuss whatever's got you upset once we get to the safehouse. Secure our client."

"We're not going to make it to the safehouse. Why do you think Brown asked for me? He knew I'd have a team along, Marshal protocol or not. Just like you did. And he was relying on that to counter whatever forces are waiting for us." He glanced back at Brown. "Let me guess. Dave wasn't the only one in the service on the take. And, now, those guys aren't just gunning for Jericho, they're gunning for you, too."

Brown's eyes widened, the color draining from his face as he looked between them.

Cannon pounded one fist on the steering wheel. "Damn it, Brown, we don't have time for you to keep bullshitting us. Who are we up against? Or would you rather I resign, right here and now. Let Art take you on alone?"

"No! Shit, he can't keep me safe. Not against...them."

Art clenched his jaw then slowly lowered his weapon. "Who's *them*?"

"It's not safe here. We need to get moving. They're probably following us. The longer we sit, the more time they'll have to snipe us. It's already dark outside. Shit, I thought you were some Black Ops soldier or something."

"Or something. How many are involved? Who's got you shitting your pants?"

Brown swallowed, looked as if he was about to puke, then swore—punching his fists into the back of the seat. "Two, that I'm aware of. They're part of some special unit. That's all I know. I swear. But they're hardcore."

SOG. Had to be. Which suggested Jericho's brush with death at the restaurant hadn't been a chance encounter. Cannon just didn't know how many or if they would focus on Brown or her.

"Well, shit." Art pulled out his phone, tapping on the screen. "Barry, it's Art. Where are the SOG teams?" He nodded. "And the other unit? I see. No, not right now. Something might be on the horizon. Thought I'd check— see what my options were. I'll call you back if I need you." He hung up. "Alpha unit's on a call up-state. Bravo's on stand-by this weekend. Which means—"

"They're already hunting us."

Cannon peeled out, fishtailing across the street then up over the curb. The headlights cut through the misty fog as the Chevy bounced across the median followed by another swerve when Cannon hit the road, heading south. "I'll get you to my office. It has pretty extreme security measures. And I've called in more backup. No one will get in. You and Brown will be safe until the feds arrive to take over—get Brown out of state."

Art gripped the handle as Cannon skidded around a corner then hit the gas, pushing them both back in their seats. "I can call in more marshals. Have them head for the office."

"That will only confuse things. We don't have names, which means no one will know who's clean and who's not since all of the SOG members are also regular deputies. That moment of hesitation is all it takes to get someone killed. I'll go after Jericho. Once I have her, you can have the entire unit brought it. Launch an investigation."

He glanced over at Art. "I know I'm asking a lot. That you're in charge. That there are protocols in place for important reasons, and it's not practical to toss them away on a whim, but... I'm asking you to trust me. Trust my team. It's our best chance at keeping any bloodshed to a minimum."

"Something tells me that's not really a concern for you."

"I won't put any of your officers at risk. But, if anyone comes looking for my team? They'll have to go through me." He arched a brow. "Well?"

"If this goes sideways, not even Hastings will be able to offer you a Hail Mary."

"Understood. Now, hold on, this is going to get rough."

CHAPTER TWENTY-TWO

Nothing. Another scan of the files, and Jericho still had what she'd started with—absolutely no new information or proof that the body they'd found burned in the car hadn't been Dave's.

Which only made her question her sanity more. The scattered memories. The nightmares. The gnawing sensation in the pit of her stomach. They all pointed to Dave being behind the escape. His hand on the blade. His bomb. And she just couldn't believe that he'd go through all that trouble—throw away his career—just to end up a victim of Brown.

But she appeared to be the only one. Art. The ME. Everyone seemed satisfied with the report. Convinced that Deputy U.S. Marshal David Faraday had been killed in the line of duty. His involvement with the Macmillans, with Brown, nothing more than an unanswered question. One they were happy to let slide.

She got it. Not only did having a dirty marshal make the service look bad, it put every case he'd ever worked on in jeopardy. If they could prove he'd been on the take since he'd started… Who knew what the fallout would be. If some of the convictions could get overturned. Thankfully, they had often worked security or retrieval—nothing directly involved with the evidence. But there were instances—joint missions—that could be compromised. Probably better for everyone to just let it fade. Initiate a discreet internal investigation, just to satisfy any lingering doubts, but nothing to outwardly convict him. Treat him as a fallen warrior and move on.

Except where she couldn't move on. Not without knowing the truth.

"Everything okay?"

She jumped when Colt appeared beside her, his head level with hers—his gaze fixed on the screen. Shit, the guy was quiet.

She glared at him. "Thought I warned you about scaring me."

He simply shrugged. Old freaking habits, her ass. She suspected they all enjoyed sneaking up on her, the jerks.

Of course, her frustration level wasn't helping the situation, any. "Guess that depends on your definition of okay. I'm fine."

"But you haven't found what you're looking for. A way to prove your partner isn't dead." Colt pointed to one of the lines on the ME report. "Looks like what the others said was right. They were able to confirm his DNA as a match to the body in that car."

"I know. It's all pretty cut and dry. But…" How did she explain it when it was nothing more than ghostly echoes inside her head?

Colt sighed. "I didn't say that to discourage you. What

I meant was—if your suspicions are correct, but his DNA was a match, then he must have changed the samples, somehow. Which explains why he'd set an explosive charge. With all the damage to the body, the ME would have to rely on matching only his DNA. The fire, alone, would have destroyed any distinguishing marks. Could cause bones to crack. And, honestly, once they matched the samples, I doubt the Medical Examiner kept searching for anything else. Cause of death was fairly obvious."

Colt glanced at her when she snorted. "What's with the look?"

She forced her mouth to close. "Nothing, I just... I didn't think anyone else believed me, other than Cannon."

"Assumptions get you killed. I agree there's a lot of convincing evidence against your theory, but you were there. If your gut's telling you Dave was the one who hurt you. That he might still be alive, that means more to me than any report. And is definitely worth checking out. Which leads me to my next question—did he try to kill you as part of a cover story or because he was afraid you might be able to prove that body isn't him? That there's something in that report you'd recognize as being wrong?"

I knew you'd figure it out sooner or later...

Jericho palmed her head, wincing against the memory trying to take shape.

"Jericho. Are you all right?"

"Fine. I just remembered something Dave said. About me figuring it out. But I don't know what *it* is."

"All right. Let's break it down. There are only so many ways to identify a body. We already know that any tattoos or birthmarks are out."

"As are fingerprints."

"Right. There might be dental evidence, but that's only if he had work done that was out of the ordinary, and the teeth weren't damaged." Colt tapped a finger against his lip. "The doctor probably didn't test for it, but you could ask them to check for anomalies in the blood. Antibodies and the like. Run any they find against childhood illnesses, or immunizations. It's a long shot, but—"

"Wait. What did you just say?"

"That we could have his blood checked for antibodies?"

"His blood."

She double checked the report then went back to the computer, clicking through folders until she found the one she was looking for.

Colt moved in closer. "What are you thinking?"

"It's a long shot, but... On one of our first cases together, we were executing a seizure of property on this douchebag drug dealer. The asshole's brother jumped us while we were making an inventory. Caught Dave with a knife to his arm before we able to subdue him. Dave bled pretty bad before they got him stitched up. There was talk of surgery, in case the blade had nicked some ligaments, but it wasn't necessary. However, I'm pretty damn sure they type-crossed his blood, just in case. It was eight years ago. If Dave *is* covering his tracks—wiping any previous identifying information from reports or records—making it match that body in the morgue—there's a chance he might not have remembered to alter the hospital's account from that file."

"You think the body they found might have a different blood type."

"I know. Pretty damn flimsy, but... Like you said. Something about that report was off, and I think that's what has been bothering me. It didn't click until you mentioned it. I swear Dave was AB negative, like me. That's why it stuck. That we could donate for each other if there was ever an emergency. But the ME put his blood type down as AB positive. Close, but..." She blew at the wispy hairs around her face. "I could be wrong. We're talking a stupid Rh switch."

She flipped through the digital pages, scouring the reports until one line jumped out at her. She inhaled, staring at the truth on the screen.

Colt gripped her shoulder. "Well, I'll be damned. You were right. The Rh listed there is different from all the others. No way that's a simple mistake. Which means..."

Jericho forced herself to swallow. To keep breathing when her chest simply wanted to stop. Lock everything away instead of facing the truth. The pain.

She fisted her hands. "Dave's not only alive, he planned this. All of it."

Colt sighed, giving her shoulder a squeeze. "We need to call Cannon and your boss. This changes everything."

He'd tried to kill her. On purpose. After eight years of having each other's backs.

"Jericho?"

Wait. Had he arranged Wilson to target that restaurant? Had all those texts been lies to keep her there? Did she really know anything about him? Or had it all been an illusion? A role he'd been playing.

"Jericho!"

She blinked when Colt shook her, looking up at him. "What?"

"Call your boss."

"He won't pick up. Not during a transport. Maybe if I call him repeatedly but... They're both essentially on lockdown. We'll have to wait until after they hand off Brown."

"Cannon will get the message. Trust me." He hit a button on his phone. Frowned. "Jericho? Did Art jam the cell service when he left? Is that protocol or something?"

"No, why?"

"Service is out."

"What?" She took out her phone. Stared at the message in the top left of the screen. "That's...odd. We should have full bars. I'll try a landline." She picked up the phone on her desk. "Something's wrong. There's no dial tone."

"Shit. We're out of here. Now."

"Just let me save this to a thumb drive." She transferred over the reports then tucked the small device down the side of her bra, shrugging at Colt's arched brow. "Can't be too careful."

"Smart. Stay close."

They headed for the exit when Six appeared in the doorway. Hair slightly out of place. Face grim. He made some signal to Colt, and the man grabbed her hand, following after Six as he angled toward the stairs. Jericho didn't ask where they were going. Why they were bugging out—using the stairs. Obviously, the blocked cell service. The dead phone lines. It wasn't a technical difficulty or a freak storm that had cropped up while they were inside. Someone was coming for them. That's why Six had ventured inside. Why they were moving quickly—avoiding the elevators. This was an escape.

The door creaked as Six slivered it open, checking inside before waving them through. Jericho waited on the landing, glancing at both men. They seemed to be having some sort of silent conversation between them. It was frustrating, not to mention creepy.

But...as Cannon had told her numerous times—sound got you killed. So, she stood there while they leaned over the rail—scanned up and down the stairs. It didn't help that they were several floors up—didn't have many options if there were people in the stairwell below them. And trapping themselves on the roof wasn't her idea of a sound strategy.

Six muttered something under his breath. "I doubt we'll get all the way down, but...we'll have to chance it. I saw three head toward the elevators. A black SUV turned toward the parking garage. I'm sure there were more men inside. Wherever we go, we're bound to meet with resistance."

He'd kept his voice low. Barely enough to reach them, which meant he was concerned people might already be heading up.

He glanced at Jericho. "Any thoughts on a different route before we commit? You know this building the best."

"It's not during regular hours, so anyone coming in needs a security code. Which, they obviously have. It also means there're most likely marshals with them."

God, was it Dave? Had he come back to finish what he'd started? There were still cameras. He knew where they were, of course. And maybe he had a way of erasing the footage. Hell, he'd altered his files. Convincingly faked his own death—would be free and clear if she'd died. He either had some mad tech skills or was in league with someone who did.

She met Six's gaze. "Also, it's Sunday. There won't be much in the way of cover in the garage. Building's usually pretty deserted. We'd fare better trying to exit on the main floor. But I assume they'll have people watching. Camped out in the lobby or outside. And we might not have a choice. There are a limited number of ways out of here."

Six nodded. He motioned to the stairs then started winding his way down. He moved fast but controlled, keeping toward the outside. The men didn't make a sound —not boot clicks. Not harsh breaths. Jericho wasn't sure how they did it. Her boots weren't silent—they weren't loud, but there was a hushed footfall every time she stepped, even consciously trying not to.

Made her wonder what kind of training they'd actually had, how intense it must have been to be this skilled, when a noise sounded from below. It wasn't much. Not really more than a scuff, but it had Six changing direction —exiting on the next floor. He didn't slow. Didn't ask for directions, which meant he was somewhat familiar with the layout. She wasn't sure how, but now wasn't the time to ask. Moving was the priority.

Six followed a couple of corridors before suddenly stopping. He pushed her against the wall with one arm, motioning some signal to Colt. The man nodded then backtracked, disappearing around the corner. Jericho flicked open the closure on her holster—readied herself to draw. Six glanced at her hand, then her side, shaking his head as he pushed back his coat—revealed the hilt of a massive Sig. Did they make one larger than a forty-five?

Something only Special Forces knew about? Top secret? Because—damn, it looked huge. Elephant-ready huge.

She tapped her badge, but Six arched a brow then pointed to her side. Sure, she was still recovering. And, yeah, it hurt like a bitch to draw—something she'd discovered last night when she'd pulled her Beretta on Brown. But, damn it, she was the law, here. Didn't any of these guys care about their own well-being? That they could go to jail for protecting her?

Judging by the look on the man's face, the answer was a resounding no. Not that she was surprised. Cannon had risked everything to come to her defense. No reason the men he trusted with his life—with *her* life—should be any different.

Jericho considered drawing regardless but decided to wait. She wasn't even sure what they might be up against on this floor. Best to give it a bit more time—see if whoever Six thought he'd heard just walked past.

Five seconds turned into ten. Then twenty. Then more. She was just about to nudge him when someone grunted followed by a hard thud. Despite the burn through her ribs, the pull on her healing wound, she drew, keeping the weapon close to her shoulder. Six snorted, shook his head, then stepped out. Just like that. Right into the middle of the hallway.

"Six. What the hell—"

"It's clear."

"Clear? How?"

She moved into the corridor then froze. Two men were on the ground, hands bound with zip ties. Colt stood over them, brushing his palms off on his pants. He smiled at her then nodded at Six.

"But…" She shook her head. "You were behind us. How did you get behind them?"

He shrugged. "Went up a floor and came down the other set of stairs behind them."

"In thirty seconds?"

"Twenty. Took ten to knock them out."

"Christ." Jericho holstered her gun. "I don't recognize them, but that tattoo on their necks is part of the fifth-street gang. They're associated with the Macmillans."

She turned to Six. "Wait. How did you know they were there? I didn't hear anything, and I was listening."

Six helped Colt move them over to a more secluded section. "Had a feeling."

Colt grinned. "Don't ask. Just trust and believe."

Six sighed. "We should take the other stairwell. Might get lucky and get a clear shot to the main floor."

"Right, because our good luck's going to start, now."

"Thought you marshals were a positive bunch. Always got your man."

"That's the Canadian Mounties. And I haven't exactly had great luck where my job's concerned, lately. Partner trying to kill me and all that."

"You've got Cannon, now. And us. Luck's already changed."

Well, damn. She couldn't argue with that. Instead, she smiled then followed them down the hallway, pausing long enough to check the stairs before heading down, again. They made good time, despite stopping at each level—listening for more men. And, for just a second, Jericho thought Six was right. That their luck had definitely changed. Until they reached the first floor and discovered there wasn't a door to the main lobby. That the stairs simply continued down.

Colt cursed under his breath. "Seriously?"

"Shit. I never use this side. I didn't know. It must be one of the secure exit points—prevent people from accessing the upper levels from the main floor. Guarantee only those with a code can access this stairwell from the garage. They probably use it for prisoner transfers to the courthouse." She matched Colt's grim expression. "I haven't done court transfers, okay? Most of the time they contract that job out to security companies they've vetted —given Special Deputy status to. We hardly have enough personnel to tackle the big stuff."

Colt raised his hands. "No blame. It just limits our options." He looked at Six. "Well, buddy? Back up, or down to the garage?"

Six looked in each direction. "It's not like we can walk out those main doors, anyway. We'd be wide open. We'd have to find a side door or service exit. But going to the garage..." He huffed. "We should... Shit. Someone's above us. Down, now."

He'd heard someone above them? Because Jericho hadn't heard a thing. Not a scuff, a creak. Not a tap of boots on the stairs. Nothing. Except her own breathing. They'd barely been moving, and yet, she felt as if she'd been running a marathon. Had used up all her available fuel. And that wasn't even accounting for the burning in her side. Without any pleasant distractions, it was painfully debilitating. Not that she'd let it stop her. But it made her acutely aware of how much of a liability she was. Why Cannon and Art had insisted she take more time to recover. She'd been fooling herself.

No, she'd been in denial. Blindly overlooking the fact that Cannon had done all the heavy lifting since she'd been hurt. He'd eliminated the threats. Been the one to hunt down the men. All she'd done was sit at the table then walk across the floor. She hadn't even handcuffed Brown. Or dragged him out to the truck.

Shit. She should have let Cannon handle all of it. Worked out a way to access the information from a satellite location. Instead, she was putting his teammates, his brothers, at risk.

Six paused at the door to the garage, glancing over at her. "You okay?"

Damn, did it show? Was she wheezing or shuffling? "Fine."

"You're in pain. Stay close. Let us handle anything that pops up. And, if I tell you to run, you fucking run and don't stop until you're out. Understand?"

"I'll stay close and try not to confront anyone, directly. That's all I can promise. Unless your lives are at risk. Then, all bets are off. I don't back down, and I don't leave friends behind."

"Cannon sure can pick 'em. Okay. On three. Our only objective is to get out. We can hunt the bastards down later."

He counted down on his fingers then opened the door. It didn't make a sound. Just a whoosh of cool air across their feet. Then, they were through. Dodging behind a group of vehicles parked near the door. There must have been some kind of meeting or maybe people had left their cars there. Gone drinking and taken taxis home, because there were more cars than she'd expected. Scattered throughout the lot. Only half of the lights were on, casting long shadows across the pavement.

The men kept her between them, shuffling to the edge of the car when footsteps sounded from farther up the lot. And not just a few. Five, maybe six people. Heading their way. Most likely fanning out and searching every possible hiding place.

Six muttered something under his breath, then he was moving. Dragging them to another section with more cars parked in a couple of rows. Giving them a bit more cover. He looked at Colt, the other man's expression just as grim.

Colt made some kind of hand sign then moved off, disappearing around the edge of the vehicles. Six crept over to the opposite side, looking out when the door to the stairs banged open—three men spilling out.

She couldn't see their faces, the low light cloaking them in darkness. But she recognized one of their silhouettes. Had spent eight years watching his back. Keeping him safe. And, now, he was there to kill her. Kill them.

Fuck that. She wasn't about to let him hurt anyone else. Defile the badge she wore with pride. Honor. She wasn't sure if she could pull the trigger—kill him outright —but she'd defend her team with her dying breath.

She nudged Six, gaining his attention. "Stop worrying about me and go help Colt. I can hold my own." She sighed when he gave her a curt shake of his head. "Six. I'll be fine. I can cover my own ass. And we'll have a better chance of actually making it out of here alive if you and Colt can thin their numbers. I know I'm not up to running around, eliminating them. But...I can handle a few threats. Handle Dave. Go...I'll be fine."

Six leaned in close. "Do *not* make me sorry for trusting you."

"I could say the same thing. We're not here to trade lives."

"Stubborn. I'll be close. Don't engage unless you have to."

Then, he was off. Gone. Slipping behind the car and vanishing. No footsteps. No loud breathing. As if he'd simply disappeared into the shadows. Become part of the darkness.

"I know you're in here, Jericho. You can't hide forever."

Jericho snapped her head around. God, his voice. It sounded normal. Like every other time he'd talked to her. As if he wasn't currently hunting her. Trying to kill her. As if they were still partners. Still friends.

She shifted, got a better sightline. The other two men split off, heading in opposite directions. Like Six and Colt, disappearing into the shadows. Only Dave stood near the exit, his silhouette openly mocking her. She'd grieved for him. Had been ready to convince herself she'd been wrong. That he'd died a hero. And, now, this.

He took a step off to his right. "Come on, Jer. Are we really going to draw this out? Play hide and seek? Let's talk."

Did the man really think she was that naïve?

He held up his gun. Made a point of showing her he was holstering it. "We'll just talk. This doesn't have to end poorly. We can make a deal. One that doesn't involve those you care about dying. Like Cannon. He's not here, is he? Sorry, but the man's too good. Too devoted to you. I had to make sure he wasn't close enough to help. But, he doesn't have to die. Just...talk to me."

Shit. Had Brown been in on this, too? Asked for Cannon just to get him out of the picture? Was he walking into an ambush, right now?

He'd risked everything to save her. And she knew she couldn't offer him any less. Besides, she had her team with her. Something Dave wouldn't anticipate, even if he knew she wasn't alone. He'd underestimate their skill. Their determination. And that would be his downfall. All they needed was a chance. A distraction so the attention was on her. Then, they could work their magic. Clear the board. And she knew just how to play it.

"I put my gun away, Jer. And the others are out scouting around the garage. It's just you and me."

Jericho took a calming breath, then stood. Gun drawn, aimed at Dave's head. She smiled when he turned toward her, keeping most of her body hidden amidst the vehicles. "Hello, *partner*."

CHAPTER TWENTY-THREE

Twenty minutes. That's how long it had been since Cannon had forced Brown to talk—confirm Cannon's worst fears. And he hadn't even reached the courthouse, yet. Was still a few minutes out. Still couldn't reach Six, Colt or Jericho.

Cannon hadn't been as quick as he'd hoped. They'd met with some resistance on the way to the office. Two vehicles had skidded in behind them. Tinted windows. No license plates. They'd followed for a few blocks before opening fire—pelting the car with a barrage of bullets. Cannon had managed to keep moving—prevent anyone from getting shot—until Rigs had made his move. Taken out their tires and left their vehicles in smoking heaps on the side of the road.

They hadn't stopped to apprehend anyone. Art had made it clear that their main objective was getting Brown somewhere safe. Art hadn't been pleased with the change in venue. Was obviously accustomed to doing everything by the book. But Cannon had discovered long ago that being a good soldier meant being able to adapt. Make split-second decisions based on current intel, and not worry about whose feelings were bruised in the process.

So, talking Art into holing up in Cannon's office hadn't been too difficult, especially after they'd been shot at. Having a few ex-Spec Op guys around to shoulder some of the duty had definitely been a selling point. While Art didn't know Cannon all that well, he knew what Cannon was capable of—what the past fifteen years of his life had most likely entailed—and the man was giving Cannon his trust.

It came with a threat, but Cannon could live with that, even if he had to pass that part of the mission off to his buddies. Because there wasn't a chance in hell he wasn't going after Jericho. Wouldn't break any rank to ensure her safety. Sure, she had Colt and Six with her—men he trusted with her life. But she was his. To protect. To die for. Period.

Not that he could do anything until he reached the courthouse—knew what kind of forces he was up against. Brown had said there were two other deputies involved, and Cannon bet his ass one of them was that Andrews asshole who'd threatened to kill them in the restaurant. Cannon had felt something was off, then. That the guy had been too twitchy, even for a special ops division inside the Marshal Service. Cannon should have trusted his instincts. Investigated the bastard. Maybe, then, he would have unearthed all of this before Jericho had nearly died. Was facing death, again.

But that was ancient history. And stressing over shit he couldn't change wouldn't help her, now. Better to shove it away and focus on what was ahead. How he'd infiltrate the building without getting himself or his teammates killed.

He had the entry code—small fucking mercy. So, accessing either the garage or the main floor wasn't an issue. Doing it without being seen, without attracting attention to himself was a bit trickier. It wasn't as if there was a ton of available cover. It was a huge building in the middle of town. Surrounded by other large buildings. A concrete jungle. He'd have to take the extra time to do a quick recon—see if he could spot any outlying forces. Eliminate them, first, then proceed inside.

It made sense. Was a sound strategy. Except where the thought of not getting to her immediately hurt. Actually fucking hurt. Right in the middle of his chest. He'd never felt like this before, and he'd done his share of rescues. Going in after captured or downed comrades. Men he'd gladly die for. But, he'd always been able to separate the man from the soldier. Push any emotions so far down they never resurfaced.

But, he'd never been in love, before. In fact, he hadn't felt much of anything since he'd enlisted. Since feeling made him vulnerable. To suddenly have his damn heart exposed was unnerving. It made him unpredictable. Irrational. Exactly the opposite of what he needed to be. What Jericho needed him to be.

Which meant sucking it up. Steering into the hard. He'd done it all his life. Surely, he could be stone cold long enough to get the job done. Switch modes. It had been natural, before. Now...

Cannon pulled over a couple of blocks away, wishing he'd had the fucking forethought to grab his vest out of his truck. But, he'd been on the Marshal's dime—had been following their protocol. Which meant he didn't get into a car armed for bear, with six different tactical knives and caches of C4. It also meant all he had was his M9, Glock 19, and the Walther stashed in his ankle holster. All were fully loaded, but if they had semi-automatics. AK's or carbines. Fuck, it could get real ugly, real fast. And with the building mostly deserted…

Yeah, not much to deter the bastards from laying down more gunfire than necessary. And Cannon knew far too well that, if you threw enough bullets at a problem, it usually solved it. Blanketing the garage or even just opening fire at her office—shooting right through the glass walls—wasn't beyond a reasonable assumption. These guys were desperate. If they thought Jericho remembered everything—knew Dave was alive. Could prove it, not to mention out the other bastards on the payroll—they had nothing to lose.

The thought got him moving. He'd do a quick circle of the block. Chances were that any exterior forces would be concentrated within sight of the building. The biggest threat was from snipers. There were apartments and some trendy hotel on the south side. Perfect place for one of these SOG guys to set up a nest. Cap anyone who made it out of the building alive. Sure, their view was restricted, but it covered the large main doors, and a couple secure exits—the ones they were probably leaving open in order to herd Jericho and the others out. The only other option was the garage entrances on the opposite side of the building—hopefully out of range and sight from the snipers—but which Cannon was convinced would be overflowing with tangoes.

But, if his buddies couldn't get out through an

alternate door—one Cannon didn't know about. Maybe in conjunction with the adjoining buildings—Cannon knew they'd never risk exiting down those huge stairs—leave themselves open. Which hopefully meant the snipers were essentially useless.

Of course, he wasn't going to bet his life on it. That they wouldn't recognize their limitations and move. Which was why he'd agreed to have Rigs back him up. The ex-Marine had a special partner along—his wife's former guide dog, Blade. The animal had been a bomb dog in Afghanistan. Had proven, time and again, he was every bit a soldier the rest of them were. Rigs planned on searching the buildings—especially the roofs. It wasn't much, but Cannon felt confident no one would get past the two of them. Not and live.

That left Cannon to focus on the immediate threats. Anyone camping out in the green space by the stairs. Waiting in vehicles along the road. The men sent to eliminate any stragglers—maybe clean up any loose ends the Macmillans no longer needed.

He headed for the main entrance, first. The street was fairly deserted, only the odd car parked along the curb. He checked each one—careful to stay clear of any sightline from the hotel on the corner—then moved on. A black van was parked near the end, a trail of smoke curling out of the window.

Idiots. Giving themselves away. He didn't miss the blacked out plates on the back, or the illegally tinted windows. This wasn't someone making a call or waiting for a friend.

Cannon approached slowly, staying low and toward the center line, away from the mirrors. The rear panel didn't have any windows—which worked to his benefit. The only question was how many were inside.

Chances were, the majority of the men were in the building—actively hunting Jericho. No way there were more than two in the van. And, if he was wrong, he'd deal. That simple. He wasn't letting anyone hurt his team —hurt his girl.

It took him three seconds to creep up on the driver— position himself to strike. Another two to smash the window—catch the guy in the side of the head with his elbow. His partner turned, cigarette hanging off his lip as he stared at Cannon. Frozen.

That just made it easier to cold cock him with the back of his gun. Knock him out. Another minute, and he had both men bound and laying in the back of the van. Weapons rendered useless.

A quick scan, and he was moving, again. Clearing the other streets, the doorways. Two guys hanging out by a tree. Armed. Gang tattoos on their necks. He didn't worry if they were involved. Just took them out. Unconscious and tied to the tree.

But that was it. All he could unearth before he was standing at the garage entrance. The fact he hadn't come across his teammates, that they were apparently still inside, was unsettling. Meant they'd had to adapt. Maybe head to the garage for cover. Would there be any cover? On a weekend?

No sense worrying, now. If his buddies were there, if Jericho was there, Cannon was going in. Full force. At least, he had on a Kevlar vest. Standard issue Marshal Service. Not as good as the one sitting in his truck— parked in the damn garage he was about to infiltrate. But it meant he could take a few hits and keep going. They'd bruise. Maybe break some ribs, but nothing he couldn't push through. Keep fighting with. And knowing the kind of help he'd already faced, the bastards would go for the torso.

Except the SOG guys. They were cocky. They'd try for the head. He'd have to be vigilant. Consider the possibility that they weren't all stationed as snipers. That one might be on the offensive—hell, maybe both. They'd be armed with multiple weapons. The one true threat involved in this undertaking. Unless Dave was here.

Fuck, Cannon hoped that wasn't the case. Discovering the truth was one thing. Having to draw down on her partner... Cannon would do it. No hesitation. But if Jericho had to take the shot...

He wasn't sure she could. Not that he'd blame her. Killing scumbags was one thing. Killing her partner, even if he was trying to do the same—it wasn't rational. And sane people clung to rationality. It could destroy her.

Well, then, he'd just have to ensure she wasn't put in that position. That he or his team did the dirty work. That she'd be free to grieve without the added guilt. Plus, Dave had stabbed Jericho. Cannon wasn't about to let that go unpunished.

He considered his options. Using the rolling door was out. Too much noise. Too slow. Instead, he made for the entrance beside it. Code-protected. Chances of men on the other side, but he was ready. Hit the numbers then went in diving. Rolling across the concrete then onto his feet. Gun sweeping the lot. His finger inside the trigger guard. A guy was off to his left. Pistol with a suppressor in one hand. Radio in the other. His attention focused on the other side of the garage. He barely turned before Cannon had dropped him, the soft whoosh from the suppressor drowned out by the thud of the body crumpling.

No worrying about casualties, here. Not when he knew they were outnumbered. Outgunned. If it came back to bite him in the ass, he'd deal with it. But, for now, he wasn't pulling any punches until Jericho and his men were safe.

He surveyed the area. If they'd been able to take the elevator or main stairs, they'd be close. The set nearest Jericho's office opened off to his left. But it was dark, half the lights shut down. And the ones that were burning seemed dull. A few buzzing periodically then winking out.

He made a low whistling noise. Waited. When he didn't get a reply, he moved over to one side, picking his way toward the back. Six or Colt would have answered if they'd heard him. Which meant either they were on the other side of the garage, were still upstairs, or...

Nope. Cannon wasn't going to consider any other option. Six and Colt were good. Two of the best men he'd had the pleasure to serve with. Lead. Call brothers. They wouldn't go down without a fight. Without making it out. Bleeding. Dying. It didn't matter. They'd drag bloody stumps to the car. Bleed out while driving if that's what it took.

And that wasn't even accounting for that weird premonition shit Six had going on. The reason they all called him Six, to begin with. The man had an eerie way of knowing when something was about to happen. Had saved all of them countless times by stopping them from walking into an ambush. Or pulling them out of danger just before it struck. Cannon didn't know if it was simply enhanced hearing. Sight. Or if Six really did possess something unnatural. Extrasensory. Cannon didn't care. Six was one of the good guys. That's all that mattered. And Cannon knew the guy would be on full alert, using all his abilities to keep Colt and Jericho safe.

A voice cut the silence, echoing in every direction. Cannon couldn't make out the exact words, but he didn't need to. He recognized the voice. Had heard the man address Jericho on more than a few occasions.

Dave Faraday.

That changed things. Complicated them.

Cannon headed toward the sound, keeping to the shadows. But that meant sticking close to the walls, limiting his view points. Several shapes moving in a line caught his attention. Men. Scouring the area. Searching for anyone hidden in or behind the vehicles. They popped in and out of sight as they ducked down, then straightened. They spread out a bit when they encountered a few vehicles parked together, the men on the ends flanking wide.

He'd go for them, first, then work his way in. Take them out one at a time. He moved out, staying low. Gun ready, when the guy on the far side dropped. Just dropped. Silently. As if he'd never been there. Just gone.

Cannon smiled. Colt. No doubt about it. The man excelled at stealth maneuvers. Had once eliminated a dozen tangoes on his own by hunting them down one at a time. Had a way of getting behind people—grabbing them without making a sound. Nothing. Not a breath of air. Not a damn scuff.

It also meant Jericho and Six were somewhere close. No way they'd leave her upstairs. The only question was whether she was hunting with them, or they'd told her to stay someplace safe. So they could take care of the men.

Not ideal, but under the circumstances, it made sense. Have them eliminate as many as possible so the race out wasn't a gantlet of bullets and tangos. Besides, he knew her all too well. She'd probably told them to go. Assured them she could hold her own. And she could—except where she was still healing. Would have to face her ex-partner.

His voice sounded, again. The words echoing, once more. Only this time, Cannon heard every one. When his name sounded through the garage, he froze. Because he knew, in that instant, she'd face him. Make him talk. Buy Six and Colt time. Fuck, sacrifice herself so they got out. Anything to put the attention on her.

A cold sweat beaded his body, the icy slide of fear clawing at him. Every instinct told him to run. Just stand up and sprint to wherever she was. Follow the voice he'd heard. Shoot whoever got in his way. He'd most likely get hit, but adrenaline would keep him moving. Pushing forward until he reached them—killed the bastard where he stood.

Which was exactly what he shouldn't do. Acting impulsively, letting his fear, his damn heart, rule his actions, would get them all killed. Instead, he headed for the other side of the building. Colt could take care of the rest of the men. Hell, he'd already downed another by the time Cannon started moving. And Six was sure to be tracking anyone else. Dave's voice echoed one more time before another one replied.

Shit. Jericho. Just as he'd thought.

Damn it, man, keep your head in the game. She's doing this for a reason. Work with her. Back her up.

No question he'd back her up. He just hated the thought of her being bait, in a sense. Of drawing all the high caliber players to her location. Though, it wasn't a bad plan. Knowing her, she was counting on Six and Colt to be there. Take out everyone else, leaving her to deal with Dave. Exactly what Cannon had hoped to save her from, but like it or not, it was their best shot.

Which meant he'd need to take care of whoever had been with Faraday. No way that bastard had come here alone. Chances were, he'd teamed up with the SOG guys. Made himself as protected as possible. Well, Cannon would see that the asshole was stripped of that support. That Dave had no one to fall back on. No team. Fucker didn't deserve one.

Cannon quick-stepped along the perimeter, constantly scanning the area. The garage opened up to the left in front of him around a corner, the voices coming from that direction. He stopped at the edge of the wall, spotted some asshole pointing a gun toward the area, and dropped him. Guy crumpled to the ground, his weapon clanking against the pavement.

Another shadow popped up. Turned. The guy's weapon in harsh relief. Assault rifle. Magazine curving out of the bottom. Cannon capped him then moved out, skimming along the curb. Another few feet, and he saw her. Standing in the center of a collection of vehicles. Gun raised in front of her. Hands gripping the handle.

They were shaking. Not a lot, but enough he noticed. Saw it in her shadow on the wall behind her. She was focused on Dave, her gaze occasionally sweeping the lot.

But she couldn't cover every direction—not if she wanted to prevent Dave from shooting her. He didn't look as if he was holding a weapon, but Cannon figured the man didn't need to. That he'd already arranged for one of his colleagues to kill her.

Not on Cannon's watch.

He slowed down. Surveyed the lot, looking for places he'd pick to hide in. No way someone trained in special operations would just stand out in the open. He'd hunker down. Get Jericho in his sights then kill her once Dave gave him the signal. Maybe they wanted to know how much she remembered? Who she'd told, first? Estimate how much damage control was needed before silencing her.

Which gave Cannon an opening. The time he needed to hunt them down. Eliminate them. There...tucked in behind a Suburban. Using the roof rack to rest his rifle. Asshole was adjusting the scope—most likely night vision. Something to give him an edge. A clear view of his target.

Cannon could take the shot, but it was risky. The darkness. The roof racks. And with only a small portion of the guy's head and arm visible. But, if Cannon missed, he'd lose his element of surprise. They obviously thought he was still engaged with Brown. That gave him the advantage.

He weighed his options then took off. Ducking behind pillars, cars—whatever he found. Just enough to blur his movement before he was off, again. Dave was talking. Trying to convince Jericho to join ranks. Weasel out what she knew. Cannon didn't have much time. He sensed it. Like a clock slowly counting down inside his head. The final tick marking the end. Of Jericho. Of

286 | KRIS NORRIS

Cannon's dreams. His chance at a life, because she was it.

He was ten feet off when the guy finished fiddling with the rifle—sealed his eye to the scope. Dave was still rambling on, but maybe getting Jericho to reveal what she knew wasn't the plan. Maybe it was just a coincidence that the fucker on the truck hadn't fired, yet. Maybe he simply hadn't been ready—until now.

Because his finger was sliding inside the trigger guard. Wrapping around the trigger—caressing it. Adjusting then settling as he got the feel he'd been looking for. There'd be a moment of stillness—as the guy drew a breath, then held it—before he fired.

Cannon aimed. He didn't have a clear shot, but fuck it. Fuck the element of surprise because he would *not* let the prick get off a shot. Wouldn't let him come close to hurting Jericho. Cannon planted his next step, used his left hand to steady his right, then fired.

It hit the guy's arm, knocking him off his mark. He rolled instantly, disappearing off the other side of the vehicle—leaving the rifle on the racks. Cannon changed direction mid-stride. Anticipating the bastard's route. That he'd try to get behind Cannon by circling around the left of the Suburban. That, or he'd simply camp out back. Wait for Cannon to expose himself then take the shot. He had to have a handgun. Possibly his service weapon, though more likely something else. That couldn't be traced.

None of it mattered. Cannon was on top of him before he could aim. Asshole was left handed, which meant Cannon had clipped his good hand. And these guys didn't train to shoot with both hands like the Teams did. Didn't worry about having to continue if their dominant arm got hurt. That they'd have to defend themselves, their team, while bleeding. Hurting.

So, getting the jump on him—cracking his head against the wall, watching him drop onto the pavement—was easy. Not finishing him off. Binding his hands and feet, leaving him alive—*that* was hard. Because, a few seconds late, and the bastard would have killed Jericho.

Cannon took a moment to study his face. Wasn't Andrews, but one of the other guys Cannon had seen that night. Which meant Andrews was still out there. Cannon didn't have any proof that the man was dirty beyond his gut feeling, but Six wasn't the only one who sensed things. And this went soul deep.

Jericho was talking, now. Her voice strained. Higher than usual. Damn, she was in pain. Probably pulling her ribs having to hold the gun aimed at Dave that long. And that wasn't taking into account her mental state. If she was losing it from the realization she might have to shoot her partner. Kill him.

But, there had to be another guy out there. And, if he wasn't holed up across the street waiting, he was here. In the garage. Hunting. Possibly targeting her, right now, just like this asshole had done.

Cannon could reach her. Take Dave out in the process, but it might not be enough. And, if Dave dropped first...

Time for Plan C.

Cannon vaulted up onto the truck, taking up the other man's spot with the rifle. He'd been right. Night vision. Thermal setting. It had the works, and just what Cannon needed to end this. He pressed his eye against the lens then started hunting.

CHAPTER TWENTY-FOUR

God, it really was him. Dave. Standing there amidst the shadows, staring at her. Smiling as if he hadn't literally shoved a knife in her side. As if they could simply pick up where they'd left off. Friends.

Jericho's stomach roiled. It made her sick. Looking at him. Hearing his voice. He'd disgraced everything she'd ever stood for. Had thrown her sense of justice and duty back in her face, and for what? Money? Some demented form of power?

Dave glanced at her gun. "I put mine away, Jer. Thinking I, at least, deserve the same courtesy."

"You fucking stabbed me. You don't deserve shit."

He winced. As if she'd actually hurt his feelings. "I didn't want to hurt you, but—"

"But what? I was worth more dead to you than alive? How much did Macmillan pay you to kill me? What was our partnership worth to you?"

"It's not like that. He didn't..." Dave blew out a breath. Visibly calmed himself. "I knew, if you lived, you'd never stop digging. Never stop searching for the truth. And, once you discovered it…" He laughed. Like it was funny. Some cosmic joke she obviously didn't understand. "They would have done far worse to you than kill you."

"Oh, so it was a mercy killing? Because you cared?"

"I've always cared. Don't get all self-righteous. Just because I decided to go down a different path doesn't mean I didn't have your back all those years. Took a bullet for you, too, once, or have you conveniently forgotten that part?"

"That Dave's gone. I don't know who you are, now. Who's standing in front of me, because the man I knew wouldn't sell his soul to the devil for money. That's why you did it, right? To get rich?"

"It was one of the perks." He rolled his shoulders, settled. "The why doesn't matter. What's important is where we go from here."

"Like the saying goes…proceed directly to jail."

"I think we both know that isn't an option. But, it's not too late for you to change your mind. There's always a place for someone of your caliber. Your skill set."

"If you believed that, you wouldn't have tried to kill me. You would have asked me, then. But we both know I'd never turn, so…"

"Then, why are you talking to me? You know I'm not alone. That you're making yourself out to be a target."

"Because I need to know one thing. When?"

"When?"

"Did you stop being a marshal. My partner. When?"

"About a year ago. Shauna and I were having issues, and… Like I said. The why isn't important."

So, it hadn't all been a lie. Those years she'd believed in him. Respected and looked up to him. He'd gotten lost.

"I want you to turn around and put your hands against that glass partition. You're under arrest for attempted murder of a federal marshal."

"Jericho...think it through. Cannon isn't here. Even if you have a couple of his buddies with you, I have twenty. Stationed around the garage. Outside. A sniper just waiting to cap anyone who walks out of here. You're not going anywhere. So...tell me who knows about this, and I'll make sure it's quick. That you don't suffer. Your friends don't suffer."

"You'd like that. For me to just roll over. Surrender. How about this? I kill you, then at least I'm not going down empty-handed."

"You really think you could do that? Kill me when I'm not even holding a gun on you? That's not the Jericho I know."

"Yeah, well, you changed that, didn't you? Now, either turn around or I'll drop you where you stand."

"Sorry. I'm going to have to call your bluff on this one, because despite everything, I know you. I—"

Movement. In her peripheral vision. A shadow shifting on top of a car at the far end of the lot. Something long aiming her way. She hit the ground—barely missed the bullet that exploded the glass of the car beside her. Raining fragments down over her head.

There was another sound. A dull whoosh, followed by a cry of pain then a loud crash. More glass breaking. She shook off the shards, glancing out only to realize Dave wasn't there.

Jericho dropped, again, rolled under the big truck

behind her just as Dave rounded the other vehicles—took a shot. It hit the pavement—bounced away. But, if she'd been a second slower...

No time to worry. To consider the what-ifs. Not when he was already closing in on her. Staying low. Out of sight unless someone got close. She had just enough time to gain her feet—dart behind another car—before he was there. Right where she'd been a second earlier. Christ, if she didn't get some distance between them, she wouldn't have time to aim. Wing him, because damn it, he was right. Even with him armed, she didn't think she could take a kill shot. Shoulder, leg. Those, she could do, but his head. Heart?

And the fucker knew it. Obviously didn't share her reservations. Though, stabbing her had probably eliminated those. And she needed to believe he'd had some. That it hadn't been easy.

Another ricochet. Then, again...

She dodged right, chancing an open space as she made for another scattering of cars. Two shots. One high, one low. Just missing her. Pinging off the car, the wall. Had they both been from him? Was there another threat? He'd claimed he had other men. Men who'd be heading their way with all the noise they'd made. The booming echo of each shot.

Twenty. That's what he'd said. Inside and out. Those were crazy odds. Astronomical. It also meant that, if they made it to an exit, they might get picked off as soon as they stepped out. Damn hard to avoid a sniper. Shots you couldn't see coming.

She needed to change tactics. Go on the offensive. Sure, she'd promised Six she wouldn't engage—had probably already broken that deal by talking to Dave, even if it had been in an attempt to buy time, especially when he'd been unarmed—but she didn't have a choice. There weren't more cars near her. And Dave was close—just standing on the other side, judging if he should follow. Chance the open space. This might be her only opportunity.

Jericho took a deep breath, hissed through the resulting burn in her side, then turned. Readied herself to make a move.

A hand over her mouth. Drawing her back against a wall of male muscle. She instinctively cocked her elbow before his scent prickled her senses. She recognized it. The row of calluses across his palm as it shifted over her mouth. The firm line of his chest. The sheer massiveness of him.

Tears burned her eyes. He was alive. When Dave had said he'd sent Cannon away, she'd feared the worst. That he was pinned down. Defending Art. Brown. That he'd die because of her.

But he was here. Warm, firm flesh against hers. His usual air of confidence slowly easing the tight feeling in her chest.

She relaxed, gaining her a chuckle.

His lips brushed her neck. "Stay close."

"But the other—"

"Eliminated."

"Outside—"

"Everywhere."

He'd taken out twenty guys? Snipers? Gang members? Sure, Colt and Six had probably done their share, but still. Even three against that many.

Considering Cannon had faced over a dozen, alone, the other night, it shouldn't shock her, now, but... She was pretty damn sure there had been other lawmen. Marshals or agents. Not the typical fare. And, yet, his three-man team had bested all of them.

Cannon eased her away, giving her a quick scan, then stood. Just like that. In plain sight. Where Dave could see him—anyone could see him. And Cannon didn't even seem concerned. Wasn't shaking or breathing hard. Didn't appear to be questioning every move like she'd been doing. Warring with any conflicting emotions. He just stood. Straight. Fierce.

Jericho edged up enough to look through the windows —gauge Dave's reaction. The man's gaze swung toward them, his arrogant smile slipping then falling. He'd obviously thought it would be her. That she'd try to deal or maybe make a play he felt confident he could counter. But all that smugness slid away. Replaced by anger. Bitterness. A twinge of jealousy.

He had his gun raised, aimed in their direction, but not directly at them. He'd been guessing where she'd hidden, and he'd missed. Which brought her to her feet. Had her shifting in beside Cannon. Staying close, like he'd asked. But she couldn't do this crouching behind some car. Avoiding Dave. Being anything less than an equal. Not and still do her job.

Cannon barely moved. Just a slight shift over— covering her a bit more. He had Dave in the crosshairs. Jericho didn't need to be looking down his gun to know it. She felt it. Sensed it. In the line of his body, the firmness of his stance. Cannon was armed, ready, and willing.

"It's over, Faraday. Your men are down. And I'll drop you before you correct your aim. Guaranteed."

Dave angled over, gun slightly tipped toward the ground. There, but not the threat Cannon's was. Jericho just wasn't sure if Dave had intended it as a show of surrender or if he was planning something. Had some kind of ace up his sleeve.

He grinned. Toothy. Smug. "Ya know, if I'd known how damn hard it would be to get rid of you, I would have put someone on it sooner. Christ, you're like a damn cockroach."

"Gun down. I won't ask, again."

Dave sighed, let his pistol rotate around his finger, tilting the trigger away from him. "It's pretty impressive you took out everyone." He shifted his gaze to her. Pinned it there. "Are you sure you got every target?"

The look in Dave's eyes. The way they strayed a bit to the left, as if trying to look behind him, had her inhaling. Focusing on the stairway door just as a guy barreled through. Assault rifle notched in his shoulder. Muzzle directed at them. He didn't have to aim. A spray of bullets would take them out. And with Dave off to their left, he'd be clear. Barely, but clear.

Cannon didn't move. Didn't shift his focus, still watching Dave when the air boomed—the sound nearly knocking her down. She jumped, spinning in time to see Six step out from behind a pillar, gun in hand. She glanced back, but the guy was already falling, red blossoming on his shoulder. He hit the pavement then stilled, nothing but the lingering echo of the report sounding around her.

Cannon grinned. "You're right. There was one left. Figured this would be enough to draw him out. Now, are you going to drop the gun, turn and surrender or do I save us both the trouble and cap your ass?"

Dave stared at the man on the ground, face white. He swallowed, coughed, then looked at Cannon. "If you care about Jericho like you claim, you won't kill her partner."

"Ex-partner, and to be honest, I never liked you."

Dave stilled, eyes wild. He seemed uncertain before grinning. He tossed the gun at his feet then held up his hands. "Fine, you win. But this isn't the end. I'll spin a deal. Turn on Macmillan. Get a new start in Wit Sec. You haven't won."

Cannon's left eye twitched, and she knew.

"Rick." She smiled when he shifted his eyes enough to make contact without losing focus on Dave. "He's not worth it. Who cares if he walks. I get you, so...he's wrong. I won."

Cannon chuckled. "Damn, I'm in trouble. Okay. We'll take him alive, but something tells me he's gonna resist arrest. Just a bit."

"Deal. As long as I get the first jab."

CHAPTER TWENTY-FIVE

"Jericho?"

Cannon sat up in bed, searching the room. He'd reached over for her—had expected to slide his hand around her waist, tug her close—but her side was empty. The sheets already cooling. He glanced at the clock, groaning. It was way too early for her to be up, especially after all that had happened.

He pulled back the covers and rolled off the bed. A pair of sweats and some socks, and he was heading out of the room, down the hallway. Six met him in the main area, coffee mug extended. Cannon shook his head, took the offering then arched a brow.

Six sighed. "Balcony. Said something about needing some air. Colt's keeping watch from outside, just in case."

"Thanks. The threat should be over, but..."

But they weren't taking chances. Not until the Macmillan empire had crumbled and the bastards behind the attempts on her life were incarcerated. Or, at least, put into Wit Sec. As much as Cannon hated the idea, he knew it was a possibility. Which was what he suspected was keeping Jericho from some much-needed sleep.

He took a swig of the coffee as he padded across the floor, slipping out through the set of French doors. She was leaning against the railing, mug in one hand, gaze focused on the horizon. The moon was still low, lighting up the water off in the distance. They'd gone directly to her apartment. Grabbed her stuff—less than he'd expected. But she'd assured him she had everything that mattered. Then, they'd come home.

Their home. And he'd see it stayed that way. Permanently.

She cocked her head his way when he shuffled in behind her, leaning into him when he palmed her waist. "It's pretty."

He nuzzled her neck, smiling at the bead of bumps that spread across her skin. "Not nearly as beautiful as you. Trouble sleeping?"

She shrugged.

"You could have woken me. Bet I could find a way to tire you out."

Her cheeks flamed, the blush spreading down her neck. "How can you have any stamina left after that marathon session?"

"Easy. All I have to do is look at you."

"Charmer. And it's not that I'm not interested. It's just…"

She sighed, the sad sound making his chest tighten. Hurt. Right over that heart she'd resurrected. The one that belonged to her.

He slid his hands together, holding her tight. "Thinking about Dave?"

Another sigh. Another tug on his heart.

"It's not your fault, you know. He chose his path. And, frankly, he didn't get nearly what he deserved."

"Killing him wouldn't have changed anything."

"He hurt you. That, alone, would have justified retaliation."

She laughed, looking back at him. "As sweet as that is, in a Neanderthal sort of way, you can't go around killing everyone who takes a shot at me. You'd never do anything else."

"Can't help it. That's just who I am, but..." He leaned in closer. Brushed his lips against her ear. "I'll try to tame it a bit. For you."

Jericho eased forward just enough to turn in his arms. Wrap hers around his neck. "I don't want you to change. Not even a little."

"Good, because as much as I claim I'll try, I'm not sure this junkyard dog can learn that kind of new trick." He touched his nose to hers. "So, what's this really about, then?"

"What makes you think there's something else?"

"Sweetheart. I've been trained in interrogation techniques. I know when someone's not telling me the whole truth. Besides, you have a tell."

She blinked then palmed his chest, gave him a shove, not that it did anything. "I have a tell?"

He shrugged.

"What? What's my tell?"

"If I tell you that, you'll try to change it."

"Cannon..."

"Just, talk to me. That's what partners are for, right?"

She stiffened, some of the color draining from her face.

Fuck. "This is about getting a new partner when you go back, isn't it?"

Green eyes looked up at him. Glassy. Wide. Before she nodded. "How am I supposed to trust anyone after this? I mean, I'll probably end up working with a number of people, but there's always a pairing that seems to stick. How can I be sure this doesn't happen, again?"

The waver in her voice. The slight hesitation when she'd talked. He'd been wrong. Or, more accurately, he hadn't looked at the bigger picture. The one that encompassed more than just a new partner. That involved believing in what she was doing. In herself.

He lifted one hand—cupped her chin. "This isn't just about a new partner. You're questioning if you still believe in the Marshal Service. If you even want to go back."

He hadn't posed it as a question. Didn't need to because the answer was in her eyes. In the way she inhaled, holding it before pushing it out. Hard. As if she needed to stem the restlessness he sensed in her.

She toed the floor, taking a few deep breaths before looking up at him. Eyes glassy. "How did you know it was time to move on? That you were ready?"

Cannon sighed. They hadn't talked too much about his time in the service. Jericho knew a lot of what he'd done was classified and refrained from asking. Anything else had been fairly trivial. A crumb here or there. Lots of words that didn't really equate to any kind of story or information. But, now, he needed to share more.

Fuck, she deserved to know everything. All the demons hiding inside him. And it wasn't as if she didn't have a decent security level. He could give her some details without breaking any kind of security agreements.

Jericho's shoulders drooped. "Sorry. Guess you can't really talk about it."

"It was after my last mission." He smiled when her eyes widened.

She touched his hand. "Cannon. You don't have to—"

"I want to. Long overdue, actually. Anyway, I'd been undercover for nearly two years. Hated it. Not having my team with me. My guys. But, I'd sucked it up. Had finally infiltrated an Islamic cell we thought was heading a major upcoming terrorist attack. They were camped out in this remote compound north of Jalalabad. Nasty place. Nothing but dirt and sand. The men were animals. Abusing the women and children. Sickened me. Had me questioning my motivations every damn day.

"But I kept trying to see the bigger picture. Made sure I only did what I absolutely had to in order to maintain my cover. Some of that shit..." He sighed. "It still haunts me. Then, finally, their head guy showed up—laid their plans out at my feet. I had everything I needed to bring them down. All that was left was to see they made it to the rendezvous site, where my Delta team would be waiting."

He took another breath, feeling some of the horror slowly fade—healed by the love in her eyes. The way she held his hand.

He paused to tuck some of her hair behind one ear. "HQ wanted the bastards alive. To interrogate. Figure out where they were getting their supplies. But, just before we were scheduled to leave, they brought in a SEAL one of their patrols had captured. Poor bastard had gotten caught in a crossfire. Been separated from his squad. Had dragged his ass twenty miles over hostile terrain. Bleeding. Broken leg. Dislocated shoulder. The guy was so fucking hardcore, I just stood there, staring. That's when the mother fucker I'd spent all that time waiting for decided to make an example of the soldier. Wanted to kill him while filming it. Televising it."

He swallowed, nearly gagging as the images and smells filled his head. Fuck, he could picture it all clearly. The pure evil in the bastard's eyes.

Jericho gave his hand a squeeze. "You stopped them, didn't you?"

"That's a bit of an understatement. Truth is, I snapped. Killed all six men in that room with my bare hands, then went after the others. There were twelve dead by the time I was done. Not exactly what HQ had wanted, but they still got their intel. Enough of a trail to keep searching. Needless to say, I was pulled out and sent on mandatory leave for a few of weeks. Was told to decompress and get my head on straight."

He chuckled. "Ended up in Seattle. I don't even know why, really. But then, Rigs called. Addison was in danger. They needed intel. Backup. Seemed pretty benign until I walked into Ice's place. She freaked. Said I smelled like death. Had this vibe around me."

He shook his head. "That got me thinking. Questioning my motivations all over, again. After working that case with the guys, I realized that's what I'd been missing during my last mission. Being part of a team. Having men rely on you—a reason to keep fighting. When I returned, I was informed I'd be going back in. Another undercover assignment. Alone. And that's when I knew. That, if I took the job—buried myself in all that ugliness, again—I'd never dig myself out. Have anything left of...me. Resigned on the spot and haven't looked back since."

He didn't add that he might have gone back. Might have caved if he hadn't met her. Found a new mission to focus on. A new teammate who meant more to him than he'd ever imagined.

Jericho smoothed her hand up to his face. "I'm glad you got out. Found yourself, again. Found me."

"Best damn decision I ever made. Now, back to yours. You know I'll support whatever you choose, right?"

"I know."

"Good. Having said that, I think you need to go back. Not because you have something to prove, but because you still believe in justice. In what being a Deputy Marshal stands for."

She blew out a raspy breath. "How can you be so sure when I'm not?"

"Because, if you were done, if you'd truly lost your faith, you would have killed Dave. Or, at least, let me. But you took him in, knowing he'd get that Wit Sec deal he wanted. That bringing down a drug empire outweighed getting your own form of justice." He reached down— brushed his finger along her jaw. "That, sweetheart, is what marshals do. And you're one of the best."

Cannon dropped a quick kiss on her pretty lips. "Besides, you're the only one who makes Art's job interesting. He'll lose his shit if you leave."

Jericho snorted. "Right."

He dragged her closer, pressing his body against hers. "But know this... I will personally be vetting every damn person he pairs you up with. And I'll be tagging along on any prison transfers or high-stakes felon arrests for a while. Best make peace with that, now."

"Glad to see you're taming those overprotective tendencies."

"You can take the man out of the military, sweetheart…"

"But not the military out of the man. Yeah, I'm seeing that. Fine, you can tag along. Just…try to behave and not scare everyone I have to work with."

"I'll see if I can tone that death vibe down a notch."

"That's my guy."

"Hell yeah, I am. Better?"

"I guess that depends?"

"On what?"

She smiled, nipped at his bottom lip. "On whether you can hold true to your promise. You said you had a way to tire me out."

"Oh, sweetheart. I know a lot of ways to tire you out."

"Then, why are we still standing here, soldier? Or are all those muscles just for show?"

Cannon shook his head in mock indignation, scooping her up into his arms. "Talk like that isn't going to get you a gentle loving."

"Gentle's overrated. It's the loving that matters. And I do. Love you."

"Love you more. Now, save your breath. You're gonna need it."

EXCERPT ~ DELTA FORCE: COLT

Five years ago, Paris...

"Okay, Sievers, out with it."

Damn. Busted.

Brett Sievers, or Colt to his buddies, his brothers, looked up from his beer, sighing when the rest of his teammates pulled up chairs and gathered at his table. The one he'd picked in order to isolate himself. So this kind of *brotherly* intervention wouldn't happen.

One night to himself. That's all he'd needed. Time to process the letter—to deal with the resulting pain. The loss—without being on display. Or having to muster up a fake form of enthusiasm he couldn't feel. Because the guys would know. Would be able to tell something was wrong. Which had meant ditching them until he could convincingly lie his way out. And god knew he could sell a lie with the best of them. Just, not tonight.

But, they'd all used their damn Delta skills and scoped

him out, regardless. And before he'd done more than order a beer.

Brett had thought he'd done a damn good job of hiding. Going to a bar that was definitely not his taste. Loud techno music, flashing disco lights, and more bodies grinding on the dance floor than was probably allowed—it represented everything he hated about furloughs. And the last place he thought his squad would hunt him down.

Or course, Six and Cannon were among the men. Bastards were damn good trackers, even in an urban environment. And they knew Brett, too well. Had spent five years watching each other's backs. There wasn't a piece of him he hadn't bared at some point—a secret he'd been able to keep. Not that they were any different.

Quieter, maybe. A bit better at pushing the really bad shit down. But, he'd have hunted their asses out if their positions had been reversed. Which might account for the lack of surprise in his gut at them appearing out of the crowd.

And that wasn't even taking into account what Six could do. Hell, knowing the man, he'd read Brett's mind or something equally creepy. There was a reason everyone called the man Six—Brett wasn't even sure he remembered Six's actual name. Casey something, he thought. Six had this way about him—sensed things a moment or two before everyone else. As if he knew shit was about to go sideways. Just this morning, he'd grabbed Brett and shoved him out of the way before one of the tent poles they'd been dismantling fell exactly where Brett would have been standing. What would have been at best, a nasty concussion. At worst, it could have killed him.

The unit had given up trying to figure the guy out. If

he had some kind of extrasensory perception thing going, or just super heightened senses. It didn't matter if it saved their asses. He could be an alien, and it wouldn't change anything. Not when he'd single-handedly kept them all from seeing an early grave. Which meant, he'd probably just done some kind of *Jedi* mind trick, or that *Vulcan* meld thing and sourced out exactly where Brett had ventured.

He took a long pull of his beer, giving the men a shrug. "Not sure what you're talking about. Just wanted a beer."

A snort from Ethan Vale, known as Phoenix. He was the newest member—still a bit green around the edges. But the guy was a hell of a sniper. Better than anyone Brett had worked with, yet, including his other Delta brothers. And Phoenix was fearless. Beyond normal in that department, as if he hadn't simply made peace with the fact he could die on any given mission, but halfway *wanted* to. It bordered on reckless—freaking creepy, if Colt was honest—but Phoenix got the job done. Kept his brothers safe, in the process.

Phoenix made direct eye contact. "Please. First, you were late for our run this morning. Then, you disappeared while we were breaking camp—right after Six saved you from getting cold-cocked. And if that wasn't enough, Cannon had to tackle your ass when that tango appeared on the side of the road and damn near blew your head off. Not to mention, you ditched us the minute we got sent on mandatory decompress." He glanced around at the gathering of men as he laid his arms along the back of the chair facing the table. "So, out with it."

Another pull. Then, another. Not that it helped. A dozen pints wouldn't be enough to drown his heart. The one still bleeding out. Fuck women.

Six sighed. "I think maybe we were wrong, guys. Let's give Colt some space."

"We weren't wrong, Six, we—"

"You heard the man." Cannon, this time. "Clear out. We'll meet for breakfast at the hotel restaurant at oh eight hundred. I suggest everyone get their run in before that."

Phoenix grunted but stood, twisting the chair the right way 'round then heading off with the rest. Six gave Brett's shoulder a pat then tagged along behind the rest of the men, quickly disappearing into the crowd. Only Cannon stayed at the edge of the table, one hand on the top, the other shoved into his pocket.

He waited until Brett looked up at him. "I don't need to have Six's radar to guess that this involves Ellis."

Brett focused on the table. If he said her name…

Cannon blew out a rough breath. "How'd she do it?"

"Sent a letter out with Hammond's squad." Though, letter was pushing it. Several lines of accusations and blame. Of how he'd never measured up—never would. And signed with her full name, not the short form he'd given her. The fucking cherry on top of the shit sundae. He tipped his beer toward Cannon. "Real classy."

"I'm sorry, man. I know she was special."

Special. That was a fucking understatement. "Me, too, I thought…"

He'd *thought* that they were serious. That the two years they'd been fighting to make them work—to not let the distance or the job destroy their relationship—had meant something. Hell, they'd talked about retiring. About moving in together. Even starting a family. She'd been so happy, planning on meeting him this week in Paris. Mapping out how they'd orchestrate leaving the service when the time came. It would kill a part of him to abandon his brothers, his team, but damn it, Ellis was worth it. Was his fucking future. His world. Everything had been fine, then...a Dear John letter to end all letters.

He'd have said it stung, but that didn't come close to how he felt. Burned. Hollowed out. Left to rot in the sun —*those* were a better description. Only, maybe, all of them, together.

Cannon nodded, tapping the table with one finger. "She say why?"

"Just the usual."

A grunt. As if the realization had hurt the other man. "She found out who your father is."

It hadn't been a question, not that it surprised Brett. "They all do in time, Cannon. You can't run from your past forever. Not when it's in your blood."

"Colt...Brett—"

"Don't. I know the score. What my old man did—I hate the bastard, would love nothing more than to cap his ass, and I'm his son. His damn blood. I'm just tired of never being good enough. Of never getting out from under his shadow. It's like my damn DNA is stained. And it taints whatever I touch. Ruins it."

"You know that's not true. Anyone who truly cared about you wouldn't put what he did back on you."

Brett snorted. "Then, I guess she never really cared."

"That's not what I meant. Fuck." Cannon took a step, stopped and turned. "Is there anything I can do? We could track her down. Get answers."

Brett raised his beer. "Got all the answers I need, right here."

Another grunt. Cannon looked as if he was going to

argue but merely nodded. "I'll be waiting up to make sure you get back. Don't make me wait all night. And Colt?"

"Yeah, man?"

"Not every woman is like her. I promise. There's someone out there for you."

"Or maybe, that's just not how my life's gonna play out."

He waved off Cannon's reply. The pep talk the other man was no doubt going to preach, despite the fact Cannon didn't seem to need a relationship. Hell, in all the years Brett had known him, he couldn't remember the guy getting serious over anyone. Ever.

Maybe Cannon had it right? Maybe that's how guys like him, like Brett, survived? Made a life in the Teams without endless regrets. They gave up on the hope of ever finding someone that meant more to them than their brothers. Their honor.

He glanced at Cannon. "It's fine. I'm fine, I just need a night."

"You sure that's the best course of action? We all have a tendency to bury the bad shit."

"So?"

"Makes it hard to feel the good."

Brett paused. There had been a tone in Cannon's voice. Sadness. Regret, maybe. Hard to tell for sure, but the guy was definitely referring to more than just Brett's troubled love life.

Not that it mattered. He'd seen the light. Found his version of Jesus. "The only good is making it through a mission alive. Seeing my brothers do, too. That's all I've got, right now. All I need to focus on from here on out. I'll be back by midnight."

Cannon sighed then walked off. Brett watched the man fade into the crowd of bodies, signaling the bartender he needed another beer. Cannon was right. Brett had spent too many years pushing the bad shit down until nothing remained. Until he was just numb. Maybe that's why he always ended up alone.

Or, maybe, he was just cursed. Destined to always be on the outside looking in. Lots of the guys made it work. Found a way to be soldiers and lovers. Husbands and fathers. Why Brett couldn't seem to figure it out was a mystery.

Or just a by-product of a crappy roll of the dice. Being related to a man the world regarded as a monster. Having to constantly rise above it—atone for sins that weren't Brett's.

Despite what Cannon had said, Brett doubted anyone could ever look beyond it. See him as anything other than a serial murderer's son. As if it was lying dormant beneath his skin, just waiting to lash out—turn him into a younger version of his father.

Not going to happen, but that wasn't something he could prove. Guarantee. And once the truth was out—there wasn't any way to step back behind the curtain. Hide it all away.

The military had—after an exhausting security check and letters of reference from the detectives that had arrested his father. The federal agents involved. They'd gone to bat for Brett. He'd always wondered if the service had secretly hoped a bit of his old man was actually inside him—the part that made him an excellent hunter. Killer. And he'd fought against those notions when it seemed his peers had bought into it, too. Until he'd made Delta Force and been assigned to Cannon's squad. After that, everything had changed. He'd become Colt—brother and valued member. The other guys hadn't done more than nod when he'd given them the obligatory speech—the one he *should* have given to Ellis—then dropped it. Permanently. As if it didn't matter to them. Wasn't something they processed or thought about when they looked at him.

And he'd had a glimmer of hope. One shining fucking moment of clarity. Of thinking he might be beyond his past. That, maybe, other people—the woman he'd eventually fall in love with—Ellis—would see beyond it, too.

Except, where that hadn't been the case. Not even close.

The bartender dropped off his beer, thanked him for the tip, then left. Brett stared at the water condensing on the bottle—watching the drops slowly slide down the side. He should have told her. He knew that. He'd had endless opportunities to just spit it out. Had actually tried on several occasions but...

He hadn't been able to bring himself to do it. Not after the way it had imploded previous relationships. Made him feel like a freak. A failure. Less of a man. And with everything going so well this time around... He'd known from the start that Ellis was different. She'd made him consider options he hadn't before—picture a life outside his unit. Outside the Teams. With more than just his brothers to keep him company.

She'd made him dream. Losing it all, now...

Maybe, he'd been secretly hoping she wouldn't find out. That, when he eventually told her, fifty years down the road, it would be so far removed, it would slip by with nothing more than a shrug and a sigh. That, for once, he could just be Brett Sievers—Delta Force soldier, and the man in love with Ellis Baker. That he would be enough. That he wasn't Daniel Sievers' son.

Brett had been wrong. Horribly wrong. And that one mistake—that stupid conversation he should have made happen. Should have found a way to get out in the open—would be his undoing. The reason he swore off women, off love. Why he'd refuse to date, again. Empty sex. Cannon seemed to get by on it. No reason Brett couldn't follow in his buddy's footsteps. Shelter that last shattered piece of his heart he hadn't given to Ellis. Do his best to keep it hidden.

He didn't know what hurt more—that Ellis hadn't even bothered to ask him, first? Had just made assumptions and left? Or the way she'd done it. As if they hadn't shared all those months together. Hadn't said they loved each other. Hadn't been on the verge of forever.

Maybe he should track her down. Make her face him. Look him in the eyes as she ripped out his heart—bled it dry. Called him a monster. It might be worth it to see her one last time, even if it was to hear the truth.

No fucking way. He'd trained for years to overcome weakness. To bury any fear. To face life expecting to die. And he'd made peace with that. But he was man enough to admit—at least, to himself—that the prospect of facing her—seeing the hatred in her eyes. The disgusted look on her face—was more than even he could bear. That she was beyond his training. His limits.

Besides, it wouldn't change anything. Knowing the truth, hearing it, firsthand, wouldn't ease the pain crushing his chest. Make it easier to breathe. To move on. And it sure as hell wouldn't fill the empty hole in his heart. Which meant, it was time to give Brett his walking papers, and focus on being Colt, instead. Hardened soldier. Loner. A man with nothing left to lose.

Colt raised his beer, watching more drops glisten in the bright lights. Whatever the reason, he'd drink to it.

ABOUT THE AUTHOR

Author, single mother, slave to chaos—she's a jack-of-all-trades who's constantly looking for her ever elusive clone.

And don't forget to subscribe to her newsletter to get the latest scoop on new and upcoming releases as well as exclusive free reads.

https://www.subscribepage.com/krisnorris

Kris loves connecting with fellow book enthusiasts. You can find her on these social media platforms...

krisnorris.ca
contactme@krisnorris.ca

facebook.com/kris.norris.731
x.com/kris_norris
instagram.com/girlnovelist
amazon.com/author/krisnorris

Printed in the USA
CPSIA information can be obtained
at www.ICGtesting.com
LVHW090959221124
797354LV00003B/6